Montana Rides!

**Center Point
Large Print**

**This Large Print Book carries the
Seal of Approval of N.A.V.H.**

Montana Rides!

MAX BRAND

CENTER POINT PUBLISHING
THORNDIKE, MAINE

This Center Point Large Print edition
is published in the year 2008 by arrangement with
Golden West Literary Agency.

The text of this Large Print edition is unabridged. In other
aspects, this book may vary from the original edition.
Printed in the United States of America.
Set in 16-point Times New Roman type.

ISBN: 978-1-60285-271-6

Library of Congress Cataloging-in-Publication Data

Brand, Max, 1892-1944.
    Montana rides! / Max Brand.--Center Point large print ed.
      p. cm.
    ISBN: 978-1-60285-271-6 (lib. bdg. : alk. paper)
      1. Montana--Fiction. 2. Large type books. I. Evans, Evan, 1892-1944. Montana rides!
II. Title.

PS3511.A87M565 2008
813'.52--dc22

2008016229

Montana Rides!

Chapter One

THERE WERE TWO MEN under guard and waiting, in the outer office of the sheriff, when he brought in the Kid. The two were handcuffed, and so was the Kid. One of the two had the malarial look of a gentleman of the Old South. The other looked like a drunken butcher. It was the fellow who looked like a butcher that said, "There he is, now."

The other, with the long and greasy yellow face, stared at the Kid.

"That's right," he said. "He has them."

The Kid stopped.

When he paused his bodyguard pushed the double muzzle of a shotgun into the small of his back. The sheriff, also, produced two revolvers by a trick of legerdemain and pointed them at the Kid's head. The Kid did not regard the weapons. He merely stared calmly, persistently, at the two in the anteroom, and they stared as earnestly at him.

"You two thugs think that you know me," said the Kid, "but you don't. Even when I was a brat I never crawled as low as you. Take your eyes off me or I'll take the scalps off your heads."

The guns of the guard and the sheriff seemed a small hindrance. It looked as though the Kid would spring straight at the two other prisoners.

Therefore they took their eyes off him. He proceeded through the door marked "Private," attended by the sheriff and the guard.

"Manacle him to that chair," said the sheriff.

The guard manacled the Kid to a chair. While he was doing so the Kid deftly removed Bull Durham tobacco and wheat-straw papers from the vest pocket of the guard. He rolled a cigarette with a gesture.

"Here's the makings in exchange for a light," said the Kid.

The guard recognized his own property, but before he claimed it he scratched a match and lighted the cigarette of the Kid's. The guard grinned, and his eyes were afraid.

The Kid paid no attention to him.

"You can leave us now, Bob," said the sheriff to the guard. "Go and wait in the next room and help keep an eye on those two snakes."

"All right," said Bob, and went out.

The Kid made himself comfortable in the chair, closed his eyes, opened them a little as he exhaled a thin cloud of smoke, and looked through the smoke at the sheriff, and beyond the sheriff through the window at the dull sheen of the desert and the painted rock of the big flat-headed mesa.

"They call you Punch, too, don't they?" asked the sheriff.

The Kid said nothing.

"They call you Punch, too. You might as well open up a little," said the sheriff. "I'm going to tell you right now, if you talk a little you go free. I haven't anything worth while against you. But if you don't talk I'll railroad you and put you away in the can for a while, to cool and ripen. You'd better chatter. It won't hurt you and it might help you. They call you Arizona, too, and they call you Montana. Am I wrong?"

"You're not wrong," said the Kid, printing his words in the air with the thin cigarette smoke which he exhaled.

"Which name do you like the best?" asked the sheriff.

"Montana," said the Kid.

"Why?"

"Well, because it's farther away, just now."

"All right. Just go on and talk," urged the sheriff.

The Kid regarded him with eyes of slaty blue, the color of the sea when clouds are gathering overhead. His face was calm. It was nearly always calm.

"They call me Punch, too," he said, finally.

"Did you ever see Gentleman Jeff and Turk Fadden before?"

"Who are they?"

"You mean to say you never saw 'em?"

"In a town this size, to a mug like you, I don't bother to tell lies," said the Kid.

Along the polished ridge of his cheek bones the sheriff grew red, but he was a man who enjoyed great powers of self-control.

"I'm speaking of the pair you just called down in the outside office," he explained, carefully.

"Yeah. I saw them last night," said the Kid. "I saw them in O'Brien's place. I saw the one with the soggy face first. He was drunk. He took a look at me and said: 'Blue and black! Perfect, by God!' "

"What did you do?" asked the sheriff.

"Nothing. I just tapped him on the chin and let him drop. He was drunk. I didn't want to do anything."

The sheriff sighed.

"When they saw you," he said, "one of them remarked, 'He's got them.' What did he mean by that? What have you got?"

"Hands," said the Kid, showing them.

The sheriff sighed again.

"That's all you know about that pair?"

"I've told you all I know. I saw the fellow with the long face, afterwards, in the crowd. That's all I know. I saw him after I pulled up the roulette outfit."

"Why did you pull up the roulette outfit?"

"Because I thought it was working with a brake. I'd lost fifteen hundred dollars. I thought there was a brake on the wheel, so I pulled it up. I found the brake, all right."

"After that you wrecked the place."

"I wrecked the place because it was a dirty dump, and crooked."

"Are you crooked, Montana, or straight?"

"I'm only crooked with crooks, mostly."

"I've got your record," said the sheriff. "It looks bad."

"Nobody has anything on me," said the Kid.

"I won't try to hold you for last night's work," said the sheriff, "unless you cover up and won't talk. I'm glad, personally, that you wrecked O'Brien and showed up his crooked roulette wheel. The whole town is glad. The town is so glad that it would like to make a hero out of you because you wrecked the joint and shot O'Brien and his two helpers. All three of them are going to get well, by the way."

"I knew that when I shot 'em," said the Kid. "I didn't want to do them any harm, but they pulled guns on me and I had to shoot. I wouldn't do a man any harm because he picked fifteen hundred berries off me. I just got curious, last night. That was all. I started to look around and they began to pull guns and things. I didn't do them any harm."

Said the sheriff: "Fifteen hundred doesn't seem like much money to you, does it?"

"No," said the Kid. "I've handled more than that."

"Let me see the inside of your hand, will you?"

"That's all right," said the Kid.

He spread out his hand. It was large, long, with tapering fingers.

"You never wore a callus on that hand," said the sheriff. "You've never done any hard work."

"Why should I be a fool?" asked the Kid.

The sheriff looked down at a paper that was lying on his desk, with short, typewritten sentences on it.

"You're between twenty-two and twenty-four years old," he said.

"All right," said the Kid.

"When you were about fifteen you started. You showed up in Phoenix. You shot two men. One of them died."

"I remember those mugs," said the Kid. "The one

11

that I wanted to kill was the one that lived. I was pretty green in those days."

"Why did you shoot?" asked the sheriff.

"Self-defense," said the Kid.

"Sure," answered the sheriff. "I know. It was always self-defense—like last night. But why did you kill the man in Phoenix?"

"They were a pair of bouncers in a big dive there in Phoenix. They started to throw me out. They were going to roll a drunk, and they wanted to have me out of the way first. That was all. The one I should have killed only got a broken leg. I was pretty green."

The sheriff moved a broad finger tip down his list.

"That same year you went into Mexico and came out on the run. Some people say you killed three Mexicans. What about that?"

"I don't know," said the Kid. "I lose my memory when I go south of the Rio Grande. I don't remember anything about that."

"All right. You were about seventeen when you met Wes Denton in the middle of San Antone and shot him to death."

"Denton's girl told me he was a snake and a bum. Besides, he was any man's kill. He had a nice record. He had a long list. I thought I'd get him before somebody else did."

"Was that self-defense?"

"Sure. I'd sent in word that I was going to get him. I sent him my picture, so he'd know. And when we met, I let him make the first move."

12

The sheriff nodded. He went on, "What about Rollie Gannet?"

"Rollie had a way of fussing with the cards. I pulled an ace out of his sleeve. It made him sore. I liked Rollie, but he went for his gun. I liked Rollie. I didn't want to do him any harm. But I was still pretty green. I aimed for his shoulder, but the bullet went too far inside." He shook his head. "Poor old Rollie!" he said. "He was pretty good at minstrel songs. I could sit up all night listening to him!"

"You killed Pudge Grace and his brother?"

"Listen to me, brother," advised the Kid, leaning forward a trifle in his chair. "You're not so dumb. You know that most of the record you have down there is hooey. It's just hooey. I had a few words with the Grace brothers and they happened to be shot before the year was out. That was all. When they turned up their toes, everybody remembered that we'd had a few words. The Grace boys had some rough friends who came after me and shot me up. But it was all hooey. Most of that list is hooey, and you ought to know it."

He leaned back again, frowning, as though he felt that he had talked too much.

"You went into Mexico to recuperate and you came out a year later. About twenty Mexicans chased over the river, gunning for you."

"I don't remember Mexicans very well, as I was saying," said Montana. He eased his big shoulders against the back of the chair and his eyes gravely studied the worn, middle-aged face of the sheriff.

13

"Mexico and Mexicans are just a cloud in my mind," he concluded.

"You killed Dick Warren in the Mogollons," said the sheriff.

"Hooey," said the Kid.

"What about Slim Jim Wrangle?"

"I don't remember him."

"No? I do, though. Well, what about Purvis and Bentley?"

"Hooey," said the Kid, frowning.

"Are you holding out on me?"

"Listen. Purvis was my friend."

"What about St. Leger?"

"Self-defense," grunted Montana. "I'm tired of this, sheriff."

"All right," said the sheriff. "I've got a lot more names on this list, though."

"I've talked till I'm tired," answered Montana. "I won't talk any more."

"Where are you heading? What are you going to do with your life?" asked the sheriff.

"Why, I'm just looking around for a good place to settle down," said the Kid.

"That's a good idea," said the sheriff. "I could give you the address of the town where you'd be at home, too."

"Can you?" said the Kid, eagerly. "Go ahead, chief! Where's the town?"

"In hell," said the sheriff.

He unlocked the manacles. The Kid stood up.

"I've taken a good deal from you," said the Kid, slowly, thoughtfully.

"Yes," said the sheriff, "I suppose you have. I may be more than half dead right now because you've taken so much from me. But I was wanting to talk to you. You don't look like a crook. You look as though you *could* go right and settle down, your poor devil."

He waved towards the door.

"That's all," he said. "You can go back to the jail and get your guns and other stuff."

"Thanks," said the Kid. "I'll remember you."

He stepped out into the anteroom and paused there for a moment, handling Gentleman Jefferson Leffingwell and the sodden face of Turk Fadden with his eyes. They did not look back. Carefully they studied the cracks in the floor.

So, after a moment, the Kid left the office and went over to the jail.

Chapter Two

THERE WAS A small passing-port let into the middle of the jail door. Through this the jailer pushed out a wallet, two Colt revolvers, two spring-holsters to wear under the pits of the arms, a knife, two clean handkerchiefs, tobacco, papers, a few odds and ends.

The Kid put them away. Then he said, "I want to see young Texas Charlie."

"You can't," answered the jailer. "Texas is in to stay for a while and you can't see him."

"All right," said the Kid. "You open that door and let me through or else you bring Texas Charlie up to the door to talk to me. Understand?"

"I understand you. You can go to hell," said the jailer.

"Do what I tell you or I'll pry your tin jail open and break you in two. I've stood a lot in this town," said the Kid, gently.

The jailer considered. While he considered, he cursed in a steady stream.

At last he said, "Well, wait a minute," and he disappeared.

Presently another face appeared at the wicket. It was a young, brown, handsome face. It was so brown that the teeth flashed very white in the smile.

"Hey, Montana!" he called, softly, joyously.

"You're going to be out of that in a day or two," said the Kid. "Where are you bound then?"

"Wherever you are is where I'm bound," said the boy.

"You can't trail with me, Cringle," said the Kid.

"Why not?" asked Cringle, his handsome young face growing very long.

"You're too young. You're going home."

"I *won't* go home," said Cringle, angrily. "The old man—"

"I know what he did to you. But he's missing you by this time. You go home."

"I won't," said Cringle.

The Kid stepped close to the door and his face darkened.

"You do what I tell you to do," he said. "If I catch you on the road I'll make you wish you were in hell. You go back home. Tell your father that you're going to walk as straight as a string for a year. For one year you're going to do everything in the world to please him. At the end of the year, if he doesn't please *you* or if you don't please *him,* you can hit the trail again and it won't be very hard to find me if I'm still above the ground. Understand?"

"Why?" asked Cringle, sadly. "Why, Montana?"

"Because I say so," said the Kid, taking the eye of the boy with a firm glance.

"I go out in style, and I come back a dirty bum, in rags. I can see the old man's face!" said Cringle.

"You're going back in good clothes, with money in the pocket," said the Kid. "Here. Take this. Jailer!"

The jailer's face appeared close to the face of Cringle.

"Here's eight hundred bucks. Hold that for the kid. When he's turned loose, let him have it. All of it. Exactly eight hundred dollars. Understand?"

"All right, brother," said the jailer.

"I won't take it," said Cringle.

"You young fool," said the Kid, "you take what's coming to you. You hear me? There's plenty of time for you to pay back that money. Use part to buy a good outfit of clothes. Use part for a railroad ticket. Go home. Just drop in at your father's house and tell him that you're stopping over to say hello—you'll soon be on your way again. You've got money in your pocket.

Then see what happens. Give your father a straight break. He's a straight man."

"Montana, do you mean me to go back?"

"Of course I do. And there's the money to take you."

"My God!" said the boy, with a sob in his throat.

"Quit it," said the Kid.

He grasped the hand of Cringle that was thrust out the wicket.

"Be good!" said the Kid.

He turned away and rolled a cigarette as he walked towards the livery stable.

There were awnings all the way down the street. Walking under them, he kept outside, as close to the supporting pillars as possible. Once a storekeeper came running into a doorway, and the Kid jumped around like a big cat. But he did not draw a gun. He never drew till he saw the flash of another hand.

When he came to the broad, dark doorway of the livery stable, the Kid finished smoking his cigarette standing on the wooden runway.

"Get my horse, Juan," he said to a Mexican.

"Si, Señor Keed," said the Mexican, and disappeared, grinning, running. For he not only knew the face of the Kid, but he knew the sort of liberality that flowed from his hand.

Some one crossed the street. The Kid turned his head a little. Then he turned entirely around.

It was the man of the soggy face, Turk Fadden. He walked rather timidly, as though the dust of the street were ice which he might break through. He lifted his feet carefully, and looked only at the Kid.

When he came close, he said, "Excuse me, Kid."

"Out, bum," said the Kid.

Turk Fadden ventured to meet those slaty-blue eyes for a moment.

"I've gotta see you. I've gotta talk to you, Kid," he said. "It ain't a frame. It's millions. It's the biggest thing you ever seen. I step you into it! Listen to me! I step you into it."

"Out, bum," said the Kid.

The face of the Turk turned gray. Beads of sweat made it glisten.

"My God! Kid," said he, "you don't know. You don't *know!* You're made for the job. Nobody could do it like you!"

He pointed across the street.

"We can step in there and sit down and talk it over. My partner's in there. He's got brains. He's like you, Kid. He's got brains. Come on, will you?"

"Out, bum," said the Kid.

He dusted his smooth brown hands together and waved the Turk away.

Turk Fadden backed up a little. He snarled: "Scared? Think we'd eat you?"

The Kid started.

"All right," he said. "I'll go have a look-see."

He walked with a leisurely step across the street. He used that leisure to scan every window that looked down on him and when he reached the swing doors of the saloon, he kicked them open, and went in with a long step to the side.

A man is never a better target than when he stands at the door of a dim room.

When he was inside, the Kid saw the long, greasy face of Gentleman Jeff Leffingwell at a corner table. Mr. Leffingwell arose and waved genially towards a chair. The Kid went to it.

"Glad to know you," said Leffingwell, holding out his hand.

"Thanks," said the Kid, disregarding the hand.

He slipped into the chair and sat well back in it. Leffingwell looked down at the hand that had not been accepted, smiled a twisted smile, and resumed his own chair. The Turk took the outer place, his back towards the bar.

"What'll you drink, Kid?" he asked.

"A small beer," said the Kid.

"Three small beers, Doc," said the Turk.

They were brought, the sides frosted, bubbles still running down the glass. The Kid raised his glass with his left hand.

"Here's everybody's luck," said he.

He let the beer run down his throat and replaced the empty glass on the table.

"You pour it, eh?" said the Turk, ingratiatingly. "I seen a fellow who put down a quart in eight seconds. I held a stop watch when he done it."

"It's a gift," said the Kid. "What eats the pair of you? How did you slip through the sheriff so fast?"

"He didn't have nothing but a guess on us," said the Turk. "But about the game—it's a big game. It's a game that we couldn't try except with you."

"Why not?" asked the Kid.

"Because you're honest."

"Quit it," said the Kid.

Leffingwell raised a hand to check the Turk.

"It's because you've got blue eyes and black hair," he said. "That's why you can make millions, and we can show you how to make 'em."

Chapter Three

"WHAT'S THE GAME?" asked the Kid, finally, when he had considered his two companions with a long, unfavoring glance. "I'm a busy man. Otherwise, I'd be glad to sit here and talk millions to you fellows all day long."

Gentleman Jeff smiled.

"Here's the way of it," he said. "We put a spot on you, and after the spot is on you're worth a few millions on the hoof."

"What sort of a spot?" asked the Kid.

Leffingwell took a piece of paper and a pen, with which he outlined on the sheet an oddly shaped blotch that contained a broad arc like a new moon with a dot near the inner curve of it.

"If you had a spot like that under the skin, you'd be worth a few millions," said Leffingwell.

The Kid started. No ordinary eye could have detected a change in him, but nevertheless the change was there. The battery was charged, yet he kept his voice calm.

"Where would the spot be, then?" he asked.

"I know a fellow," said Leffingwell, "who has about seven millions in land and cattle. Then he has some mines in the mountains, and some oil has been struck on holdings of his, too. He has the seven millions, one wife, one daughter, but no son. A long time ago, some greasers got mixed up with him. You been much south of the Rio Grande, Kid?"

"I've been in old Mexico a little," said the Kid.

He looked straight into the face of Leffingwell, and his eyes were a dull, slaty blue which revealed nothing at all. He might have been asking for a cigarette. He might have been looking at a distant scene through a window.

"When a greaser gets off you he gets off you for life," said Leffingwell. "He gets through with you. He wants to take your heart out through your backbone. Know that?"

"I've heard people say that," said the Kid. "But what about the mark under the skin?"

"This rich bird that I'm talking about had a son," said Leffingwell, "in the old days. But he got crossed up with some Mexicans, and one day they took the boy right off the place and disappeared with him. The old man has been looking for the brat ever since. Never has found him. And that kid they're sure to know because there was a birthmark on him. There was a birthmark on his left shoulder —it looked like a star and a crescent. It looked like the design for a Turkish flag, you see?"

The Kid drew in a quick breath—of cigarette smoke.

"I see," said he.

"They could spot the brat. He'd be twenty-four years old, now, and he'd have blue eyes and black hair! He'd likely be big. His mother is tall. His father is tall. Only the sister is on the small side."

Leffingwell was silent. He twisted suddenly in his chair.

"Rush on some more beer!" he commanded. "Tall ones, this time."

The Kid sat back. He continued to smoke, and through the smoke he studied the dark and distant mind of Leffingwell.

Turk Fadden leaned forward across the table until it creaked under the weight of his elbows.

"Lookat!" said Turk. "Lookat—what a cinch!"

His face was tilted down, but his smile and his red-stained eyes were visible, looking up like a beast into the face of the Kid.

"Does my mug look like the family picture?" asked Montana.

"No," said Leffingwell. "Not much like, not much unlike. They're a little thinner and longer in the beak. But what does that matter, brother?"

"How would the spot come on me? Like a birth-mark—and made to stay?" asked the Kid. "Tattoo?"

Leffingwell grinned at Turk Fadden, and Fadden grinned also, never taking his hungry eyes from the face of the Kid.

"Tattoo is the trick," said Leffingwell. "I've been in the South Seas. I know how to do the thing. I know birthmarks, too. I've studied 'em since the big idea came. For six months the Turk and I have been watching and waiting for the right *hombre*. A man with the nerve to put the thing through. A man with the blue eyes and black hair. A man we could trust to give us our split."

The Kid considered for a long time. He disregarded the beer that stood before him. Leffingwell took the glass, spilled the contents half into his own and half into Turk's glass, and ordered a fresh supply for the Kid. This, too, remained untasted.

"People have been telling me," said Montana, sneering, "that I ought to settle down."

He allowed another long pause to intervene. Several times Turk Fadden would have spoken, but Leffingwell found his eyes and stopped him. They were like people in a train who have talked themselves out.

"The old man in this picture," said the Kid, at last, "what sort of an *hombre* is he?"

"Mean," said Leffingwell instantly, as though afraid that another opinion might be expressed first. "Mean. Hard as a razor and sharp as a razor. He wouldn't give a nickel to all the beggars in the world. He wouldn't give a damaged nickel. Everybody hates him. He's mean as a snake."

Relief spread gently through the set face of the Kid.

"Well, that's all right," said he. "The old man would be hard to fool, eh?"

"He would be. It would take brains—and nerve—to fool him," said Leffingwell.

Montana nodded and cleared his throat.

"What split would you boys get?" he asked.

"One-third for Turk, one-third for me, one-third for you, Kid."

"No. Fifty-fifty," said the Kid.

"Hey, wait a minute!" said Turk Fadden.

"Shut up, Turk," said Leffingwell. "The Kid's a gentleman. He wouldn't argue about it unless he was right. We'll make it fifty-fifty. As much for you as for Turk and me together."

"What makes you think that I'd go straight?" said the Kid. "What makes you think that I'd come clean and give you any split at all?"

"Because we could tell the right news and open you up wide any time we pleased," said Leffingwell.

"Yeah, we could do that," remarked Turk Fadden, licking his lips.

"Suppose that you decided to step down on me. Any time you pleased you could always blackmail me," said Montana.

"Nobody would bother you, Kid, unless he had to," said Turk Fadden. "We ain't cats. We only got one life apiece. Why would we wanta bother you, Kid?"

The Kid considered this remark.

He merely said, softly, "Everybody says that it's time for me to settle down."

Then he rose from the table and paced up and down the room for a time. He paused near the table, and said, gently, to the empty air, "What a dirty deal!"

"You know how it is," remarked Leffingwell. "A fellow has to take the hands as they fall."

The Kid looked carefully at him, then looked carefully away. He sat down again at the table.

"What's the name of this family?" he asked.

"That's all right," said Leffingwell, smoothly, quietly. "We're going to tell you everything. But the first place, we want to know about how you stand. We know that you're as good as your word. Everybody knows the story about you and McRay and how you came back for him. But before we talk everything straight out, we'd like to have your word."

"I see," said the Kid. "I might let somebody else do the tattooing job on me, eh?"

"Well, every man gets some funny ideas," said Turk Fadden, with an apologetic laugh.

"We'll just shake hands all the way around," said Leffingwell, holding out his long, greasy, yellow hand.

Montana looked at it for a second or two. Then he regarded the faces of his two companions.

"I'll give you my word, Leffingwell," he said. "I'll give you my word, Fadden."

Anxious as the pair were to put their deal through, this assumption of a greater cleanness, a high superiority, made Fadden turn red and Leffingwell green.

"We oughta have an agreement," insisted Fadden. "We oughta have a signed agreement that can't be broke."

26

"You fool!" commented Leffingwell. "A gentleman's word of honor is good enough for me. Besides, documents like that can always be found by those that shouldn't lay eyes on them. You ought to know that."

"Aw, have it your own way," answered Fadden. "What do I care? I was just thinking, was all."

"We'll drink on it," said Leffingwell.

"No, I'm not drinking," said Montana, disgust twisting his lips a little. "But what's the name?"

"The name is Lavery. It's the Richard Lavery ranch down in the Bend."

The Kid whistled.

"I've heard of that. The Lavery place, eh?"

Leffingwell smiled with contentment. He could not help putting out his chest a little.

"When you play with me, brother," said Gentleman Jeff, "you don't play for small stakes. The sky is the limit. Savvy?"

"And old man Lavery is hard-boiled, eh?"

"Like leather."

The Kid fell into a muse. The disgust twitched his mouth more than once.

But at last he said, "Oh, all right."

"That's good," murmured Leffingwell, with a sigh.

"It is," agreed Turk Fadden, rather sullenly.

"I'll go through," said Montana. "After all—they tell me I ought to settle down." He laughed, "I'll settle down, all right."

Chapter Four

THE BEND WAS far away in miles and far away in time; and under the heat of the sun there was still a faint prickling under the skin of the Kid's left shoulder where Leffingwell had done the tattooing, as Montana approached the Lavery ranch.

He paused on the shoulder of a bald, scalped mountain beside a mescal pit, a twenty-five-foot circle of stones heaped high to the windward and lower to the lee. Cactus was still growing plentifully all over the breast of the mountain, so that it was easy to imagine how the Apaches or Comanches of the old days had made the great roast and gone off for a forty-eight-hour debauch on the fermented juices, a silent ecstasy of dreams and wild visions. From this high point it seemed to the Kid that he was looking down into the past, for looping across the valleys and swaying up the distant heights he could trace with his eye a broad, dim chalk mark across the mountains. The lasting grains of that chalk were composed of the bones of men and beasts, for this was the road that the Apaches had followed for centuries when they rode under their "Mexican moon" to ravage the southland, bringing back multitudes of cattle and not a few slaves.

Montana drew his eyes away from the distant time and looked down into the present moment where the Lavery house stood on an upper terrace of the valley of the Lepanto.

The whitewashed 'dobe walls shone like marble. Since it was the Lavery house, it was big, of course, but it looked like a bit of doll's furniture compared with the enormous steps by which the slope of the valley came down to the edge of the creek. Everything about that valley was big, from the red rock walls of the east to the gray rock walls of the west. Straight on the valley held, diminishing, but splitting a slash through the heart of the mountains and running on towards the Rio Grande.

Ten thousand square miles of mountains came lunging and springing on his eye like waves of a sea; their violence made a joyous mental uproar, and it was a pleasure to let the vision slip away down the valley of the Lepanto towards the Rio Grande, where the huge limestone wall of its cañon was divided and the old stream came lazily through.

The Kid, when the full picture spread out before him, regarded it for a long time, thoughtfully. Then he spurred the mustang ahead. It was not a big horse, nor a fine one. It was the sort of range mustang that has a roached back and a ewe neck and a lump of a head. But it had four legs of hammered iron, and red fire in either eye. Montana cared neither for looks in a horse nor for a smooth gait; he simply wanted motive power that would get him over as many leagues as possible in the course of the day's march. He had changed horses and paid boot three times during this long journey.

This was new country. It had a new air. Its dimensions were new. The whole feel of it was new, so he went on at a dog trot. It was the morning of the day. The western wall of the valley burned almost a pure white and the grass that covered the western slopes was luminous as green fire, while all the eastern side was red shadow and dull green shadow, when the Kid rode up to the ranch house. The dimensions of it had been growing steadily, during the last two miles.

No one was visible around the house. The Kid watered his horse at a trough fed from spring water that gushed out of the end of a long pipe, painted red with rust. He put saddle and bridle on pegs in a long shed; the mustang he turned out to graze in a pasture near the house. Then he went to the kitchen door. Through the screen, when he brought his face close to it, he could make out a one-legged man wearing a blacksmith's leather apron, and washing pans with a great rattling at a sink.

The Kid pulled open the screen door.

"Chuck?" he said.

The cook offered no greeting.

"Peel those potatoes," he said.

There was a big dishpan filled with potatoes sitting on a chair near the stove.

The Kid saw half a loaf of bread, a pint tin cup, and a great pot of coffee steaming on the back of the stove. He put the loaf under his arm and filled the cup from the coffee-pot.

"You work before you eat, bum," said the cook.

"That's not Western manners," said the Kid, amiably, gently.

"This ain't the West. This is the Lavery place," said the cook. "Put down that chuck."

"Pick your home town in a hot spot and go there," said the Kid.

The cook picked up a gridiron two feet across. Yellow-dried hot-cake batter stuck in strips to the edges of it. With a powerful under-arm sweep, he hurled the sharp side of it at the head of Montana.

The Kid ducked. The gridiron struck the wall, broke in two pieces, and jangled down against the floor. The whole kitchen gave out a metallic vibration. The Kid sat down, tilted his chair against the wall, and began to eat, while the cook stumped past him, picked up the broken pieces of the gridiron, and examined them.

He returned to the sink and continued to wash the pans. The Kid went on eating. Finally the creaking of saddle leather and the trampling of a horse approached the house.

The cook went to the window, stuck out his head, and said: "Mr. Lavery, there's a tramp in here that's throwed a gridiron at my head and broke it and made me give him a handout. I'm glad you've got back."

The Kid got up, went to the stove, filled his cup with coffee and stepped outside, holding the stump of the loaf in one hand and the coffee in the other. He saw the big man on a big cream-colored horse. Richard Lavery around the eyes looked as sad as a Christian martyr. Around the mouth and jaw he looked as savage as a viking. His hair was gray, but he wore a pair of saber-shaped mustaches sloping past the corners of his mouth. His horse was a charger fit to carry an emperor. Richard Lavery looked, in fact, like an emperor dressed in old ranch clothes.

He took out a handkerchief and wiped his black mustaches until they were bright and sleek.

"I'm looking for a job. I hear that you can use any sort of a man, up here."

"Can you handle a rope, work cows, build fence, ride range, and shoot coyotes?" asked Richard Lavery.

"I can shoot coyotes," said the Kid.

The rancher considered him, without a smile. It seemed that his lean, handsome face was not made for smiling. He had the appearance of a man who had just ruined some powerful enemy and competitor or was about to ruin one.

"I can use any kind of a man up here if the man can use me," said Lavery. "Come along."

The Kid finished his last bit of bread, swallowed the powerful coffee, reentered the kitchen, and placed the empty tin cup on the table. The cook was smiling to himself. He did not lift his grizzled face from the sink where he was washing the pans.

The Kid went outside and followed Lavery to the largest of the sheds near the house. It was filled with all manner of farm implements, from gang-plows and rusty fifth-chains to mowing-machines, big rakes, picks and shovels, a pile of thin casing for wells, Jackson bucks, sacks of nails, and a hundred other articles, new and old, sound and broken. The shed was a hundred feet long and crowded, except in one corner where a blacksmith shop had been fitted up.

"Take a pick and shovel and come with me," said Lavery.

He rode half a mile from the house, with the Kid following, a pick and shovel over his shoulder. At the mouth of a narrow gulch Lavery paused. A foaming stream of water ran down the gulch. It was fed by a small cascade at the farther end, and down the side of the cliff, near the mouth of the little valley, there was a white mist of water falling, also. The rock-cut ravine was twenty feet deep and ten feet wide. Above the level of the gulch spread out eight or ten acres of fertile ground which had been planted out as an orchard, and which flourished. The sleek green of the fruit glistened from the well-pruned branches.

"Dam the mouth of that ravine for me," said Lavery. "This runs dry, part of the year. When you get that water dammed, you eat and get your pay and start as a regular man on this ranch."

He turned his horse and rode off. His back was straight and his shoulders squared.

Montana looked at the pick and shovel, then at the depth of the gulch, the width of it, and the white rush of the currents. He threw in a large rock. It went bounding down the current, throwing up flags of spray.

So he sat down and made a cigarette. His face was calm. There was a dreaming light of pleasure in his eyes. He remembered that the eyes of Richard Lavery, also, had been of a slaty blue. His smile grew more contented.

When the cigarette was finished, he went back to the ranch and entered the great wagon-and-tool shed. He rolled out a light buckboard and loaded it with twenty sections of the thin well-casing. From the blacksmith shop he got a complete soldering outfit, lamp and all. He took a smaller pipe with a joint in it and a coil of heavy hose with a nozzle fitted to one end. Then he harnessed his mustang, hitched it to the tongue of the wagon, and made it drag the load to the mouth of the gulch.

He laid the sections of well-casing in a long file up the side of the gulch, right in the path of the descending shower of water that helped to feed the stream below.

It was hard work. The rock was slippery; the sections of the casing were heavy; the ascent was almost perpendicular. It took him hours to lay those pipes end to end and solder them strongly. But he did not stop working. The lunch hour passed. He merely tightened his belt and kept on. He laid heavy sections of rock against the sides of the casing. Presently he had a pipe line two hundred feet long, laid up against the wall of the gully. It was not at all a permanent structure, but he hoped that it would serve his turn, for he could not eat on this place until the task was done; and if he spent a year simply shoveling earth and gravel and rock into the mouth of the ravine, the force of the water would sweep the stuff away as fast as he dropped it.

When he had the casing in place and wedged as securely as possible, he fitted the smaller pipe into the lower end of it, soldered that more strongly than the rest, and then joined the length of big hose to the pipe.

That done, he climbed to the top of his line of well-casing and laid a series of heavy stones so that they gathered in the spray of the waterfall and formed a funnel to shunt the stream into the mouth of the pipe line. The water was now dropping down a closed flume. The air no longer could strike it to white feathers. It became a heavy force that made the pipe line quiver, then work like a great snake.

The Kid climbed to the bottom of the line, picked up the hose, and opened the nozzle wide. He had forgotten to count on one item, in his little scheme of hydraulic engineering. The released head of water kicked the hose out of his hands. The stream struck his breast and staggered him. The hose fell to the ground, spitting, hissing, leaping, writhing like a python gone mad, beating the heavy brass nozzle against the ground.

The Kid saw that his whole work would quickly be torn to pieces by the forces which he had managed to lock up in it, so he sprang at that dancing nozzle and, mastering the vibrations of it, held it firmly with both hands. It was like a kicking fire-hose. When he played it against the gravel of the side wall, it struck out a shower of stones and mud.

He used that stream like a surgeon's knife on a great scale. First of all, he undermined an immense, over-hanging brow of rock and stratified gravel. He cut deeply into the base of this projection until it sagged with unsupported weight. A great crack opened from top to bottom, along one side. Then the whole mass was loosed and poured with a roar into the gulch beneath. Fifty tons of detritus he delivered at one load and completely blocked the lower part of the little gully. More material followed. He washed the bed of the stream full of gravel; he caused it to heap up above the floor of the small ravine. Still he kept that pow-erful hydraulic tool at work.

The whole mouth of the little valley was a scant twenty feet across. He undercut and dropped the upper slopes that impended over the entrance until the dam was a dozen feet high, a solid mass above the floor of the ravine. A smile of malice crooked the lips of Mon-tana as he saw the backed-up water rising rapidly.

He turned off the hose. He dismantled the pipe line. By the time he had reloaded the wagon, already the bed of the ravine was filled and the water was pouring swiftly over the fine orchard land, scooping it up like dry sand, running terrible trenches deep among the roots of the trees.

Then he hitched the mustang to the tongue of the wagon and returned towards the ranch house in the ruddy glow of the end of the day. He unloaded the well-casing. He restored the unused pick and shovel. He put away the hose, clean and neatly coiled. He replaced the small pipe and the soldering outfit. There was little to tell how he had been employed except the mass of solder that was used up.

The heart of the Kid was at peace when he stepped out of the wagon-shed and walked towards the house. It had been a hard day's labor, but it was according to the desire of his soul!

Chapter Five

A DOZEN MEN loafed around the kitchen veranda. Some of them had finished washing up; some were busy at the runner towels; others were brushing their wet hair to sleekness; others were still at the basins making puffing sounds, sputtering the water over the ground.

Everyone stopped operations to look at the stranger. With calm eyes they observed him, and with calm eyes he regarded them. They were hand-picked. He could see that. They were men who would not say "no" to another hour of work, another round of cards, another drink. And, young or old, they were as tough as seasoned hickory.

Everyone spoke or nodded. The Kid nodded in turn. He filled a basin and began to soap his sore hands. The coolness of the water pleased him, but that pleasure did not compare with the content that was in his heart.

One of the men said: "Something funny. The orchard creek's runnin' dry. There ain't a drop in it this afternoon."

"Lavery'll like that," said another.

They talked of other things, but the Kid kept smiling faintly. His jaw muscles were working. His striking muscles throbbed up and down the length of his arms.

He was brushing his hair as sleek as the others when Richard Lavery walked out of the house.

He went straight up to the Kid.

"You don't eat till you dam the orchard creek," he said.

The Kid squinted into the fly-specked mirror in order to draw straighter the part of his shining black hair. He finished carving the line and parting the hair to either side with hand and brush.

"Go look-see," he said, at last.

He (lid not turn his head, but he could feel Richard Lavery looking at him. He could feel the spreading of the swift silence through the group, the eyes that fastened on him.

He liked that. The pleasure of it tucked his stomach up against his backbone. It made him feel that he could bite straight through an inch bar of steel.

Then Lavery turned, with a faint grunting sound. A moment later he was on a horse and galloping off.

The bawling voice of the cook shouted: "Come and get it! Come and get it!"

The men stood up and began to file into the dining room. When the Kid reached the door the cook, who was standing by, put a hand against his breast.

"You don't feed till the boss takes you on," said the cook.

The Kid walked on. The cook staggered, swore, and then said: "All right; it'll be later."

Several of the men turned around and looked the Kid in the face. They had eyes as uncompromising as the eyes of fighting dogs but the glance of the Kid was soft, almost tender. One word from the cook would start a fight, it was plain. But the cook said only: "It's all right, boys. This is Lavery's job. We'll see what happens, later."

Those cowpunchers smiled grimly and went to their places at the table. There was only one place left for the Kid, so he took Lavery's armchair at the head of the table.

Silently the others considered him and his chair. His blue eyes grew softer, more luminous, as he glanced back at them. Then he commenced to help himself.

The clatter of knives and forks was gathering momentum still when the pounding hoofs of a horse swept up to the house. Heavy heels struck the side veranda. Into the doorway strode Richard Lavery, calling:

"Tumble out, all hands. Get picks and shovels. Crashaw, bring along some dynamite and caps. Move, now! Head for the orchard. It's being drowned and ruined."

There was a rushing and stamping of feet. Two or three chairs overturned with a crash. With that departing tide of men went Lavery, also.

No one was left except the cook, who began to pant heavily.

"You think you're hell, eh?" said he.

The Kid smiled tenderly on him and reached for a redder slice of steak.

"All right," said the cook. "It'll come later!"

The Kid said nothing at all.

He was eating leisurely. The steaks were thick and tender. They were well cooked, crusted brown-black on the outside and full of rich juices that spurted under the knife.

An hour went by. The meat was cold. The fat had congealed to gray glass on the platters. The cornbread no longer was steaming. Only one of the apple pies had been touched. And Montana had made a cigarette. He smoked it, leaning back in his chair, sipping coffee. It was good coffee, sweet, oily, strong.

There was a heavy, distant explosion. That meant that they had finally blasted the dam to turn the water loose and free the orchard from the flood. The strong sweep of the water would saw straight down through the dam, down through the crowded debris in the gulch, and in not many minutes it would undo all the labors of the Kid.

He smiled again.

The door to the kitchen creaked open. The cook looked in and saw the cold food, the smiling face of the Kid.

"Ah, blast your heart!" he said, and closed the door again.

Returning voices at last came towards the house, but when they were close they grew silent.

40

Montana smiled again, rose, refilled his cup with coffee, sat down, and made himself a new cigarette.

He was smoking that when the men poured over the veranda like thunder and came crashing through the doorway into the dining room. Richard Lavery came first.

"Stand up!" he commanded.

His dozen hard men paused behind him, slowly spreading out to either side like clouds behind a thunderhead.

"I'm not through eating," said the Kid. "I'm not through my after-dinner cigarette, either."

"All right," said Lavery. "Take him!"

They hardly began their rush. They hardly had time to more than lean forward when they saw two long Colts glistening in the hands of the Kid. The right-hand gun spoke and the sombrero was flicked from the head of Lavery.

"The next time it won't be just a hat," said Montana.

He swung his left-hand gun a little to the side, carelessly. All movement ceased. Only the kitchen door swayed as the cook stood there, opening his eyes and his mouth.

"It's all right," said Lavery. "He can't get out of the room."

"Not till I'm through smoking," said the Kid. "Not till you've told me that I'm a permanent hand at forty dollars a month. I built your dam for you! That was all you wanted."

He leaned back in his chair. He abandoned the left-hand gun to remove the cigarette from between his lips and smile his gentlest, bluest smile upon them all.

They hardly looked at him. Instead, they regarded Lavery. He was red and purple, in patches.

"Sit down, men," he commanded. "It's not over, but sit down."

The Kid crushed out his cigarette on his plate as they settled themselves in the chairs. He had a man on his right and on his left, very close. Either of them could snatch at a gun, if either of them chose. But they only scowled and busied themselves in reaching for the cold, greasy food. The coffee, even, was only tepid.

There were chairs for everyone except Richard Lavery himself. The cook had to bring him a kitchen chair. He sat at the other end of the table, far away. The vast effort at self-control took the red out of his face and left him gray.

"I think you're only a young fool," said Lavery. "You've half ruined my orchard, but I think that you're only a young fool. I'm going to try to keep reasonable. What's your name?"

"You can take your choice," said the Kid. "Some people call me the Montana Kid, and some call me the Chicken-feed Kid, and some call me Oroville Kid, and some the Smiling Kid, and some just call me the Kid. I'm not one to pick and to choose. I answer to almost any name except—Fool!"

He waited an instant.

Then he stood up and slowly, deliberately, put away

42

his guns inside his coat. His eyes picked up the glances of the hardy men of Lavery, one by one, until those glances wavered.

He said: "I've finished eating and I've finished my after-supper smoke, so I'm going out to have some fresh air. It's a little close in here for my kind of a man."

He turned his back on them and sauntered slowly towards the door. He heard a rumble and a stir behind him. Then the voice of Lavery snapped: "Sit fast. This is my business. I'll settle it in my own way!"

The Kid opened the door and walked out into the sweetness of the mountain night.

Chapter Six

IN THE EAST there was a moon with a body as curved and hollow as the hull of a Chinese junk, but although it was not much past its first phase, it cast enough light to show the Kid the valley as a thing of dimly glistening plateaus and cavernous darknesses down to where the river was gleaming.

A rider loped up the valley trail to the water-troughs, and dismounted with a flutter of divided skirts. Montana approached.

"Hello!" said he. "Are you part of this outfit?"

"I'm Ruth Lavery. Are you a new hand, or just here for the night?"

"I'm Montana, and I'm a new hand."

"I thought Dad was full up," she commented.

43

"Yeah. But I'm an irrigation expert. I irrigated the whole orchard, today."

He chuckled. She pulled the bridle over the head of the mustang and held it by the mane while it drank. "Why should the orchard be irrigated?"

"I don't know. I just follow orders."

"Where are all the rest?"

"They're eating. They were working extra late."

"But not you?"

"No, not me. Your father didn't want me for the extra work. Here, I'll put that horse out to grass."

"Thanks," she answered, and looking upwards muttered: "There's that beast of an owl again! I wish—"

The Kid pulled a gun as he saw the broad silhouette shooting soundlessly overhead. He fired twice, with a slight interval between, as though he were gauging the distance in some manner; then he fanned the hammer with his thumb so rapidly that three more explosions followed in almost a single roar.

The owl staggered in the air, swooped in a half-circle, then landed with a soft thud hardly twenty steps from them.

"You got it! That's shooting!" said the girl.

She ran towards the owl, but the Kid took the horse to the pasture, turned it into the field to graze, and then put away the saddle and bridle. When he returned, Ruth Lavery was crouching close to the great bird. It looked almost as large as the girl. It swelled. The ruff of the neck feathers stood out. It hissed like a snake,

44

but it was dying; it kept from falling only by stretching out its great wings.

"Kill it, Montana," said the girl. "Look at those eyes! They're like night lamps. It looks like a fiend, doesn't it; but the poor devil is suffering. Kill it."

"No," said the Kid. "It's dying fast enough and I've wasted five shots on it. Besides, I don't mind watching it die."

She looked suddenly, silently, up at him. The moon glinted on her cheek bone and jaw. She was pretty, but she looked like her father.

"I saw an owl prong a rabbit in a field one day," he explained. "I heard the rabbit screech. This is the first owl I've killed since that day."

The wings of the big bird crumpled. It tipped forward to the ground.

"You're pretty hard, Montana," said the girl.

He picked up the owl by both wings. For its size, it was amazingly light. The wind kept the feathers trembling.

"That rabbit screeched like a woman," said the Kid. "I don't mind seeing owls die, since then."

"Where have you been hearing women screech?" asked the girl, slowly rising to her feet. Montana considered her for a long moment.

"Well, I'll carry the owl in for you," he said.

"It's yours," she said. "You shot it."

"You ordered it out of the sky," said the Kid, "and I'm only a hired man. I guess the Laverys have sky rights as well as water rights all over their land."

"That—" she began. Then she changed her voice. "Have I stepped on your toes?" she asked.

"You've just been a little natural," he answered. "You've just been a little Laverish."

This angered her, but still she wanted to justify herself.

"About the women screeching," she said. "I don't know. Maybe you *have* been where women screech a lot."

"Down in old Mexico a fellow hears a lot of things," he said, "but it's all right. If you stepped on my toes, I guess I stamped right back."

"You did," said the girl.

He took off his hat.

"I'm sorry, Miss Lavery," he said.

Now that the shadow was removed, she could see his face. He counted a second and a half while she looked straight into it. He knew all about his face. It had done a lot for him in his life.

"What do you say we quit?" said Ruth Lavery.

"That's all right with me. Do you want this owl?"

"I do," she answered. "That's the murderer that's been killing our chickens, I think."

"No," he answered. "An owl like this catches things that sleep out or move around at night. It kills rabbits and mice and all sorts of things like that. It does a lot of good."

"Why did you kill it, then?" she asked.

"You told me to," said the Kid.

This was not exactly true, but she chuckled.

"All right," she said. "You're the sort of a fellow who has to win, I see."

He walked with her down the side of the house, past the windows of the bunk room and the dining room. They turned the corner and came to the wing which was occupied by the Lavery family. The doors and windows were open to the cool of the night. Through the windows he saw that everything inside was soft colors and pools of light.

"Bring it into the patio, will you?" she asked. "I want mother to see the spread of the wings. It's a beauty."

They crossed a living room and entered a patio garden where a fountain was leaping up out of the shadows and into the moonlight, leaping and falling and leaping again. There was table for two laid near the fountain, with a lamp shining on it. On the verge of the lampshine a gray-headed woman lay in an invalid chair.

"Mother, you should have eaten!" cried the girl. "I didn't dream you'd wait. I got off to take a look at the tracks of a whole herd of deer and that rat of a roan broke away from me. It was more than an hour before I could catch it again."

"It's all right," said a deep, husky voice. "I didn't worry a great deal."

"This is Montana, our new man," said the girl. "He shot this owl just now. He *can* shoot. Look at it. Look at the neck feathers and over the shoulders. Isn't it lovely?"

The Kid held it up by both wings. Where the lamp-light struck, the feathers showed a mottling of gray and tan in delicate patterns, but the Kid felt that Mrs. Lavery was looking not at the dead bird, but at him.

"Get ready for dinner, Ruth," she said. "Will you stay a minute more, Montana? I want to see the eyes. They're enough to frighten one, aren't they?"

The girl was gone. Her feet rattled across the gravel, thudded over the floor of the house, and were lost to hearing with the slamming of a door.

"They've frightened plenty of things," said the Kid.

She touched the gloss of the wing.

"You're much younger than most of the men my husband employs," she said. "You're not more than twenty-four, are you?"

"No," said the Kid. "I'm twenty-four."

He shifted back a little, glad of a ghostly arm of shadow that crossed his face. He was pleased enough to have most women look into his face, but not this one. There was too much hunger in her eyes and inexhaustible pain.

"You come from Montana, then?" she said, smiling, nodding a little.

"I don't know," said the Kid. "As much Montana as anything. I'm one of the drifters."

"Well, you're young and strong. That's the time for drifting, I suppose. Have you been away from home long?"

"Home?" said Montana, truthfully. "That's where I draw a blank. I've always been on the loose."

"Ah?" she said, with an intake of breath. "My poor lad!"

It was hard for him to keep smiling. It was hard for him to meet her eyes. They were not a slaty but a luminous blue like the eyes of her daughter. She had been beautiful, once; the skeleton of beauty was still there. Pain that had worn the soft flesh away had left something of the spirit to take its place. The Kid wanted to go away. He wanted to turn his back on what he was feeling.

"Oh, I've had a pretty good life, all the way from Mexico to Montana," said the Kid. "You know. People are good to a kid that hasn't a proper name or a home and all that sort of thing."

"Ah, I hope they are good," said Mrs. Lavery. "I've thought of that very thing, more than once. Even when you were a little thing were they good to you? Were they specially good to you even when you were just a baby? Or have you always been a hardy fellow?"

She smiled at him. The Kid had faced guns. He faced that smile, also.

"Far back as I can remember, I was a tough little *hombre*," said he, "but people were pretty good to me. About the first thing I can remember was trying to wring the neck off a big turkey gobbler. He gave me a whanging with his wings and scratched me up a lot. I should have got a beating for that, but I remember that I got the gobbler, instead—roasted! People are like that. They're good to a kid."

She laughed. There was a drawling sound of content in her laughter. There was a drawling pleasure in her eyes, also. She shook a finger at him.

49

"You were a rascal, I see," said she, "but I'm glad to know that people were kind to you."

Hurrying steps came towards them. It was Ruth Lavery in a dress as gay as a bit of mist that the sunset colors. It was bright even through the shadow. In the lampshine it cast a glow on her brown face. She was very pretty. When she turned her head her throat was a thing to see, but she never would be a beauty like her mother.

A heavier step came out of the house at the same moment.

"Hello, Richard!" said Mrs. Lavery. "Was it a good day?"

The Kid turned.

"You?" said Lavery. "I might have guessed, I suppose. Get out!"

Chapter Seven

THE KID PUT both wings of the owl into one hand, his left hand. He looked at Lavery as he said, "Shall I put the owl down here, Miss Lavery?"

Over his last words rushed the voices of both the women. Mrs. Lavery was saying, "Richard, you mustn't!" And the girl exclaimed: "Father, I asked him to come in! I never heard of such a thing! I *asked* him to come in!"

"Ask him to get out, then," said Lavery.

"Hush!" said the mother. "There must be some explanation. Richard, please tell us why—"

50

"Don't bother about that," said the Kid. "I'm going. It's all right."

"I won't let you go till I hear something else!" cried the girl. She stepped in front of him and faced her father.

"I asked him to come in. You can't order him out like a dog," she cried.

"Ruth!" said the mother.

"I don't care," said the girl.

She shuddered. Her head went back. Her hair almost touched the face of the Kid and Richard Lavery looked steadily at her. No one could tell what was locked up in his mind behind the iron of his face.

"This fellow is a thug and a gunman," said Lavery. "He's probably made a bet that he could stay a few days in this valley whether I wanted him here or not. With one of his fool practical jokes he half ruined the orchard today. I'm telling him to get out of the valley. I'm warning him that the other men know he's an intruder and not wanted. Ruth, stand away from him and let him go."

The girl twisted around and took hold of the arm of the Kid. Her face was sick. Her eyes were big. She looked more like her mother, for a moment.

"Will you come outside with me, Montana?" she asked.

"Certainly I will," said the Kid.

"Stay where you are, Ruth," said Lavery. "If you cross me now, I'll—"

"Richard!" cried Mrs. Lavery.

There was something in her voice that made all three turn suddenly towards her. Her husband strode suddenly to her and crouched by the chair, holding her hands.

The Kid muttered: "Go back to her. Go quick!"

"No," said the girl. "I'm going to—escort you out—"

He went with her through the living room. On the ground outside, he dropped the weight of the owl to the ground. She still had her hand on his arm so that he could feel how she trembled.

"It's all horrible and shameful. I don't know what you've done. I don't care. I know you were my guest and I know you were insulted. I'm sorry. I apologize."

"Don't you apologize," said the Kid. "I'll tell you something—"

He made a pause. "You don't need to apologize. But,—! you're a fine sort. Good night."

He went around the corner of the house and, at a little distance from it, he looked through the open door into the bunk room. All the men were there. Half a dozen were playing cards. Others were in their bunks, all facing towards the door. The stage was set to wait for the entrance of a leading character.

"Oh, go to blazes, everybody!" whispered the Kid. "I can't go through with it, anyway!"

He went out to the pasture, found his mustang, brought it in, got his saddle and bridle in the shed, and made ready to leave the place. The sound of the mother's voice was never out of his ears.

So he rode grimly past the house. He was just opposite the door of the bunk house when he heard the voice of a man burst out with laughter.

He checked the mustang and waited. Several other voices joined. The Kid forgot all about Mrs. Lavery and her daughter. He remembered only Richard Lavery's iron face and the twelve good men and true who punched cows on this place and now lay in wait for him.

He turned the horse, rode back to the shed, put up saddle and bridle, and threw his blanket roll over his shoulder. He put the glad mustang back into the field and returned towards the house. He walked straight up the side of the wall, keeping close to it, stepping as soundlessly as a cat. Then, turning, with one long stride he was up the steps and inside the bunk room.

Every man was facing him and every man stirred just a little, as a hand jerks when a fly lights on it. One man stood up. That was Ransome, lame in one leg, fifty-five years old, with a bald, blond head and a bulldog face.

The Kid did not speak. He did not hurry forward. He came to a dead halt, surveyed every face, and then went slowly forward. Behind him, guns were out. He knew it.

Towards the farther end of the room near the window—cowboys are mortally afraid of a draught indoors—he found an empty bunk. On this he rolled down his blankets. He kept his back turned for a long time. Then he straightened, stretched his arms over his head, and yawned.

The game of cards had stopped. The men were looking at one another. Electric currents of tension were passing from mind to mind and from soul to soul. Here and there a hand was gripped into a fist, but no guns were in sight—now.

The Kid took out the makings and sifted tobacco into a wheat-straw paper. His coat was open. His hands were a thousandth part of a second from the two heavy guns that hung under his armpits. He looked down towards the wheat-straw paper, but he was seeing anything that happened in the room, particularly anything that chanced to move with speed. Above all he was aware of Ransome, still fixed statue-like in the middle of the floor.

Ransome said, suddenly: "The chief don't want you here. Get out!"

Montana went on rolling the cigarette with a consummate care, making the little cylinder perfectly symmetrical.

Ransome called: "The chief don't want you and we won't have you. Get out!"

The Kid said nothing. Some one sat up in a bunk and twisted around. That was the cook. He was grinning, but nobody else smiled.

"Well, boys," said Ransome.

Every man in the room arose. Ransome walked straight towards the Kid. If he had come slowly the rest would have followed, shoulder to shoulder, but he went too fast, so they made only a few steps, then paused to watch.

Ransome came up to the Kid, swung his hand with a broad, clumsy gesture, and struck. The Kid saw the blow coming for eternities. He had time to finish his cigarette, put it in his mouth, dodge the blow, and pull two guns. But he stood fast. He was seeing everything with wonderful clarity as though the sun had shone through clouds upon a winter landscape.

The flat of the hand struck his cheek with a resounding whack. His head was jarred. His skin burned. But he only stared straight back into the savage eyes of Ransome, who was shouting, "Get out, I say!"

"You shouldn't have done that," said the Kid.

There were ten guns or more in the hands that were ranged around the room. The Kid regarded not them but the foreman. Ransome went backwards a step, looking Montana up and down, then he turned about and went back towards the table, slowly, so that a limp appeared in his walk.

"Put up your guns, you dirty hounds!" said Ransome.

They were agape, but they began to put away their guns. They were paralyzed by something that they did not understand.

Ransome put his fists on the table and leaned on his arms.

"No," he said, " I shouldn't have done that. Not at my age!"

The Kid sat down on the edge of the bed, lighted his cigarette, and began to undress.

"No," said Ransome, "I shouldn't have done that. And I shouldn't have *had* to do it. But there ain't any men any more. Except the murderers, there ain't any men any more."

He walked out of the room. The door of the bunk room was never shut in such summer weather, but Ransome seemed to forget this. He slammed the door shut behind him as though he wanted to close the thought of the bunk room out of his mind.

The Kid went on undressing. He took off his coat and hung it up. He took off the two spring holsters from beneath his armpits and laid the guns under the blanket at the head of the bed. He pulled off his boots, stripped, took up a blue-striped flannel nightgown, and dropped it over his head.

He walked in his bare feet to a shelf that was hung from the wall, heaped with newspapers and magazines. He picked out a newspaper, yellow at the edges, carried it hack, got into bed, shook out the long sheets of paper, and began to read.

Now and then he put out a hand and flicked ashes from the end of his cigarette to the floor.

He could hear the others moving, but there were no voices. It was the silence of a church or a funeral.

Every instant of this time, he knew, was being photographed in the brain and soul of all the men who were there. He knew that they felt small and young and weak. A savage complacence grew in him. He forgot the stinging of his cheek.

Bunks began to creak. Men were getting into bed.

He sat up, threw the butt of his cigarette out through the window, lay down, and turned away from the light.

He closed his eyes. He wanted to smile, but he controlled his face as though some one were bending over him, taking note of his facial expression.

He made himself breathe deeply. He smoothed the furrows of his forehead. He made every muscle of his body soften, relax, prepare for slumber.

After a time some one muttered, loudly, "Oh, well—"

The lantern was blown out. A puff of darkness swept over the room, but the Kid was already sound asleep and smiling a little, unconsciously.

Chapter Eight

IN THE MORNING the Kid was the first up, for he was one of those natures that require little sleep. As he walked out through the grayness of the room he heard a man groaning. That was Ransome. His bald, blond head glistened a little as he turned it rapidly from side to side, moaning in his sleep.

The Kid observed this phenomenon for a moment with a stony face. Then he went outside into the dawn, pumped some water into a basin, scratched his beard, and looked towards the kitchen door.

"Hey, cook!" he called.

"Yeah? yeah?" answered the cook.

He came to the door and pushed it open.

"Can I have some hot water for shaving?" asked the Kid.

"Well, of all the nerve!" said the cook.

The Kid began to laugh. He took out a little roll of

canvas, spread his shaving-kit, and worked up a lather with the cold water. He shaved himself without stepping to a mirror. He even found the exact edge of the thick hair above his cheek without the use of a glass.

When his face was clean he passed his hand over it, felt the draw of the damp, smooth skin against his finger tips, and was pleased.

He went out to the field, caught the mustang, saddled it, watered it, tethered it for future reference.

The other men were up, now, getting ready for breakfast. He made it a point to keep away from them. He waited until the cook bawled out, "Come and get it!" then he went in, last of all. The men were sitting down. Again there was no place for him, but the rancher's chair at the head of the table was again unoccupied. He walked to this and sat down.

For breakfast they had fish, fried potatoes, hot cakes, molasses, and coffee. The Kid was a big eater. He helped himself plentifully.

Suddenly the voice of Ransome said: "You oughta know, Montana, that Lavery has gone to town. Maybe knowing that'll do you some good. Maybe I oughtn't to tell you, neither, but I dunno why I should hold out news on you—not to favor nobody on *this* man's ranch!"

He looked around the table slowly. He looked at every face. The men bowed their heads and continued to eat.

The Kid said. "Thanks, Ransome. That news ought

to do me some good, but I'm just a fool. I'm going to stay and see what happens."

Two or three men cleared their throats, which nervousness had caused to contract. That was the only comment.

"I want to tell you something," said the Kid.

Only Ransome looked towards him, as though it were patent that the Kid would speak to no one but him.

"Fire, my boy," said Ransome.

"When you walked down the room last night," said the Kid, "you made a big mistake. You walked too fast. You walked away from a lot of fellows who were ready to follow you to hell and back. But you walked away from them. It looked as though you wanted to play a lone hand. Afterwards, you told them to put up their guns and you're the boss."

Ransome opened a mouth filled with food and gaped. He looked askance, rolling his eyes at the Kid, then down the line of faces opposite him. All heads were down. Every face was suddenly flushed and all brows were knit.

"Well, I'll be hanged!" said Ransome. "I didn't think of that. Well, I *will* be hanged."

"No," said the Kid. "You're not the one that'll be hanged. I'm the one. You've crowded all these fellows against the wall. They've *got* to kill me, now! You've crowded them so hard they've got to."

"I give it up," said Ransome. "You oughta know. About things like that you oughta know. I'm just telling you that the chief has gone to town, though. He didn't think he could depend on what would happen to you out here, it looks like."

Two or three of the men raised their heads. Their faces were redder than sunburn. They looked into the eyes of one another. They felt more manly. They felt that they had been redeemed by praise from a great enemy. Every man at that table felt that he, personally, might soon be so crowded that he would have to kill the Kid. But every man felt that the job might wait awhile. The Kid knew that they were fighting-stuff. It was true; and the Kid knew it! That knowledge was enough to justify their manliness. What do you want, after all? The world with a fence around it?

As they filed out, after breakfast, Ransome said to the Kid: "I'm sorry about last night. You can go to blazes for all of me, but I'm sorry about last night."

"That's all right," said the Kid. He put his hand on the powerful shoulder of the foreman. "I know I can go to blazes for all you," he said, "but it's all right."

Ransome went outside with him. They stood shoulder to shoulder, rolling cigarettes.

"What do you think, anyway?" asked Ransome. "You think you can fight the whole world?"

"No, I can't fight the whole world. I might kid it a little, though," said the Kid.

"Yeah. You're kind of funny," said Ransome. "Whatcha gunna do today?"

"Ride with you and learn something about cows, if you'll let me."

60

"Ride with me? All right. You ride with me, then," said Ransome.

So the Kid rode with him all day.

When he started off in the morning every man watched him. Every man saw that he could handle a horse like an Indian and every face darkened.

They came to a cow bogged on the edge of a "tank."

"Tail that cow out," said Ransome to the Kid.

"How do you tail out a cow?" asked the Kid.

There were two other punchers in that group. They stared. Imagine not knowing how to tail out a bogged cow! Ransome grinned and explained. The Kid tried. Everything went wrong. He couldn't get the cow's tail properly caught over the pommel of the saddle. He got covered with mud. He was mud from head to foot. His face was caked with it.

Ransome and the two punchers laughed and laughed.

The Kid waded through the next stream they crossed. He ducked under and came up free from mud. The men laughed again.

"Well," said the Kid, "I had to get clean some way, didn't I?"

They looked at one another, still laughing.

"He had to get clean some way, eh," said one.

They laughed again.

"The sun will dry me pretty soon," said the Kid.

"The sun will dry him pretty soon!" they said, and roared with mirth again.

Everything that the Kid did pleased them because everything he did was a failure.

Ransome told him to rope a heifer that seemed to be bothered with specially thick clouds of flies. The Kid chased that calf for two miles, trying his rope again and again but never managing to more than slap her with it. And the three men sat their horses in the center of the circle and actually laughed till they cried.

The Kid gave it up. He came back and said: "Ransome, I'm beaten. I can't do it. Hang it, I always thought throwing a rope was dead easy. I see I'm wrong."

"Throwing a rope is easy—for some folks," said Ransome. "Buck, go daub your rope on that calf."

Buck loped his cutting-horse towards the calf, shaking out the noose of his lariat. The heifer, taught by fear, bolted. The cutting-horse followed its doublings and dodgings like a shadow. The noose shot, caught hold, and the calf went down with a whang as the cutting-pony sat down against the slack. The four feet of the calf were tied and Buck was smoking a cigarette when the others came up.

Said the Kid: "That's the slickest thing I ever saw. Will you teach me how to do that, Buck?"

"Sure I'll teach you," said Buck.

"How long will it take?" said the Kid.

"Oh, about twenty years is all," said Ransome.

And they laughed again. The Kid joined in the laughter, too, gently, shaking his head.

"I'm no good," said the Kid. "I couldn't do a man's work on this ranch."

"Yeah, you could learn, though," said Ransome. "If you wanted to, you could learn."

"I'll tell you something," said the Kid. "Why shouldn't I try? I'm sort of tired of a lot of things I've been doing."

They did not laugh at this. They looked at one another fixedly.

After a time they started repairing a line of fence where the barbed wire sagged. The Kid worked seriously. He worked until all four started home for lunch.

"Say, Kid," said Ransome, "how did you build that dam in one day? You tell me, will you?"

"Well," said the Kid, "it was like this. I got a lot of well-casing and made a regular flume and washed down the whole side of the hill with hydraulic power. I put all the stuff back in the shed. You'll see the solder sticking to the joints of the casing."

They laughed again, more heartily than ever.

"You could have a steady job with *me*, brother," said Buck. "That is, if I had a ranch big enough to hold you!"

When they got back to the ranch house, the cook was asking for wood, roaring for it from his door.

"Pack in some wood for him, Kid," said Ransome.

The other cowpunchers were standing about, washing up. With curious eyes they watched the Kid hurry to the woodpile and run the load into the kitchen and thunder it down into the woodbox.

"Is that enough?" asked the Kid.

"The woodbox'll tell you when it's full!" roared the cook.

The Kid labored for ten minutes, filling the box until he had corded the wood high on top of it.

"That about right?" he asked.

"Aw, get out of here!" said the cook.

The Kid went outside. The men were laughing. Buck was talking to them and they were roaring with mirth. The noise died away a little when the Kid appeared, but merry eyes were still fixed on him. He pretended not to notice. He began to sing as he washed his hands and face.

When they went in for lunch there was an extra plate and chair for the Kid.

Chapter Nine

AFTER LUNCH MONTANA built fence—an arduous and disgusting labor—most of the afternoon. The weather had turned humid and close towards the middle of the day and the heat still was increasing when he came in with Buck across the valley. They found most of the other punchers already in the "lake." It was merely a big pool behind a ledge of harder rock that stretched across the creek as a natural dam. There was a good depth right up to the shore and a number of high rocks from which one could dive. Obviously it was meant for swimming, and Buck and the Kid had their clothes off in no time and joined the rest at the sport.

If the Kid and his guns had filled the eyes of the ranch hands since his arrival, he filled them still more now that he was stripped. When he stood on top of the thirty-foot red rock, laughing and waving the rest out of the way, he looked to them like a great golden-brown seal. And when he went smoothly into the lake from the height and, slipping far under the surface, upset Stew Ransome, the content and the delight of the cowpunchers were past words.

Their shouting was still filling the valley when the cook came down to them, riding on a mule, with the stump of his wooden leg hooked over the pommel of the saddle. He was putting the mule to a trot that bounced him here and there on the saddle. He called out and waved both arms, from a distance. When he came near he shouted: "Lavery and the sheriff and a coupla deputies have reached the house. Vamoose, Montana!"

The Kid stood up at the edge of the lake and put his hands on his wet hips.

"Tell them the water's fine down here," he said.

The cook went back up the slope with his head turned over his shoulder like a dog that has been sent home from hunting. As for the other punchers, they gathered about the Kid and tried to persuade him to common sense. They swore that Richard Lavery was a grim fellow who would not be denied his own way.

But the Kid left them still talking and, diving into the water, he went across it to the farther shore with a powerful crawl stroke that threw up a bow-wave before his face. Those who tried to follow him were left far behind. He stood up on the red rock, again, still laughing, panting, with the ripple of his muscles showing through the sleek of his brownness. Then Richard Lavery and two strange men who carried rifles balanced across the pommels of their saddles came out from the rocks. Lavery's voice called, "There he is—there on top of the rock!"

He pointed. The sheriff was so sun-blackened that the gray of his beard looked white against his face. He picked up his rifle and held it at the ready. His eyes sharpened, like the old antelope-hunter that he was.

"Stick up your hands!" he shouted.

"All right," said the Kid.

He put his hands high over his head, tilted forward, and flashed down through the air in a perfect dive, bright in the sunlight and still glistening through the shadow until he clove the water. It thumped together behind his feet.

The sheriff watched the golden streak sliding far underwater and coming up near the shore.

The Kid rose where the stream was hip-high and stood there with his chest going up and down, every rib showing at the depth of the inhalation, all the belly muscles pulling taut.

"What's biting you?" asked the Kid.

"You're wanted," said the sheriff.

"By what, grandfather?" asked Montana.

The ranch hands came up dripping from the lake. With solemn faces and lighted eyes they listened to Montana. It takes a public disaster to make a sheriff a popular man.

"You're wanted by the law," said the sheriff, in a dry voice.

"What law?" asked the Kid.

"My law—the county law—the state law," said the sheriff. "You're under arrest for—"

"All right," said the Kid. "You and your law go to blazes. I haven't finished my swim."

He turned about.

"Come right up here," snapped the sheriff, "or by the nation, I'm gonna put a bullet right through the sleek of you."

"You try it!" said the Kid, without turning his head, stepping onto a rock at the edge of the lake.

"Put down the gun, Marston!" said Lavery. "Don't shoot!" He was shouting out the words now. "You— you—come back here, a minute!"

The Kid turned a little.

"What's the matter, Santa Claus?" said he. "What's biting you?"

Lavery had flung himself from his horse and was running forward.

"Stand fast there a minute!" he was crying.

"I'm tired of the face you wear,", said the Kid. "Back up or I'll take *you* for a swim. Back up!" he added, his voice ringing out suddenly. "If you put a hand on me I'll tear the arm out of you!"

Richard Lavery stood close, pointing a trembling hand at Montana.

"There's something on your back—where did you get that?" he asked.

It was on the tip of the Kid's tongue to say, "By a tattooing-needle," for he knew perfectly what was meant, but he merely frowned.

"What's on my back? Water?" he asked.

He slicked his black hair and flipped water from his hand to the ground.

"There's a mark on you," said the rancher.

"It's not *your* brand," said the Kid, sneering.

"On your left shoulder," said the rancher. "There's a mark on your left shoulder blade. Will you let me see it again?"

"I'm not a prize steer to be looked at," said the Kid.

"Wait a minute, Kid," said Stew Ransome. "There's something behind all this. The chief means something. Great Scott! there's an idea just jumped into my own head! I've heard something—why didn't I think—"

"All right, Stew, all right," said the Kid. "*You* can treat me like a mustang on a rope, if you want to. But not that—"

He filled in the blank with a grim look at the rancher. And then, as he turned, Richard Lavery gripped the arm of Ransome.

"How does it look to you, Ransome?" he asked. "Is it under the skin?"

Stew Ransome peered closely.

"It's under the hide, all right," said he. "There's a kind of a transparency of the skin and the smoke of the mark comin' up into it. Why?"

Lavery put his hand on a rock and then sat down.

"Wait a moment," he said.

Everyone had drawn in close. The sheriff and his deputy were still on their horses, rifle in hand. The cowpunchers stood solidly banked around the central spot where the Kid confronted Lavery, with Ransome between them.

"What's the big idea?" asked the Kid, sternly. "What's knocked the old boy out? Has there been a fall in the price of beef? Is that the news he read on my back?"

Ransome was almost as drawn of face as Lavery. He gave the Kid one sharp glance.

"You shut up," he said. "Something's happening—maybe! I've got a crazy guess. How are you chief?"

Lavery stood up with a manifest effort. His eyes were wild.

"Boy," he said to the Kid, "what marked you on the back? Tell me the truth of it."

"No branding-iron, anyway," said the Kid. "What's the matter with you? What's the matter with all of you? Are you loco? Did you never see a birthmark before?"

"Do you hear, Ransome?" said Lavery. "It *is* a birthmark!"

"Quit it," said the Kid. "I'm tired of being looked at."

The sun and wind had dried him. He strode suddenly to his clothes, bursting the closely packed group asunder. He began to dress, facing them, frowning disdainfully.

"Watch him," said the sheriff to the deputy. "Get his guns!"

The sheriff kept his rifle at the ready.

"There'll be no monkey shines," he commanded.

"This is the queerest game I ever took a hand in," said the Kid. "What sort of cards are you using?"

Lavery had followed him. He came right up to the Kid and put a grip on the rubbery muscles of his forearm. The Kid looked down at the trembling hand and then up at the face of Lavery.

"What the hell is biting you, Lavery?" asked Montana.

"You're exactly twenty-four?" asked Lavery.

"I suppose so," frowned the Kid. "What are you trying to hang on me?"

"Were you born in May?" asked Lavery.

"I don't know," said the Kid. "Take your hand off me. I'm sick of this business."

"You're fatherless and motherless?" asked Lavery.

The Kid stared at him and made no answer. One of the cowpunchers broke out with an excited oath and was still. Everyone was still.

Lavery said: "Will you tell me another thing? Where do your first recollections begin?"

The Kid made a long pause, still frowning. He shook off the hand of Lavery with a sudden and violent gesture.

"I remember back to Mexico, and what of it?" he demanded.

Richard Lavery pulled himself up straight. He turned around to the sheriff. His voice had the self-control of the sick-room.

"We'll go up to the ranch," he said. "I don't need—

ah—I don't need your guns, it seems. The fact is that perhaps this young man may have a claim to this ranch, whether I want him on it or not!"

The Kid was pulling on his boots. He stopped the work.

"What the devil do you mean by that?" he asked.

"You don't know your father and mother," said Lavery, in the same subdued voice. "Your memory begins in old Mexico. You're twenty-four years old. Well—twenty years ago my four-year-old son was kidnapped by a gang of Mexicans and carried across the Rio Grande. And he had eyes and hair the color of yours—"

"Oh, hell!" said the Kid. "What's this going to be? Is this something out of a fool book?"

"Fiction is a half-wit compared with truth, my boy," said Lavery. "On the back of my little son there was an oddly shaped birthmark. It was a crescent and a spot—black-brown."

The Kid had one boot on and one boot off when he jumped up to his feet. Everyone was leaning forward, hushed, taking notes on an historic occasion. And it was worth remembrance that Lavery was trembling like a leaf. It was worth remembrance that the Kid was sneering.

"I think I see the way this bird flies," said the Kid, grimly. "I'll tell you something. There's none of your blood in me, Lavery. If there were, I'd cut myself open and let it out! What's a mark on the skin? It's the feeling in my bones that tells me I'm no kin of yours!"

Chapter Ten

IT WAS AN odd thing to see Lavery take this blow and merely nod under the shock of it, with his mouth pulling a little to the side. Stew Ransome said: "Shut up, will you? Shut up!"

"Oh, all right," said the Kid, to Ransome.

He sat down and pulled on his other boot. He was silent. He had the face of one who is cursing his luck. When he stood up he looked sullenly towards Lavery.

"Well?" said the Kid.

Lavery answered: "Even if I'm right—and I can't be wrong—you'd better come up to the house with me and talk things over."

He took his horse by the reins and led it slowly forward, turning a little to wait for the Kid to join him. The Kid made a pace or two after him, then looked back towards the semicircle of cowpunchers whom silence had covered like the shadow from the western rocks. The Kid walked on beside Lavery with long strides.

Lavery kept looking ahead of him. The sheriff and his deputy fell in behind, very much—with their balanced rifles—as though they were driving in two criminals.

"You never suspected who your father and mother might be?" said Lavery.

"No," said the Kid.

"Down in Mexico?"

"I kicked around from pillar to post. I've always been drifting."

"The sheriff has heard something about you. He knew you by my description. You've been a rough fellow."

"Yes, I've been rough."

"They've laid a list of dead men at your door," said Lavery.

"Yes," said the Kid.

"Is it true?"

"Yes," said the Kid.

Lavery stopped short, but he did not look at Montana. Then he walked forward again, laboring up the slope as though the breath were gone from him.

There was no more talk between them until they came up to the house. Lavery left his horse at the hitching-rack. He turned and looked across the valley that was his as far as the eye could reach.

"My father was a little wild when he first came West," said Lavery. "He was a little too quick with his gun—and a little too straight with his shooting. Perhaps that explains a few things about you. Well—we'd better go inside. I'll tell your—I'll talk to my wife."

They went into the living room. Lavery made a curt gesture. He seemed unable to look at the face of the Kid. "Sit down," he said.

He passed out into the patio.

The invalid would be there, of course. The Kid thought about her. Suddenly he picked up his hat from the floor where he had dropped it and strode towards the outer door, making his step soft. He came to the veranda and the flare of the red-gold sunshine. There he paused, looking over the blue and silver mountains.

He turned back, sat again in the chair, and dropped his sombrero on the floor beside him.

After a moment, Ruth Lavery came in, singing. She had on a thin deerskin jacket that was rubbed pale at the cuffs and elbows. Her boots went up sleekly, without a wrinkle, under the edge of her short skirts.

"Oh, what in the world!" said she. She stopped. She came hurrying on again as he rose. He looked down at the floor.

"Why are you here?" she asked, anxiously. "You and father haven't—you haven't—"

"I haven't hurt him," said the Kid, sullenly. "Not with a gun, anyway."

She sat down on the arm of a chair. He slumped back into his former place and eyed a crack that made a long, straight line of darkness across the floor.

"What's the matter?" said the girl.

"I don't know," said the Kid.

"But what's happening?" she exclaimed, rising.

He held up a hand to silence her. Just then a woman's voice cried out in the patio. It was a short, gasping cry and it lengthened into a long scream.

The girl went like a flash, snatching open the patio door, shouting: "Mother! I'm coming!"

The Kid got up and strode after her, changed his mind, dropped both hands on the back of a chair and leaned his weight on it.

74

He pulled out a blue polka-dotted silk handkerchief and mopped his face. He mopped the back of his neck. Then his face was ready for more drying. He rubbed the silk through his damp fingers, but it would not take up the moisture properly.

He heard a step come quickly from the patio. It was the girl's step. He was rather surprised that he should be able to identify it so readily, but, for that matter, it was his business in life to pay heed to small things. Life depended on eyes and ears more than upon a straight aim, as a rule.

She came into the room towards him and stopped at his shoulder. He heard her breathing. Finally he turned around and looked down into her eyes. They were wide open, without a shadow of guard in them. Women had looked up at him like that before, but never with this clear and happy light. He thought to himself that he could stare right down to the bottom of her heart—and count the pebbles there! It was a fool idea; as if she were a trout stream.

"Well, Dick?" said the girl, holding out a hand.

He felt himself hardening to iron, body and face. Some of the expectancy faded out of her face. The hand which she had held out dropped back to her side.

"She wants to see you," said Ruth Lavery.

"All right," said Montana.

She turned away and went to the patio door. When she paused and looked back, he had not moved. She came to him again.

"I'm guessing at how you feel," she said. "It must be frightfully queer. Try to let yourself go. Then everything will be easy."

He raised his hand.

There was no flinching to her. She went on: "It's because of father. He's rather hard. You think you hate him, but wait till you know him. He's as gentle as a baby, underneath. Or maybe it's the other way around. You've been a pretty free hawk in the sky and you don't want to be tied down to chickens and geese." She managed to laugh. Then she added: "But try to let yourself go. Father's heart has been aching for twenty years. And poor mother— But we're not bad stuff, as people go. And we'll all love you, Dick, so that you can't help feeling the same way about us. I loved you right away. I loved you from the first minute."

"Thanks," said the Kid. "You're swell. That's all. You're wonderful."

She went slowly towards the patio door again, looking back at him over her shoulder.

"All right," said the Kid. But he did not move.

She waited by the door, saying nothing, smiling, simply waiting for him.

At last he went as far as where she stood. She gathered up one of his hands in both of hers, searching his face, loving all that her eyes saw.

"Father and I may not be much, but mother is pure, clean, clear heaven. You'll see. You'll be easy with her, right away. She understands everything."

His lips mumbled: "I'll go right up to her and put my arms around her and kiss her and call her 'mother.'"

She answered his whisper.

"That's the thing to do. Do that, Dick. Dear old man, I know it must be hard. We've been waiting for you twenty years but this is all new to you."

He started. He was not aware that he had spoken his thought aloud.

"Well, I'll try," said the Kid.

He stepped out into the patio and saw that Mrs. Lavery was lying in the same invalid chair, which had been pulled back to the shadowy side of the patio for the afternoon. He saw Richard Lavery standing beside the chair like a soldier. To Montana she held out her hands, smiling.

The Kid walked straight up to her, took her hands, and leaned to kiss her.

He could not manage it. He was like one who cannot finish a bow. He began to shudder. Her eyes were exactly like those of the girl, blue, luminous, so clear that he could look straight into her soul.

"It's all right," said Mrs. Lavery. "Sit down here, my dear. Hold one of my hands, if you don't mind. I understand. Don't force a single word or smile. All in one day—it's a frightful lot to happen."

He sat down beside her. Richard Lavery cleared his throat but said nothing.

"What I wanted to say," said the Kid, "is this—suppose that I were all wrong. That it were all a mistake—"

She kept smiling at him. Her eyes were like the eyes of the girl. They were quietly loving all of him that they saw.

"Go away for a little while, Richard, will you?" she said.

"I'll go," said Lavery. But he hesitated.

The Kid stood up and faced him, eye to eye.

"I'm sorry about things," said the Kid.

"Sorry?" said Lavery. "Good lord!" Suddenly his glance burned. "I should have known from the first!" he said. He made a gesture with his hand and then went suddenly out of the patio.

The Kid sat down again. Mrs. Lavery tapped a little gong that was beside her chair. A Chinaman came out into the patio. He had a frightened round face but he kept smiling, nodding, looking at the Kid. Already he had heard, it seemed.

"See how quickly news travels!" murmured Mrs. Lavery. "Sam, we need something to drink. What will you have—Dick?"

Her voice betrayed her only when she spoke the name, for the emotion welled up there and clung to the sound of it.

"What will you have? Whisky?" said Mrs. Lavery.

Suddenly he was able to grin.

"Not the sort of whisky you'd have in the house," he told her. "Not unless you poured some lye into it."

"Brandy?"

"Yes," said he.

"Brandy, Sam," she ordered.

She released his hand. He pulled out the handkerchief and dried his face again and the backs of his hands. Her glance followed every movement.

Sam came in with a bottle of cognac and two glasses. He poured out a full glass for the Kid; he put a mere splash in the glass of Mrs. Lavery. As he went off again she raised the drink and smiled at the Kid over it.

He raised his and tried to smile, but he could only twitch his lips.

So they drank, silently. He put down the glass, bowing his head, considering the cold burn of the drink and the fumes that he began to breathe. Then he took the two glasses and put them on the table. Most of her small portion was still left.

He came back and sat down beside her.

"You don't have to talk," said Mrs. Lavery. "And you can go, in a moment or two. Just let me say a few words first. Last night I yearned over you. My heart opened for you, my dear, dear lad. When I heard everything that had happened since you came to the ranch, it made me laugh. And of course the son of Richard Lavery could be nothing but a big, bad, bold young man! What else could he be? Now go away, Dick. I know you want to. Such things must be hard on a boy like you."

He wanted to do something about her. His hands were empty and they wanted to take hold of her. But all he did was to stand up, stare into her face for a moment, and then leave the patio.

Chapter Eleven

EVERYTHING WAS HARD, but strangely enough the hardest thing of all was to be with the cowpunchers. He and Lavery had breakfast and lunch with the men. They had supper in the patio, during the good weather, with Mrs. Lavery and Ruth. Those suppers were a test to the Kid, but the meals in the big dining room were almost worse. He had to steel himself. He had to make conversation and be affable and gay. They were all suspicious. They were all waiting for him to "put on airs." He understood exactly what was going on in their minds. It made him despise himself. Somehow, the lie he was acting with the Laverys was not as bad as the lie he was acting among those fellows who were his peers. He wooed them constantly.

He practiced at least an hour a day under the tuition of Buck, learning how to handle a rope. He worked seriously, listening to crisp advice and clear-cut example. Under a veteran cowpuncher called Hooker Thomas he studied the fine art of riding range and knowing cows and their ailments from a distance. From all the men he could learn something. Honest work had always seemed to him a simple matter of back muscles and patient endurance, but now he discovered, with a shock, that all of these fellows were experts. He went out deer-shooting with several of them and Richard Lavery. They had a lucky day, but he could hit nothing. His artistry with guns was confined to the use of the revolver, but these fellows were at home with a Winchester and six-hundred-yard targets. The crowd brought home five deer, neatly cut up, but he had not contributed. He never had killed a deer before. He felt that he never *would* be able to kill one unless he were able to stalk it to point-blank range. He could not skin a beef, either. He did not know how to cut up meat. A hunting-knife, to him, was something to be used on living meat. It was a tool that one dexterous Mexican had demonstrated on the Kid's own body, for instance, and that was a lesson that he had never forgotten.

Cattle, rifles, skinning, the care of hides, the nature of the range he worked on, day by day. Then there were accounts. Richard Lavery took him into the office and showed him the great ledgers over which a bookkeeper worked, and the Kid studied these, too. He surveyed prices, shipments, ranch supplies. He had to learn selling-values. Richard Lavery said he would send him up to Chicago one day, to study the game from the buying end.

The Kid did all of these things with all of his might, but the shadow remained on his brow.

Then came Saturday night. There was a dance in town, a regular cowboy dance where men would try to be clean but not dressed up. He was to take Ruth, as a matter of course. There was a fine light rubber-tired rig and a span of good trotting-horses—a present to Ruth on her eighteenth birthday.

He and the girl wrapped themselves in dust coats

and drove the seven miles to town. He let the horses go full blast. They pulled till his shoulders ached into the middle of his back, but he enjoyed having his hands on something.

He pretended that the horses were all he could give attention to, and the girl was contented and silent beside him until they were almost in sight of Bentonville. The church steeple glinted far away in the moonlight.

Then she said, "It's hard, Dick—terribly hard, eh?"

"What?" he asked.

"Everything," she answered. "You're finding everything pretty hard. Aren't you?"

"A little," said the Kid.

"What would you be doing if you weren't here?" she asked.

He answered, rather savagely: "I'd be playing poker with crooks, working up new towns, riding like the devil out of towns that were getting too hot for me, hunting up some trouble, here and there, spending a good while every day with the Colts. That sort of a life. Looking at mountains and wondering what lay on the other side of them. Staying up late. Sleeping till noon. Never giving a damn."

She was silent for a long time.

"You brought guns with you tonight?" she asked.

"Yes," said the Kid. "Everybody packs guns, I suppose."

"Yes. As far as the coat room. They check their guns with their hats and coats."

"I'd better check my hands than my guns," said the Kid. "Trouble is never far away from me in a crowd. Not in this man's country."

"You're a long way off from any of your old stamping-grounds," she suggested.

He answered, roughly: "I've killed men, and dead men have friends everywhere."

"All right," said the girl, quietly.

Then he said, as they turned into the smoothness of the village street, "I'll leave my guns in the rig under the seat, if you want."

He felt her turn suddenly towards him.

"Well," she said, "you'll have to make a beginning sometime."

"I'll begin tonight, then," said Montana.

They passed through the town. The dance was in an old barn, on the farther side of Bentonville. There were sheds around it, already filled with horses. Ropes had been strung from tree to tree and to these ropes teams and riding-horses were hitched. A few lanterns hung here and there, making pale globular regions of light. In one of those regions the Kid halted the team, tethered it.

He took off his coat, unfastened the armpit spring holsters, and laid them with the two big guns under the lap robe which was folded beneath the seat.

When he turned the girl was waiting for him. In the lantern-light and the shadow of the moon her face was dim, but he saw that she was smiling at him.

"That takes the real nerve. I'm proud of you," said

Ruth Lavery. "Kiss me, Dick, will you? And tell me I'm beginning to be almost a sister to you. Kiss me, Dick, will you?"

She pulled at the sleeve of his coat and stood tiptoe.

"No," said the Kid.

"Well, I'm sorry," said she. She stepped back. "Why can't you?"

"I don't know," said the Kid.

"It's all right," she told him. "I don't care. I'll make you care more about me, one of these days. You wait and see. Come along. Everybody is going to be excited about you tonight. Everybody will be looking. I hope—I hope I won't burst, is all I hope! Dear old Dick! You wait and see. You'll like these people."

They went towards the entrance of the barn. Music of horns and violins snored and sang inside. A big gasoline lamp turned down a cone of white light over the door. People were coming into that light in thin streams, in hurrying couples.

"Hey, Ruth!" cried a chorus, suddenly.

They came swarming, laughing, reaching their hands for her. She was saying. "Yes, here he is. This is my big brother, Dick. Dick, this is Mary Walters, and here's Len Walters, and Cherry Mayberry, and—"

He stood like a stone, smiling faintly. Their faces were rubbed to a blur in spite of the brilliance of the light, for just at the door of the dance-hall he could see the long, lean, greasy face of Gentleman Jeff Leffing-well.

Chapter Twelve

THEY ALL POURED in a jumble into the dance-hall on the floor which had been polished by the pressure of loose hay for many a year and now only needed to be rubbed up before each dance by scattering powdered wax over the wood, putting a bale of hay over a thick felt, and then dragging the bale over the floor with a team of cheerful volunteers.

The Kid looked over that glistening floor on which the images of the dancers glided like reflections in yellow, muddy water, and wished that the floor had been smaller and the crowd larger. There were a hundred couples, perhaps, but the crowd would not be thick enough to let him hide in it.

Entering, he shook hands with Gentleman Jefferson Leffingwell openly and cheerfully, but in passing. A twitch of Gentleman Jeff's eyelid indicated that he understood and would be patient. Then a dance ended, and another began. The Kid was dancing with he hardly knew whom. He was one of those slow, smoothly moving, rhythmic dancers that women prefer to all others. He used only a few simple variations as he glided around the floor, keeping close to the edge of it. He seldom spoke. Presently his partners would be silent, also, feeling that he was deep in the music, and entering it in their own turn. He stood straight, but he kept his eyes turned down. There were rollicking cowpunchers whirling the girls in circles or skidding through many intricate figures, using the floor as though they were skating on ice. Even the elderly men and women stepped a great deal more rapidly than the Kid. The very slowness with which he moved picked him out from the rest of those brown faces, laughing, with shining eyes; and his easy grace had in it a suggestion of something foreign and almost dangerous.

He escaped from the floor when he could and entered the adjoining saloon. The lanky form of Gentleman Jeff Leffingwell came instantly out of the corner shadows. He waded through the closely packed double line of drinkers at the bar and came back with two glasses of beer in his hands. The Kid joined him at a window where the cool of the night wind breathed in on them.

"You've done a wonderful job," said Leffingwell. "I heard a cowpuncher talking about you this afternoon. He was from the Lavery place. He says that you're the worst ranch hand and the best fellow in the world. Oh, they're all glad that you're the heir to the estate. It was a great idea, Kid, it was a wonderful idea to go at Richard Lavery like a wolf at a house dog. You couldn't have done it better. We don't need to step out with the cash in the till. You've done it so damned well that we can make the biggest play of all and try for the whole thing. Suppose you go right through with it. Suppose that you put the thing across for life? What's to stop you?"

He was in an ecstasy. The great breath of ambition

flared his nostrils. "It's worth waiting for," said Leffingwell. "We'll carve up the whole wad of the Lavery
millions!"

"No," said the Kid. "It's a bust. I'm not going
through with it."

Leffingwell looked at him, took a quick swallow of
the beer, and looked out into the open night. He began
to drum his bony fingers on the top of the window-
sash. "You're going to sell us out, eh?" said he.

"I'm not selling out. I'm stepping out," said the Kid.

"I don't give a damn what your reasons are," said
Leffingwell. "If we knew you were going to chuck the
game, we could have got somebody else to go through
with it. You're not the only man in the world with
black hair and blue eyes and some nerve! You're cutting our throats!"

"Don't say that again," murmured the Kid.

Leffingwell brought his glance back from the darkness to the face of Montana.

"What's happened?" he asked.

"The Laverys happened. To me. I can't crook them.
They're white. When you sprang the idea on me, you
told me that Lavery was an iron man. He is, but he's a
white man, too. His wife is an invalid. His girl is as
clean as a whip. I won't go through."

Leffingwell licked his lips without removing the
gray that had settled on them like dust.

"There's another reason," said Montana. "The real
Dick Lavery may show up any day."

"He's dead," said Leffingwell. "You're talking like

a fool. That kid was murdered. If he'd been alive the greasers that stole him would have sold him back to Lavery for a hundred thousand dollars!"

"You don't know Mexicans," said the Kid. "A Mexican can hate you so much that the mere killing of you doesn't take the weight off his chest. But it isn't a matter of thinking. I *know.* When you first broached the idea of the birthmark I remembered something."

"When I talked about that mark I saw the knife go into you," said Leffingwell. "What was it?"

"I was down in Santa Katalina, once," said the Kid. "You know that town in Mexico?"

"I know it," said Leffingwell. "It's famous for the water-lilies they find in the river—and the dead men."

"The Rurales had been making a raid and they were coming in with one prisoner. The Rurales are a tough gang, you know, but they made a lot out of that one prisoner. They had a halter around his neck and they were making a regular parade into the town. Everybody turned out, yelling and cheering, but the prisoner was only a young fellow. He was carrying half a dozen wounds. The blood was black on him, here and there, and in places it was still running red. He walked right along with his head in the air. His clothes had almost been torn off his back in the fight. I was three feet from him when he went by. On his left shoulder I saw a birthmark. It was a curved streak with a black spot beside it."

Leffingwell groaned.

"If the Rurales had him, why didn't they hang him?" asked Leffingwell.

"They put him in jail and trusted his wounds and two guards to keep him there. He killed one of the guards, cracked the skull of the other, and climbed a wall that would have made a cat dizzy. That was how he got away. The Lavery blood is a pretty good strain, Leffingwell. I'll tell you the name he goes by, down there. They call him Tonio Rubriz."

"Hold on," said Leffingwell. "That's the son of the bandit, Matea Rubriz."

"He is," answered the Kid. "That's why those hard-boiled Rurales were making such a fuss over bringing him in. Mateo Rubriz must have done the kidnapping. Lavery loses a son; Mateo gets one. That's the sort of mathematics that a Mexican can understand."

"They'll never know what happens up here," said Leffingwell.

"They will, in time," said the Kid. "A story like this yarn of Lavery's heir turning up and being known by his birthmark is pretty sure to travel wherever people sit around and talk. It may take a year or two years, but pretty soon Tonio Rubriz is going to hear it and wonder why *he* wears the same birthmark. A week after that, he'll be up here, making inquiries. Probably he'll leave Mateo Rubriz behind him with a cut throat."

Leffingwell said through his teeth: "You could have thought of all this when we laid the deal in front of you!"

"I was going to make a quick clean-up and step out," said the Kid. "I didn't know the Laverys were white."

"And *now* you're going to tell the Laverys the truth?"

"I am."

"They'll be pleased," sneered Leffingwell. "They'll lose you out of their family and get a greaser cutthroat instead!"

"It isn't Tonio's fault. Mateo educated him to raise hell, I suppose."

"And Turk and I get nothing but a loud laugh out of the best idea I ever had?" said Leffingwell.

"You'll get something better than a laugh. Go down to Santa Katalina and find Tonio. Tell him the truth. Do you think he'll be grateful? And doesn't Mexican gratitude turn into money?"

"A nice, simple, easy idea," said Jeff Leffingwell. "All that I have to do is to go to Santa Katalina and find an outlaw that the Rurales have been trying to catch all these years. I might get in gunshot of Tonio Rubriz, but I'd be a dead man before I could talk to him."

"I'll go with you," answered the Kid. "I'll tell the Laverys the truth tonight and start for Santa Katalina tomorrow."

"You collect the hard work and I collect the gratitude. Is that the idea? You're a funny *hombre*. What do you get out of this?"

"I get a chance to breathe freely again. That's all I want. And the next time a thug like you, Leffingwell, tries to talk to me, I'll see if lead can stop him."

"You're a funny *hombre,*" said Leffingwell, shaking his head. "You remember the way a greaser walked through the street with his head up and his wounds still bleeding. And you find the Laverys are white. So you chuck the sweetest chance to make a big clean-up that you'll ever have in your life. Well, if you'll do what you say about it there's no money out of my pocket."

"It takes a week to get to Santa Katalina," said the Kid. "I'll meet you there."

With no farewell, he turned on his heel and walked off, putting his half-finished glass of beer down on a table.

As he pushed back the swinging doors he saw a horseman sitting still just beyond the sidewalk. Something came gleaming into the hand of the rider. The Kid side-stepped like a boxer; the bullet, as the gun exploded, tore the air beside his face. A second shot went wild, for the mustang had begun to rear. The Kid ran dodging in, like a snipe flying up the wind. The gun spat almost in his face. He caught the rider by the revolver hand and the nape of the neck and crashed him to the earth. The weight of the fall ended the fight.

The Kid, arising with the Colt in his hand, was now aware of the uproar of voices, the running of feet. Saloon and dance-hall emptied into the street. People were packed around him. The dust cloud and the dim lights blurred their faces like something seen in a dream, just out of focus.

A loud voice was shouting above the clamor: "He

just sat there and waited for young Lavery. I never seen a colder try for a killing. If Bentonville's got one rope and two ounces of manhood in it, the dirty sneak will be lynched."

The Kid had heard lynching-talk before. He had even been the focal center of it. Now he leaned and picked up the fallen man by the scruff of the neck and held him in a shaft of light that came from the window of the saloon. He saw a gaunt face and a pair of pale, wandering eyes to which the wits were just returning.

"I've seen you before," said the Kid.

"You never seen me. You seen my brother. He was the Jim Wrangle that you murdered! If that fool of a cayuse had held still, I would of sent you after him."

At this plain avowal a deep-throated, angry murmuring came from the crowd.

"Get back on your horse," said the Kid. Wrangle obeyed, but he failed to pick up the reins. He sat with his head bowed, his hands folded on the pommel of the saddle. The Kid gave the Colt back to him.

"There are a lot of angry fellows in this crowd, Wrangle," said the Kid. "You'd better move along."

Comprehension could not come at once over Wrangle. Then waves of light entered his mind one after the other. Staring wildly at the Kid as he gathered up his reins, he muttered: "You sound white and you act white. So lemme warn you that there's another here in town who's going to try you. Where I've missed you, he won't miss!"

He never would have made his way through the mob

except that the Kid walked before him until the horse was clear of the thick of the men. Then he was able to gallop rapidly away. Nothing but hoots and whistlings followed him.

The Kid turned back and found Ruth Lavery in the throng, working eagerly to reach him.

"Shall we get back to the ranch?" she asked.

"We'd better go back," he agreed.

The people milled in confusion on the spot. Eyewitnesses were telling over and over exactly how that bit of history had been enacted. A big man with a pointed beard and sharp-ended mustaches gripped the arm of the Kid.

"That was a big thing to do, but it was a fool thing to do, young man!" he said. "That's a thing to please everybody but your family and the insurance company."

The Kid escaped. The shifting of the throng that wanted to see him, the eagerness with which they pressed forward, formed the screen behind which he managed to get away. They untethered the team. She sat in the seat upright and stiff as he drew the lap rug over her knees.

"Take the guns again, Dick," she said. "God forgive me for putting you into such danger. But even if you'd had a gun—I don't think that you would have used it."

He said nothing. He simply buckled the spring holsters in place again and they drove off, taking a cross-lane to avoid the throng in the main street. They were out of Bentonville with the bright sweep of the stars overhead and the mountains crouching small and black on the edge of the horizon.

"Will you tell me, Dick?" she asked. "If you had had the guns, would you have used them?"

He squinted at the pale road that wound before them. The buggy was jumping impatiently at the bumps and swaying in the ruts.

"Yes," he said, "I would have used them."

The echo of his voice was the shivering of her body.

"There's something else a good deal more important that I might as well tell you," said the Kid.

She waited, merely turning to watch him.

After a moment he said through his teeth, "No, that'll have to wait."

He had not been able to speak. He gritted his teeth, but still the confession would not come up in his throat.

Chapter Thirteen

WHEN THEY GOT to the ranch house the horses were steaming. They were wet to the tips of their ears. The Kid had hardly spoken since they left the town.

"I'll help you put up the team," said Ruth Lavery.

"No," he answered. "I'll do it."

Before she got out of the rig she put a hand on his arm and murmured: "I know you're thinking of all the trouble that may come up at you out of the past, but you'll beat it. Everybody is behind you now. Nobody else in the world would have let that wretched murderer go as you did. It was a grand thing to do, Dick!"

"I'll tell you why I did it," he answered, grimly. "I was remembering how his brother looked and what he said after I'd shot him. It took Slim Jim Wrangle awhile to die."

She waited, as though expecting to hear more, or as though gathering her strength after the shock of what she had heard. Then she climbed down to the ground.

"I'll make some coffee and scramble some eggs. Shall I?" she said.

"Not for me," said the Kid.

"Good night, then, Dick."

"Good night."

He went out to the barn and put away the two driving-horses. As he turned back to the house his own mustang came down to the fence and stood in the moonlight, pressing against the barbed wire, pointing its ears at the Kid.

He looked at it for a moment, and then went on. He opened the front door and closed it softly, for Mrs. Lavery was a very light sleeper. The windows in the living room were closed. In the warm air was the half-sickly sweetness of willing flowers.

He went up the stairs without lighting a lamp to take with him. His feet found the steps and the turns with a flawless certainty. He did not have to touch the rail of the balustrade for guidance. When he came into the upper hall door of his room was open and lamplight shone softly through it. Perhaps Ruth had lighted the lamp for him. But when he went to the threshold he saw Richard Lavery standing in front of the open window. It was late, but the rancher was fully dressed.

He turned around so that the Kid could see the gleam of his eyes and the luster of the black mustaches.

"Ruth told me what happened," he said. "It's the sort of thing that I would have liked to do if I had the nerve. It's a thing that tells me you're a Lavery. Your mother is awake, too. She'd like to talk to you; she heard Ruth chattering at me and called us in. She knows the story, too."

"I'm sorry about that," said the Kid. "Did it upset her?"

"Nothing can upset her now except bad news about you. In these few days you've made her ten years younger and stronger. There's color in her face! No, Dick, she wants to see you not because she's alarmed but because she's so happy to have such a son. Come in with me now."

The Kid walked over into a corner of the room, drawing down a great breath.

"Wait a minute," he muttered.

Something gleamed in the corner. He moved the lamp until he could see a filled gun-rack sitting there with a pump gun, a pair of "tailor-made" double-barreled shotguns, two big-caliber rifles for large game, and a dainty thirty-two repeater with a little twenty-two beside it for tricks or practice.

"I thought you might want a gun-stand of your

own," said Lavery. "I got your measure and those stocks ought to fit you all right."

The Kid said nothing. He put down the lamp again slowly, with a strained face, as though he were afraid of dropping it. Then he stepped back rather hastily out of the brightness of the light.

"I've got to tell you something," said the Kid.

"Go on, Dick," said Lavery.

Montana cleared his throat and frowned.

"Take your time," said Lavery. "I think I know what it is."

"Do you?" said Montana.

"It's some wildness out of your past. Well, my dear boy, that simply means that you're a Lavery. There's nothing you can tell me that will topple over my faith in you. If there were mistakes in the old days, there'll be a chance in the future to make up for 'em. And I'm here to help." He went to the Kid and faced him closely. "What are fathers for?" said Lavery. "Great God! what's the use of blood if it doesn't tie fathers and sons together? There's nothing you can say that I'm not ready to hear."

The Kid pulled back his head and closed his eyes.

"All right," he said. "I'll talk in a minute."

"Take your time. Take your time," said Lavery. "Or is it something that it would be easier to tell your mother?"

"Ay. Perhaps," said the Kid. He went down the hall to the door of Mrs. Lavery's room. Lavery knocked and pushed it open a crack.

"Here's Dick come to talk to you," said he.

"Come in, Dick!" called Mrs. Lavery.

Montana stepped into the doorway. Lavery murmured: "I'm a happy man, Dick. There are plenty of men in the world brave enough to kill, but precious few brave enough to let their advantages go by! Good night!"

The Kid muttered a vague answer, entered the room, and closed the door. He stood before the whiteness of the bed on which the light of the bedside lamp struck out a glistening arc. She held out her hands to him. She always did and he always knew that she wanted to put her arms around him. He sat beside the bed and took one of her hands and leaned his big head and shoulders towards her.

"I want to tell you something," he said.

"I want to hear it," said she, smiling. "I want to hear all about it, from the moment that scoundrel appeared out of the night."

"It isn't—" he began.

She sat up.

"Suppose one of the bullets had gone true? It would have killed two people in one, Dick. I couldn't live if I lost you again."

He stared at her. It was true that she had changed since his coming. There was more color, more substance.

"It isn't about tonight," said the Kid. "It's about—"

"Then I don't want to hear it!" she interrupted. "What I want to know is how the blood runs in the heart and the brain of a hero. I've been lying here with tears in my eyes, crying for joy, thinking what a meager soil I am to produce such a glorious tree. Sometimes it seems to me that you can't be mine. But I know that is only the effect of the twenty years you were lost to me. Talk to me about tonight, Dick."

He was silent, looking into the soft brightness of her eyes.

"Unless there's something else—that you worry about," said Mrs. Lavery. "*That* I'd like to hear, too, so that I could help. I was robbed of your boyhood and all the years when you would have come to me for help. I never can have those years back and the loss of them has been an open wound that my life nearly slipped away through. But now the wound is healing and the life is coming back. Still I want to be of use to you. Mothers are made of tough stuff. They're a durable metal when their children need them. So if there's trouble in your mind tell me about it, my son!"

The door to the Kid's conscience, which he had opened wide, was slammed shut by the last two words. He stared at her until he realized that sorrow and a certain grimness were appearing in his face. Then he glanced down at the floor. Instead of saying what he had come to say, he merely answered her, "The fact is that there's trouble and it is going to take me away on a trip."

"A trip? Where? And what trouble?" she cried.

The Kid said nothing.

"Can't you confide in me, Dick?" she pleaded.

Montana looked up at her but without speaking.

"You haven't known me long enough," said Mrs. Lavery. "That's the trouble. The hearts of women and men are different stuff, and I haven't been able to open yours. Some day I shall, if praying will do it. But if you must go—will it be for long?"

There was not enough air in the room. The Kid could not breathe.

"It won't be long," he lied.

"Then go, my dear," she said. "All my trust and my love and my faith will go with you. When do you start?"

"In the morning—early."

"Then it's good-by?" she asked.

"Yes," said Montana.

He swore to himself that he would put his arms around her and kiss her good-by as a last act of treason. But he faltered. He could only press her hands against his face before he went rapidly from the room.

Chapter Fourteen

IN THE PALEST gray of the morning the Kid leaned above the bunk of Ransome. At his whisper the foreman rolled from the blankets to his feet, stepped into trousers and boots, and stole outside. There was just enough light to set the windows of the house glimmering. The Kid said: "Ransome, I'm coming clean to you. I'm no more a Lavery than you are and the birthmark is a neat little job of tattooing."

It was early in the day, but Ransome brought a gnawed plug of Star chewing tobacco out of a hip pocket, bit off a corner of it with one grinding of his jaws, and then spat into the dust.

"Go on," said Ransome. He rested his hands far back on his hips and looked up at the Kid, with the tobacco quid making a mound of his left cheek.

"I'm leaving," said Montana. "I have an idea that I can turn up the real Lavery, but something may happen. If there's no word of me inside of six months, you tell Richard Lavery what I've told you. Because if you don't hear from me in six months I'll be dead, Ransome. I'd break the news myself, but it might upset Mrs. Lavery like a bullet through the head. Understand?"

"Like a book," said Ransome. He stared at the Kid. "Wherever you're going, you don't want company?"

"Thanks. It's my job. I've been a snake all my life and now I want to see if I can crawl straight for a while. So long, Ransome. Say *adios* for me to the boys."

"So long," said Ransome. He shook hands. "You ain't been a snake," he said. "You just been too young to be careful."

The Kid went to his saddled mustang and mounted it, waved his hand, and cantered to the house. He left it there with thrown reins and entered the darkness of the house. Upstairs he tapped on the door of Richard Lavery's room, entered when the voice spoke, and in the dimness saw the rancher sitting up in bed.

"I've got to leave for a while," said the Kid. "I can't tell you where."

Lavery got out of the bed. He merely said, after a moment, "Do you know when you're coming back?"

"Not the exact day," said the Kid, his face twisting a little as he realized the degree of the understatement.

Lavery took his hand with a mighty grip.

"I hope I know enough not to ask fool questions," he said. "I'm with you, wherever you go and whatever you do."

That was ended. The Kid left that room and went down the hall to the door of Ruth Lavery. She opened it almost instantly after he tapped.

"Yes, Dick?" she said.

"I've got a call that takes me on a long trip," said the Kid. "I've got to say good-by."

She leaned suddenly against the edge of the open door. But it was only for a moment. All the Laverys seemed to be soldiers ready for anything at a moment's notice. She stood before him again and held out her hand.

He took her by the shoulders. They were as strong and firm as the shoulders of a boy.

"One of these days—" said the Kid.

His voice trailed away into vagueness.

"Think about us sometimes," said the girl.

"I'll think about you every day of my life," said the Kid. "Good-by!"

"And you'll never come back," said Ruth Lavery.

"One of these days—" said the Kid, huskily. "Well, good-by!"

"Good-by," said the girl.

As he turned away he could see that she was wilting, growing smaller, and he hurried his departure. It was strange that she, of them all, should be the one to know that he never would return.

When he got down to the horse the dawn was hardly brighter than when he had first saddled the horse.

"Anyway," said the Kid to himself, "it didn't take long."

He turned off onto the mountain trail. At the top of the first high slope he turned and looked back out of the upland brightness into the dusk that still covered the lower valley. The windows of the house shimmered through that morning twilight. The Kid looked well upon the whole scene, writing it down in his heart. Then he rode on into the pass.

The old trail which the Indians had followed when they rode south had turned through this pass and so down into the valley which was now the ranch of Lavery's, but since Mexico was the actual goal of Montana he preferred to cover his direction by going back for a distance into the mountains. After that, he could cut to the left and cross the Rio Grande at one of many fords.

The dead had fallen more thickly in the iron throat of this pass, it seemed, as though the great stone walls had stamped out the life and the spirit suddenly. There were great thigh bones of oxen and many nameless fragments which helped to make up the white of the chalk mark that was so visible from a distance. From a ledge ten feet above the floor of the pass the skull of a horse showed its teeth at Montana and he had not the heart to grin back.

The hoofbeats of a galloping horse came dimly up from the valley and entered the pass with a mighty clangoring that seemed to ring before the Kid and behind him. He pulled up his mustang and saw Richard Lavery come pelting around an elbow turn, taking it so fast that he was aslant in the saddle. He pulled up beside Montana with a nod of satisfaction.

"You're bound for trouble, Dick," said he. "So I simply left word that I was called away on a short business trip. I'm going to see you through this."

"Thanks," grunted the Kid. "But the ranch needs you."

"The ranch does well enough under my foreman. I'm riding with you."

"Not on this trail," answered Montana.

Lavery dropped his right hand on his hip and shook his head.

"It's no good, Dick," said he. "If ranch life is dull for you, I'm going to find the taste of the sort of thing you like. Then maybe I can learn how to dish it up for you at home. You can't dodge me."

"You're feeling young, eh?" said the Kid, scowling.

"Like a boy!" answered Lavery.

"Well, I'll make you old again. Listen to me. You know Mateo Rubriz?"

104

"The bandit? Of course I know him. Rubriz? Is he what's on your mind?"

"He has a son," said Montana. "You've asked for this, and now you can take it. He has a son with a birthmark on his shoulder—something like a crescent moon with a dot inside it."

"You?" exclaimed Lavery. "You mean that Rubriz is the man who stole you, Dick?"

"Can't you get it straight?" demanded Montana. "Ever hear of tattooing? It's only a picture that I'm wearing under my skin. And I happened to have the hair and eyes to go with it. Your boy is Tonio Rubriz. If the Rurales haven t hanged him yet, maybe the yarn I can tell him will turn him into a gringo. That's all."

The mind of Lavery seemed to stagger and his hand made vague gestures in sympathy with that mental wavering.

The Kid went on, his voice hard and brutal: "Your wife isn't tough stuff. If her son that's come to life fades out into a lie, she'll snuff out. You know that. So I'm going to try to get my hands on that Tonio Rubriz and bring him back up here to fill my boots. You go back home and hold your wife's hand till the good news comes back. I'm on my way. I would have kept this dark, but you forced my hand."

"It was a plant," said Lavery, "and you couldn't go through with it?"

"There are a couple of white women back in your house. Go home and take care of 'em," directed Montana.

"And let you ride south, my lad, to deal with Mateo Rubriz?" exclaimed Lavery.

"Don't be so fatherly," said the Kid. "If you tried to come along, you'd only be in the way. I don't want a lot of sympathy. I want a clear track. *Adios.* I'm gone."

"Suppose you were in my boots, in a spot like this, what do you think you'd do?" asked Lavery.

Montana stared at him. He started to speak once or twice, but merely moistened his lips.

"All right," he said, at last. "Come along and be shot, for all I care."

Chapter Fifteen

FROM THE WINDOW of her room Ruth Lavery had seen the mustang of Montana climb into the pass. She could see him pause on the lip of it, as if to look back, and that moment of delay was for some reason a comfort to her. As he disappeared she was about to leave the window when she made out another horseman rushing up the slope towards the mouth of the pass and speeding into it without delay. It was her father. She knew that by the slight angle at which he slanted in the saddle.

At once she was puzzled. Richard Lavery was not the man to pursue another for the sake of speaking a last word of farewell. Neither was he apt to ride in this manner to give even his son a thing that had been forgotten and left behind.

She went downstairs and found Stew Ransome sitting on the chopping-block behind the kitchen, drawing long, translucent slivvers from a stick which he was whittling. By the irregular rhythm with which he champed at his tobacco, by the corrugation of his brow, but above all by the fact that he was whittling with his sharpest knife, she knew that all was not well with him.

"Stew," she said, "what's up?"

He finished the sliver he was cutting, shifted his quid, looked up at her, and by way of tipping his hat, barely touched the brim of his sombrero with the tip of his finger.

"That reminds me of a story," said Ransome.

"I don't want to hear a story," said the girl. "I want to know what's in the air."

"Buzzards high up, hawks lower down, and some crows flapping around close to the earth," said Ransome.

"Listen to me, Stew," said the girl.

"I'm listening," he said.

"You're not," she assured him. "You're just watching me and thinking up some way of dodging my questions."

"How would I be thinkin' up a way of dodgin' your questions when I dunno what your questions are gunna be?" asked Ransome.

"You know what they'll be, though," she said. "I'll tell you right now what you're thinking about."

"Go on and tell me, then?" said Ransome.

"You're thinking about the pass," she said.

He was so startled that he cut right through the slender stick he was whittling. He held up the stub of it and shook it at her. "Look what you've gone and made me do," said Ransome, gloomily. "This here would of made a boss handle for a bull-whip, with some leather wrapped around it. It's as round as though it was machine ground. Pass? What the devil would I be thinking about the pass for?"

"Because Dick and my father have both ridden into it," said the girl.

"Have they?" murmured Ransome.

"Move over, Stew," said she.

He moved over on the chopping-block and she sat down beside him. She put a hand on his arm.

"Look me in the eye," she commanded.

"There ain't hardly room for more'n one on this here block," said Ransome, darkly.

"Look me in the eye like a good fellow and tell me what's up," said the girl.

"Up in the air," said Ransome, "there's buzzards and hawks and crows—"

"If you won't talk to me I'll go and have a look-see," said the girl.

"At what?" asked Ransome.

"Just at what's up in the air. Will you saddle up the mare for me?"

"What you want the mare for?" asked Ransome, his head jerking back a little as he spoke.

She stared hard at him, then rose and went with a sudden decision to the nearest shed, out of which she took a saddle and bridle, and threw the coil of a lariat over her shoulder.

Ransome leaned his elbows on the pasture fence as she passed in through the gate.

"What would you be wantin' the mare for, Ruth?" he demanded. "Here, I'll take and catch her for you if you gotta have her."

She said nothing, but, dropping the saddle and bridle near the gate, she advanced into the pastures. The horses knotted together in a far corner, waiting for her with lifted heads. As she came near, they scattered fanwise, right and left, some charging almost straight at her as horses will always do when they are pretending to be frenzied with excitement.

She made a few running steps to the left, shot out the rope with a good clean swing of the arm, and landed the noose around the neck of the black mare as that piece of shining satin tried to sneak away next to the fence. The instant the roughness of the rope prickled on her skin, the mare checked her galloping, planted all four feet, and skidded to a halt. Ruth Lavery led her to the gate and threw on saddle and bridle.

"If you gotta be riding, I'll cinch up that saddle for you," said Stew Ransome.

She maintained the dignity of her silence, put her knee against the tender ribs of the black, and made the little mare grunt as the cinches were hauled in.

"You gunna punish the mare with cinches drawed up like that?" chuckled Stew Ransome.

He opened the gate as she led the mare out.

"I may be away awhile," she said.

She swung up into the saddle and looked down at him. He had taken a firm grip on the bridle reins. The mare vainly tried to toss her head free.

"Tell me something, Ruth!" pleaded Ransome.

"All right," she answered. "If I'm away for a while, you tell the folks that I've dropped over to the Sanderson place, will you?"

"The Sanderson place ain't up through the pass," said Ransome.

"I'm taking a long way round is all," said she. "Let go of her head, Stew."

"Ruth," said he, "I wish you wouldn't be so doggone bull-headed!"

"I'm not," she answered. "I'm just a little curious. So long, Stew."

And she sent the black off at a good brisk gallop, heading straight for the pass.

When she came into the pass she checked the black and listened carefully, in hope that she might either hear the voices of the two men talking together, or else at least the clangor of hoofs in the far reaches of the gorge, but she heard nothing except the panting of the mare.

So she went on again until she came out of the pass and saw, far beneath her, the yellow winding of the Rio Grande and two horsemen fording it at the shallows, crossing their legs across the withers of the mustangs in order to keep out of the wet. And all at once her heart began to hammer at her ribs as she saw that they were actually bent for the Mexican side.

No matter how narrow that water might be, it was bad business for anyone to bother with the Mexican side. Her father had told her so a hundred times. She could roam where she pleased, but never across that muddy little strip of water. Another race with another way of thinking lived there. It always seemed to her, when she looked far south, that the mountains which lifted yonder were of strange shapes and sizes.

The two riders were her father and Dick. She had no doubt of that once they gained the farther shore and set off at a trot. She could distinguish her father's slant in the saddle almost as far as she could see him.

She told herself that she would ride at least as far as the bank of the stream, and then turn back. So she went down to the edge of the water. A boatman, pulling up-stream in the shallows, turned his head, let his skiff drift backwards, and watched her vaguely. And for some reason that blank gaze of his spurred her into the ford, because it roused in her mind a savage discontent. If she had been a male no one would have tried to appoint bounds for her, and now that her father and brother were rollicking far south into the heart of unknown adventures, why should she be left behind?

She rode right into the water. The mare almost had to swim in the center and the flaps of her divided skirts were drenched. But now the bank shoaled up before them and they lifted to the dry land, where the mare shook herself like a cat.

A wind had risen, blowing all the south full of a dim,

russet cloud of dust, while behind her the northern mountains were perfectly clear. That was an omen to warn her back.

Then she thought of Stew Ransome. When she returned he would say that girls were safe to have around. They never would go more than one step into dangerous country!

This reflection made her set her teeth. She decided that she would ride as far as the mouth of a valley that opened between two hills; so she cantered the mustang easily onwards. Her heart kept swelling. Something tightened in her throat. She kept glancing over her shoulder to make sure that no one was cutting in between her and the river to shut off her retreat. And for the first time in her life she was glad of the little thirty-two revolver which was stuck into a holster and fastened to the side of her saddle.

Then, when she came to the valley, she laughed at herself. For it was a pleasantly green strip laid down between two brown, rolling ridges. No water flowed through the center. It was simply a thin seepage of moisture from the higher strata of rock, perhaps, that gave life to the roots of the grass. The dust cloud which still colored the sky above her was not apparent in this hollow, so she rode on, putting the mare to almost its best pace. Her father and Montana could not be far ahead, now, to judge by the rate at which they had been cantering.

She passed the mouth of a ravine that entered the hollow from the right, and as she did so she had a view of half a dozen riders coming out of the draw. They were all Mexicans. The smallness of their mustangs proved their race, and something about the narrowness of their hips, the shortness of their necks, the way the huge sombreros seemed to fit right down on their shoulders. They were so many black silhouettes against the light.

One of them must have called to her. At any rate, a sound like a voice kept ringing and re-ringing through her brain, and when she looked back, sure enough the troop was spilling out of the mouth of the ravine at full gallop and rushing after her!

Instead, of spurring the black mare, she took a steadying grip on the reins. There was nothing to be afraid of, she told herself, for this was a free country, a civilized country. Certain stories that drifted north over the border, certain revolting tales, were merely the exaggerations of men and story-tellers. Men are always ready to believe the worst—about Mexicans.

She had reasoned herself into almost perfect calmness of mind when she felt the tremor of the approaching charge. She would not look back. But she could *feel* a quivering of the ground, or was it in the air. Then a yell crashed on her very ears, roaring all about her.

It swept away every scruple of her self-assurance. It tipped her forward in the saddle with flogging whip and digging spurs. The black mare straightened out to full racing speed, the hills right and left began to jerk away behind her.

The valley forked. Which way had her father ridden? Oh for a glimpse of those two men who would scatter these renegades like chaff! Which way had they ridden?

To the right seemed luck, and that was the course she took.

Chapter Sixteen

SHE KEPT TELLING herself that everything was all right. It was a good Mexican joke to frighten a gringo woman; and if she had not fled they would never have followed. But she also realized that the longer they pursued the more serious they would become. She wanted to pull up the black mare and ride straight back through them, yet she knew that she would never have the courage to do this.

She wanted to draw well ahead of them, then turn right or left in a wide detour that would bring her, sooner or later to the blessed sight of the waters of the Rio Grande and the happy shore beyond the stream, but she was in another valley whose floor was level drift sand and whose sides were flat-faced rocks.

She went on for an hour. She could hear nothing behind her now, so she pulled up the black mare. The little horse dropped her head at once and began to blow with rapidly pumping sides. This was bad. It meant that the mare was soft; that the sleek of her body was mere grass fat and not good condition; and if the Mexicans chose to keep coming they might run her down. Mexican horses, she knew, cannot run fast but they run forever. She listened to the dripping of sweat that fell from the belly of the mare into the sand. Then, looking back, she saw the Mexicans swing around the next bend of the ravine. They had their horses at a steady lope, but they freshened that to a run at the sight of her, swinging their hats.

She put the mare away at a brisk gallop again. Time meant nothing in Mexico. Those fellows might hunt her all day long, and if the chase lasted like that they would do something about it when they caught up with her. Some one had told her that Mexicans are seven-eighths Indian. She grew so sick that she was afraid she would faint.

Then she made another plan, on a larger scale. Before her a group of ragged mountains had turned from blue to brown; now they were close at hand. That, she was reasonably sure, was the San Carlos Range. Somewhere in the core of it lay the little town of Ormosa and if she could get to that she ought to be fairly safe. It was a robbers' roost, but she would be safer there than alone in the naked wilderness. Or, when she entered the mountains, she might be able to fade away from the pursuit in the intricacies of the ravines.

One day she would sit at her father's table and be laughed at for this plan of hers, but ridicule in the future meant nothing compared with the fact of the present. One sweaty cowpuncher with a white skin would have seemed to her, now, a gift fresh from the hand of God.

They were climbing. She had to let the mare pass from a canter to a trot. In the eagerness of her fear she kept thrusting far forward in the saddle. A cold hand pressed on the small of her back. She began to remember small, distant moments of her life. She recalled that people are said to see all their past when death is near by. Mostly she was remembering bits out of her childhood. The days of childhood are dull because they are endless, but it seemed to her that that was the only happiness because it was the only safety.

Then, at last, she reached a labyrinth of intermingling cañons. Such relief came over her that she found she was moaning a little with every breath she drew. The mare could judge as well as she. She let that nodding, laborious head take whichever way it chose, left, right, right and left. Sometimes they were in sand; again they went over flinty rock where surely they would leave no trail.

They went on endlessly, like this, always eating nearer to the heart of the range, so that above the walls of the ravines she saw the big shoulders of the upper mountains walking slowly by. Before long that day must end and she would be stranded without water. But that was nothing. She could travel by the stars. She would drink of the cool and secure blackness of the night as of water.

A straight, narrow valley opened before her now, a rocky terrain where an army could have hidden. In one of those nests of boulders she halted the black mare. The breathing of the exhausted horse rocked her in the saddle; there was a horrible rattling, stertorous sound in the throat of the mare. And then, as she looked back, she saw half a dozen riders winding among the rocks in the lower ravine! The men looked bigger than the horses and the horses were moving with active, tireless feet, as though they were on the way home.

This time she could flee no more. She knew it by the way the mare swayed on her widely braced legs. All the rest had been merely a flourish and a gesture, but now the gun was pointed at her head. She must hide. Not among the rocks that had seemed, a moment before, sufficient to hide an army. Not among the rocks, because the Mexicans would find her by an instinct, but in one of the great crevices which made recesses in the wall of the cañon. There was no use in searching long. She entered the first narrow mouth of a little cañon to her left. The floor of it was polished rock that could hardly take a hoofmark. Twice the ravine made elbow turns, then ended in a sandy, circular area spotted by a few gaunt skeletons of the ocatilla and the evil-smelling creosote bushes. The walls of the amphitheater rose up in sheer lines for thirty or forty feet. The sandy slopes began again above their edges.

Well, if she had searched for a day she could hardly have found a better hiding-place.

She dismounted, stripped the saddle from the back

of the mare, and sat down on a rock. The heat of the rock stung her even through her strong riding-dress, for the westering sun was still high enough to look right into the hiding-place.

The place was perfect. Perhaps it was too perfect—so perfect that it might be known. And Mexicans always know their native terrain as a fox knows its hunting-range.

All was quiet. All was so quiet that the noise of the sweat that dripped from the belly of the mare made the girl angry. She stared fiercely at the bedraggled little horse. There was no sympathy in her. When she got home she would sell that mare for a song and get a real mustang, tough, savage, wicked, unbeautiful, but efficient. A horse is a machine that ought to get one places. Pretty things are weak. That was the trouble with herself, thought Ruth Lavery. She looked down at the slender round of her wrist with disgust. A man could smash that fragility between thumb and fore-finger, she felt.

A touch of wind cooled her wet face. Her lips were covered with the dry salt of her sweat. She scrubbed them clean with her handkerchief. The saline taste set thrilling agonies of thirst at work in her throat, but she merely smiled at such minor torments as these.

The wind came again, and on it the dim murmur of voices that laughed in the distance. That was both a shock and a relief—the sense of their nearness and the proof which laughter seemed to give that they were only casually hunting, with no understanding of how near they were to their quarry.

Something stirred on the sandy slope above the cliff on her left. It was a coyote that had pounced on something small. That small life squeaked out a note as thin as a ray of light in utter darkness. The coyote champed, licked the red from its lips, and then canted its beautiful gray head to the side and looked down at the human with a half-whimsical and half-hungry interest. Something made the girl turn her head. When she looked again the coyote was gone.

Now the faint sound that had made her turn developed into a big cock road-runner which stalked into the little arena, looked about it for an instant, then made for a shattered boulder. Out of the crevices slid, a moment later, a small diamond-back. It coiled at once, the sun fingering with glintings and shimmerings of light the rich cinnamon color and gliding over the row of diamond-shaped spots that ran down the back from head to tail. The belly scales were a bright, horrible white.

It paid no heed to the human near by. That was hardly strange, but it was wonderful that the shy road-runner should go about its work unperturbed. It seemed to the girl that by sitting motionless for a short time she had made herself a natural feature of the place. That was why she was seeing so many things. She wondered what she might find in her own setting if, every day, she sat still as a stone among the people she knew. What savage, what foolish, what monstrous things might appear to her? Or out of her own nature might step what terrible and unknown influences?

The road-runner was moving around and around the snake, lowering and raising its splendid tail, flaring its short wings with a shimmer of metal green on the top feathers, and making all the while a sound that was absurdly like the cooing of a dove. It was no bigger than a small crow, this famous warrior in feathers, but its legs were as long and strong as the legs of a grouse. From tail to the erectile crest it was a decorated brave, as though nature wanted to show all possible honor. It was all buff and bronze glossed over with green; the edges of the wings were delicately bordered with white and black; but about the eyes there was a special pattern of Prussian blue in front and brightest orange behind. The long tail was a balancing-tool; so were the wings. Really, the road-runner was no more than a big, wicked beak and a pair of legs that served as mechanical springs to hurl the lance.

It came in smaller circles close to the rattler and the diamond-back struck. The bird jumped. The blow passed under it.

Instantly the diamond-back recoiled. The cock stood dangerously close, ruffing out its neck feathers, bowing up and down in savage curtsy.

That was the whole story of the battle. It was the same thing over and over for half an hour while with unwearied eyes of horror the girl watched, until at last the rattler, after striking full length, lay for the exhausted tenth part of a second stretched in helplessness. That instant the powerful beak of the cock struck behind the head. The rattler, in its agony, coiled by jerking its tail up to its head. It writhed in a confusion of coils. It lunged at the bird with repeated strokes. And now, like a fine fencer waiting to send home the death blow, the road-runner avoided these deadly lunges by neat fractions of an inch.

Suddenly it was in again. Its beak seemed to linger in the wound it inflicted. Its head wrenched twice at the life of the snake. And again it was out and away from the flying coils.

That was the story for the next half dozen chapters, always with the same climax, the same ending, until the diamond-back as it coiled, with flat head retracted for the stroke, began to stoop its weapon towards the ground, as though slowly returning the bows of its enemy. One of those curtsies ended with the head motionless on the ground, and with that the road-runner walked calmly forward and began to make a meal. The rattlesnake stirred no more. It was horribly as if the snake had not died, but simply had surrendered.

The girl turned her head from that monstrous happening. She had seen and heard nothing, but when she looked up she saw a tall young Mexican on the slope above, standing where the coyote had stood. He had a round face stuffed out sleek with fat except where vicious wrinkles were incised about the eyes. When he saw her look up he took off his hat and laughed as he bowed to her.

Chapter Seventeen

THE MEXICAN, STILL laughing, bowed himself out of view behind the rim of the rock. She heard his voice calling out in triumph. The sound of it started her heart beating again, but she kept gasping for breath as she saddled the black mare again. She knew that she was trapped, but she had to do something; otherwise the grip that fear had on her throat would have stifled her.

A moment later she was jogging the mare down the winding little ravine that led towards the outer valley. The little black had regained both wind and spirit, like a true mustang. She was pricking her ears, stepping daintily, playing with her bit and putting the stiff of her tongue against it. So a wan ghost of hope had started up in the girl once more as she came to the verge of the outer valley.

There it disappeared, for a pair of Mexicans sat their horses right before her. They were smoking cigarettes. When she appeared, they looked at one another and laughed.

One should treat a Mexican with authority. She put some more weight into her stirrups to stop the shaking of her knees: "Rein back your horses and let me through," she said. "You've started enough trouble for yourselves already, today."

One of them took off his hat and bowed over the pommel of his saddle to her. When he took off his hat a shag of hair fell over his forehead. His shirt was black-spotted with grease. The fringes of his gloves had been worn away. His face looked fat with bloat and his body was starved like a sick dog in winter.

"A girl ought not to be out in the mountains alone," he said. "But we'll ride along and keep you company, eh?" He started to laugh so that he could hardly speak.

Another fellow came in view, jogging an active little gray horse, now washed almost black with sweat. He looked young, not more than eighteen or nineteen, but he was better dressed than the others and he had an air of authority in his treatment of them. He was a big youth, with a blunt, wide face. He rode straight up to her and looked her in the face till her eyes widened, began to sting, and she was forced to glance down.

"You see?" he said to the others. "A gringo never can look you in the eyes. Not even a rich man's daughter."

They all laughed. "Who is she?" asked one of them.

"Señorita Lavery," said the youth. "You are Señor Lavery's daughter, I think?"

"Yes," she said.

He took the reins out of her hand and pulled them over the head of the mare. Then he called to the rest of his companions:

"This is money; this is not just a woman. Mateo Rubriz will give us a sackful of pesos for her. We go to Ormosa! Quick now! Into the saddle and away. Hey, Juan! You have the freshest horse, because you weigh nothing. Ride on to Ormosa and find Mateo

123

Rubriz, or Tonio. We come after you as fast we can."

One of them was a little hunchback, pale as grease. He was on a ewe-necked beast that looked more like a goat than a horse, but it still could raise a good gallop. The hunchback cantered up the slope and disappeared. The rest of them gathered around Ruth Lavery like an escort.

They began to talk about her ransom. What would they ask from Rubriz? What would Rubriz get from her father? And the terror got out of her head and heart as she listened, and sank like water to the level of her stomach. She still felt sick, but she could think. Mateo Rubriz she had heard of; everyone in the Southwest knew about him. He had raided north of the Rio Grande twice and kidnapped his man on each occasion. He was the fellow who had caught the nephew of the President of Mexico, received a ransom for him, and then turned him loose in the desert after cutting the soles of his feet to strips.

She stared right ahead of her at a void of thought. The voices sounded in her ear with dull and hollow vibrations.

There was comfort in listening to what they said, because they reasoned like children. As for the amount of money that Rubriz would pay, a fellow of his dignity could not afford to pay less than a hundred pesos per man in return for their gift. That would be eight hundred pesos. Surely Rubriz would give them that much, and the thought of a hundred pesos for the work of one day made them all drunk with joy, except the youthful leader of the gang. He kept his eyes before him and said nothing.

They talked about what Rubriz might collect. One fellow suggested a thousand dollars, as a great round sum that made his eyes big. Another laughed at this suggestion and calmly named a million. They all applauded this as cheerfully as though they, not Rubriz, might have the chance to collect the ransom.

That thought kept sticking in the mind of the girl. Now that she had seen these faces they seemed better to her than unknown Mexicans. She said to the young leader: "Why do you take me to Rubriz? My father will pay you if you bring me back safe. He'll pay you *more* than eight hundred dollars. Why do you take me to Rubriz?"

The youngster puckered his eyes at her for a moment. He looked her up and down then took a long, hard squint into her eyes.

At last, without a word, he drew a forefinger across his throat and then turned away.

The man of the fat face and the skeleton body was more talkative, however. He rode up beside the girl and explained: "Mateo Rubriz is no fool. He knows that two robbers take more than one, so wherever he goes he will be the only robber. Well, that shows he has good sense. You cart see that? Other robbers have tried to come into the San Carlos Mountains. They are good mountains. You can see for yourself how many places there are to hide in them. But even when they have only come to hide, for a while, Rubriz hunts them out and kills them and takes their horses and their money. He gives their women to his men and puts the money into his pockets and drinks some more red wine. Red wine is good for the stomach, señorita."

He rubbed the flat of his paunch as he said this, and laughed with eyes that expected sympathy.

They were not all evil, these ragamuffins.

If only the night had not been coining down! They entered a ravine already thick with shadows; the peaks above were rosy gold with the sunset. When they came out of the ravine the gold had left the mountains. There was only a band of dirty orange around the horizon. The big stars came down in the sky. Then the host of their smaller companions shouldered after them. The Milky Way banded the heavens with cloud. And the Mexicans became silent.

It was cold and she was tired. Now and again a childish impulse of sulkiness came over her. But then she remembered how the yellow waters of the river had run by her at the ford, and she knew that everyone would agree that this was her own fault. Or if she had not fled, in the first place, there was not a chance in a hundred that the idle young pack would have taken after her.

She could see the bigness of their sombreros. She could see the nodding heads of the horses, here and there. Still they climbed through winding passes until at length, out of the night below them, a scattering of lights shone like spangles of gold on black velvet.

"Ormosa," said one of the men.

They were halfway down the slope when the sound of horses came up towards them. A man's voice began to call: "Pedrillo! Pedrillo!"

"It's Juan!" said the leader. "Hai, Juan!"

Two riders came out of the dark. The hunchback hurried up first.

"I found Don Tonio!" he exclaimed, breathless. "He says that if it is true his father will pay a great deal of money. He knows the name of Lavery. He is pleased! Tell him, Pedrillo, that we want *two* hundred pesos apiece."

The second rider pulled up his horse. The party halted, clustering closely around this newcomer. He rode a tall horse. He was himself tall in the saddle.

"Light a match and let me look at her," he commanded.

A match was lighted and held almost under her chin. Beyond the blinding flare of the light she looked into the dim face of this Tonio Rubriz. He was young and handsome. There was strength in his shoulders. Even by that dull glow she was sure that his eyes were blue, not black.

The match died. It burned the fingers that held it and it was dropped to the ground.

"Very well," said Tonio. "This is the sort of a face that the gringos call beautiful. And a gringo father will pay very well for her."

"You are pleased, Don Tonio?" asked one of the men. "You will speak to your father about us, then?"

"You may all be damned in hell fire," said Tonio

127

Rubriz. "I'll never speak for you. If there were half a man among the lot of you, you would not have chased a woman all day. Men like the crew of you shame my country."

"Hai, Tonio!" yelled the hunchback. "I thought you were pleased?"

"To catch a Lavery, because my father hates the name," said he.

"You will not set her free, Tonio? I have lamed my horse chasing her!"

"Oh, you shall have money, you shall have money," said Tonio Rubriz. "My father will see to that, and he's the master. Bring her on after me!"

He turned his horse.

"Señor Rubriz!" called the girl. "Señor Rubriz, if you will send me back at once, you will be paid whatever is right. If you will—"

"Tell her to keep her mouth still," said Rubriz. "Tell her that I have sworn to speak to gringos only with a whip."

She caught her breath. Somehow she had been building greatly on the youth and the pride in his face and on what he had said before. Now she rode on silently behind him, with Pedrillo still holding the reins of the horse.

They did not go through the town. Instead, they turned to the right and after a short time came to the wooded throat of a ravine. There a voice challenged them sharply.

"Tonio!" said young Rubriz, in answer. He said to

the rest of the girl's escort. "Stay here. There will be money sent out to you, I suppose. Manuelo, take the gringo horse and lead it to the house. I don't want to touch leather where gringo hands have been before me."

A man loomed from among the brush, took the reins which Pedrillo surrendered, and led Ruth Lavery out of the narrows of the ravine into a more spreading valley. Trees spotted it with black clouds, here and there; the lighted windows of a house were not far away, a low, large house in front of which they stopped.

"Lead her in," said Tonio. "Take her by the arm and lead her in."

Tonio walked ahead. Manuelo followed, gripped the girl at the elbow so hard that her arm was kept straight. One smoking lantern lighted a hall that had the mask of a puma grinning on the wall. Saddles, bridles, coats, hats hung in crowds from rows of pegs, and the head of the great cat glared over them.

Tonio stopped at a door and rapped once on it.

"Who is it?" boomed a resonant voice in Mexican from the other side of the wall.

"Tonio," said he, and threw the door wide.

He stepped in, with the girl following. She saw a long room half filled with swirls of smoke, and at a table sat a man with a broad, muscular face. Around his throat was tied a rag of red silk.

"I bring the daughter of Lavery," said Tonio.

The man at the table was playing cards. Now he

rose. The pack streamed out of his hands and, fluttering, dropped towards the floor. He slowly pushed out his arms as though he were embracing a mighty thought. And he began to laugh. Joy stuffed his throat so full that his laughter made no sound, and his head kept bobbing back as the mirth shook his body.

Chapter Eighteen

MONTANA AND Lavery, as they came through the hills, found themselves at the head of a small ravine with a little white town stuck in the middle of its throat.

"We'd better climb the ridge and cut around that village," said the Kid.

"Climb the ridge? It's steep enough to slide down," answered Lavery. "Afraid somebody'll recognize you, Montana?"

"I am."

"And if they do?"

"Then there'll be music in the air. But we'll take a chance and go ahead if you want to."

"All right," said Lavery. "It's all a chance, anyway. What devil have you raised in Mexico?"

They rode on towards the town.

"A devil with money in his pocket. They have a price on me," said the Kid. "I suppose that I'll be passed over the counter sooner or later, but I hope there'll be some bargaining first."

"Is everybody in Mexico on the lookout for you?"

The Kid explained: "It's like this. Mexicans like bargains. Bullets are cheap and my scalp would sell high, and I've been too well advertised. I've played tag with the Rurales a good bit, and when they play the game it's likely to be a thousand miles between the start and the first King's X."

"They're a tough lot, those Rurales," said Lavery. "Perhaps we'd better try to climb that divide, after all, and cut around the back of the town."

"Oh, there's no fun changing your mind after you've made it up," answered Montana. "You understand—if they come kiting after me they'll be after you, too?"

His eyes were quizzical as they studied the face of Lavery. The big rancher smiled. "That's all right," he said.

They entered the town. It no longer seemed so white, for the wash had dried and peeled away from the 'dobe bricks at the corners of the houses, and the rain had washed the feet of the walls to mud. The odd, spicy fragrance of Mexican cookery, both sharp and oppressive, hung in the air of the street. In a doorway squatted barelegged women rubbing out cornmeal to make paste for tortillas, or sewing, or simply with folded arms, staring at the nothingness of life. Children came out in little swirls of dust to see the strangers. Chickens scuttered out of the way, but the pigs in their dust wallows would not move.

"Nothing but the noise of cartwheels makes 'em stir," said Montana.

They reached the little central plaza of the town; they were halfway across it when from the gaudy front of a little fonda stepped a very tall and a very short man in gaudy uniforms with rifles slung at their backs.

"Rurales!" said the Kid. softly. "Don't hurry your horse."

They rode straight past the pair. The tall fellow had a scar that ran a seam from his chin up the left side of his face, lifting the corner of his mouth and dragging down the corner of his eye. He put a hand over his mouth like an Indian surprised, and stared at the two riders.

Lavery could count the steps the horses were making; ten strokes of his heart to one stride. Then, behind him, he heard a voice peal out: "El Keed! El Keed!"

"Ride like hell!" said the Kid, and got his own mustang into a racing gallop in half a second. The rifles began; the air was instantly full of that music of which Montana had spoken and that voice behind them kept screeching, as though a knife were being jabbed into the man who yelled: "El Keed! El Keed!"

They rounded a corner and tried to fade away into the horizon.

But Mexican horizons are wide and Rurales have the patience of buzzards and the speed of hawks. They followed all that day. Montana "borrowed" fresh horses three times.

Lavery protested only the first time.

"Take horses without paying for them?" he exclaimed, as Montana cornered a herd in a field.

The Kid pointed back to a dust-cloud that was

rolling towards them through a gap in the hills. Two Rurales were helping to raise that cloud of dust, together with a crowd of adventurous Mexicans who could be depended upon to shoot straight and fast.

"We can't become horse thieves!" shouted Lavery.

"Stay honest, then," answered Montana as he shied his rope at a bronco, "and get yourself hanged with some honest Mexican rope."

Lavery said no more. He roped a good mustang for himself and changed saddles faster than he ever had turned the trick before. A Mexican cowhand had spotted the thieves, and now was couched flat on the ground behind a big cactus, taking pot shots that raised little puffs of dust at the feet of Lavery or went by his ear with a thin, ghostly whoop. But try as he would, he was ten seconds behind Montana in getting his fresh horse under way.

In the middle of the day they "borrowed" mounts again; but still, as evening drew on, they could see the persistent dust-cloud rolling towards them. The Kid's horse played out. He roped a wild roan mustang in a mesquite tangle and fought the brute an hour before it submitted. That roan had the gait of a mule and the manners of a mountain lion, but there was no wear to it. Even while it fought, it kept jumping in the right direction. It loped the rest of that day and most of the night. In the hours of darkness they entered the grand confusion of the San Carlos mountains. There, in a wilderness of rocks, they trusted to have lost the two Rurales, the tall cadaver with the scarred face who had

133

started the yelling and his companion who had done the shooting. At any rate, they did not appear during the following day when the Kid left the mountains and journeyed down the slopes towards Santa Katalina, that lay in a loop of its river like a white lump of chalk.

"That's where I saw him walk through the street with the Rurales all around him and the crowd yelling. He was dripping blood. The Rurales had nicked him in a dozen places, it looked like. I could see the mark on his back as clear as day," said Montana.

Lavery wiped the dust off his cracked lips, uncorked his canteen, took a swallow of lukewarm, alkaline water, and nodded. He said nothing at all, but kept studying the white, sprawling outlines of the town like an artist who wants to remember sketching material. Then he rode on with Montana into the town.

They entered Santa Katalina in the smoky dusk of the day, stabled the horses, and sauntered under the big green trees of the plaza. Three sides of that plaza were bounded by the broad sweep of the river; along the other side a row of eating and drinking places was retired behind a big 'dobe arcade, so clumsily and irregularly built that it looked as though the hands of children had done the work. Little iron tables were strewn under the arcade and out among the trees of the square. The Kid drifted among those tables, with Lavery tagging behind.

Finally the goal was sighted.

They were apart by themselves at a little round table

close to the flank of a huge tree, drinking coffee and Mexican "hot water" and smoking cigarettes. Gentleman Jeff Leffingwell, by a few strokes of art, had transformed himself into a Mexican caballero. But Turk Fadden was his unchangeable self, sodden, leering, brutal, a caricature out of a grim book. But even he looked more in place in Mexico.

They jumped up when the Kid approached.

"I was thinking that you wouldn't show up," said Turk Fadden.

"This is the day," answered the Kid.

He brought up Lavery with a gesture, saying: "Here's a friend of mine that I want you to meet. Mr. Lavery, this is Leffingwell and this is Fadden. I've told you about them."

Turk Fadden turned red, but Leffingwell was instantly at home.

"A pleasure to meet you, sir," said he. "You know, sir, that when a man is living by his wits he sometimes turns his attention to some queer bits of practice. But now to have an opportunity to rectify a crime, to heal the wound caused by a brutal act, to cause the pain of twenty years to vanish, is a matter, Mr. Lavery, which I can only say moves me to—"

"Listen," said Montana. "Lavery is not that kind of a fool. But he'll pay you and the Turk like a king. Cut out the bunk and sit down, everybody."

Leffingwell was not affronted. He merely laughed and then did the honors.

"Sit down here on my right, Mr. Lavery," he said.

"And you here, Montana, because I dare say that you'll prefer to have the tree at your back. These men of action, Mr. Lavery, are bound to take certain precautions, eh?"

"Tripe!" said the Kid.

He signed to a waiter and ordered tortillas, chile con carne, coffee. Lavery took the same.

"That's a light meal," said Gentleman Jeff. "You ought to try—"

"We eat light on purpose, down here," said the Kid. "A full belly makes a fellow sleepy, and even the snakes know that it's dangerous to be sleepy in Mexico. What do you people know?"

"About Tonio Rubriz?" murmured Turk Fadden, lowering his voice, and glancing askance.

"*You* tell me, Leffingwell," said the Kid. "Turk can't help talking as though he were still in the penitentiary doing the lock-step."

"You always have your little jokes, eh?" said the Turk, sneering and scowling.

"Shut up, Turk!" said Leffingwell. "I'll tell you, brother," he added to the Kid. "It'll be easier to pick red-hot iron out of a fire than to pick Tonio Rubriz out of his place."

"We'll have to handle him with fire-tongs, then," said the Kid. "Go on."

"He lives up in the mountains, in a town called Ormosa. I mean he lives in it or near it when he's not sifting through the passes on some raid or other. The people love that *hombre*. The Rurales hate him.

136

Everybody is always talking about him behind the hand. The Mexicans like anything that's against the law. You know that. Maybe that's why they like Tonio Rubriz."

"They like him because he's a Lavery," said the Kid. "What do they think about old Mateo Rubriz, these days?"

"Old Mateo's poison," said Leffingwell, "and everybody agrees that he is. But there's one good thing about him, and the greasers forgive him everything because of it. He loves his son." He made a gesture as of apology to Lavery, who was silent as a stone, listening, watching eyes.

"He loves a meal ticket," said the Kid. "Of course he does."

"I dunno," said Turk Fadden, gloomily, "how you can ever get at Tonio."

"I'll go up to Ormosa and ask for him," said the Kid.

"You'll get a knife stuck between your shoulders if you do," said Leffingwell. "They don't talk about Rubriz, up yonder."

The food came. The Kid began to eat with a great appetite.

"You have to know how to ask your questions in this man's land," said the Kid. "I know the right way of doing it."

"After all," said Turk Fadden, "we come on a wild-goose chase, Leffingwell and me, unless Mr. Lavery sees that we get something out of it?"

Still Lavery said nothing.

"When Tonio Rubriz finds out that he's really Dick Lavery," said the Kid, "he's going to have you right there in Ormosa to thank for unraveling the mystery."

"He won't have me," said Turk Fadden. "I ain't gunna try—"

"All right," said the Kid. "If your skin isn't tough, you can't handle the roast goose."

"I like your way about things," said Leffingwell, with his greasy smile, "but—"

The Kid rolled some beans inside a tortilla with wonderful deftness, conveyed the morsel to his mouth, and wiped his hands. He pushed back his chair at the same time.

"You'll find me in Ormosa," he said. "I've got to start, because company is coming this way. Lavery, jump!"

He rose. Two men who were walking among the tables suddenly began to run towards him at full speed. One was very tall, with a scarred face, yellow and hollow as death. The other was short and chunky and wore a glistening mustache. Their uniforms shone in the lamplight.

Chapter Nineteen

THE TALL MAN, running in the lead, flipped out a revolver and began to fire every time his right foot left the ground. The Kid shot him through the head. He went down in a loose sprawl. His companion tripped over the body, capsized a table, and lay across his friend beneath the wreckage.

The Kid lifted his coffee cup with his left hand. The gun still weighted down his right as he finished the drink, and said to Leffingwell and Turk Fadden: "You'd better get out of this. That second Rurale is not dead and you'll be held as confederates in the crime. I'll see you tomorrow in Ormosa. Come on, Lavery."

He put up his gun, placed money on the table, and walked away. A crowd was gathering around the two fallen Rurales. The Kid passed straight through that crowd and took pleasure in the way the people shrank to either side, avoiding him. He was so pleased that he was still smiling when he reached the stable.

It seemed to Lavery that the tumult which lifted behind them was growing louder, rushing on them at the speed of a galloping horse, but the Kid kept on walking at ease. In the stable, he was not saddled until Lavery had been waiting for a nervous half minute at the door of the barn. Then Montana came out, smiling a little, and canted his head to one side as he listened to the distant shouting, the hoofbeats that scattered here and there.

He said nothing to Lavery, but mounted, and Lavery followed out of the town. All he could be sure of was that the Kid was happy—very happy in a world of which Lavery knew nothing.

When they were so high in the hills that Santa Katalina in the plain was a little star-cluster of lights, hardly separable, the Kid made camp with Lavery in a small ravine. It was a dry camp. The horses had nothing; the men had only one canteen of water between them, but Lavery felt that he could endure anything rather than the silence of the Kid, who sat up with his back against a rock and looked at the stars and the slow wash of moon-shadows among the trees and the boulders. However, Montana was not talking.

In the morning he was a little less taciturn after their tired horses had climbed into view of Ormosa.

"I'm going ahead to see how things are," said Montana, making his usual cigarette during the pause. "You wait till dark and then drift in to take a look-see for yourself. You'll find me there, likely."

"I'm going in with you," insisted Lavery. "You've taken the brunt of everything, so far. Now I'm going in to do my half."

The Kid looked him over without curiosity or anger.

"You stay here till night," he said, and rode off. Lavery stayed.

Ormosa lay in the center of an amphitheater which was a mass of exits and entrances, for into the hollow led a dozen narrow ravines, choked with pine trees. On all sides above it, went up the mountains, bald and towering. There might have been a hundred people in Ormosa, and twice as many dogs. Goats, and pigs almost as lean and nimble, strayed in the streets. The mustang of the Kid kicked at them as it went by. The Kid laughed.

There was a tavern in Ormosa. The Kid walked into the little fonda which occupied most of the ground floor of the inn and laid the length of his quirt across the top of the bar. The sound was like the report of a gun. It brought up to their feet half a dozen wild fellows who were sitting in a corner, playing cards. They looked as rough as the mountains about the town but more unshaven.

The bartender remained calm. He simply picked up a rifle from the shelf and stood with it at the ready.

Said the Kid, "Which of you knows Tonio Rubriz?"

Still faces and uneasy eyes greeted the question. Slowly the men began to turn their heads and look at one another.

"Which ever of you knows him, tell Tonio Rubriz that I am staying here at the tavern for a day or two. If He does not come to find me, I'll go to find *him*. Landlord," he continued to the man behind the bar, "your best room!"

The proprietor fought the Kid with his eyes for a moment. The Kid threw the lash of his whip over his shoulder and waited. Finally the Mexican put down the rifle, muttering. He led the way out of the fonda across a patio where chickens were scratching in the dust, and went up a flight of stone steps to the second storey. There he showed a big, naked room with a goatskin on the floor, and another flung over the bed for a covering.

"This is hardly fit for my dog," said the Kid, "but I shall use it. I shall sleep until dark. At that time bring me a good platter of roasted kid, some red wine, and bread. Give grain to my horse. If the pigs squeal or the children yell in the street, quiet them with a whip. I wish to be quiet."

The patron regarded the Kid for a long moment from beneath thick black eyebrows. Then he withdrew, his slippers making only a whisper on the floor.

The Kid threw himself down, folded his hands under his head, and stared at the ceiling. He smiled, for it was like old times. He stroked the sleek of his throat with a lingering touch. Then he closed his eyes and, as he had promised, fell asleep, and did not waken until a footfall came through the hall.

The Kid sat up. It was dusk. The room was dark. The chill of the mountain air had poured into it. Already the stars were so bright that he could see the black of the mountain-sides against that golden stippling.

A foot kicked the door.

The Kid stood up, placed his hat on his head, touched the guns under his arms, and set his bandana straight.

"Come in!" he called.

The door swung in heavily, slowly. First entered a boy carrying a lantern which he placed on the center table. After him came a woman with a dark, pretty face. She had a great tray of food in her arms and she slid it onto the table beside the lantern; then she looked up with a flash of teeth and eyes.

The Kid stepped to the table, looked at the roasted meat, breathed the fragrance of it, opened the flask of wine, tasted it, and nodded.

"Tell Tonio Rubriz that I'll be ready to see him in half an hour," said the Kid.

Then he fell to on the supper and ate heartily. He finished the meat and the bread and the wine, made a cigarette, and had begun to puff at it luxuriously when he heard an outcry of voices in the street, a trampling of horses, a yelling of fierce laughter, a calling upon God in good American.

The Kid went to the window. Most of the street was darkness, but here and there the pale gold of lamplight stole across it in a nebulous haze. In one of those mists of light there was a whirl of several horsemen who handled their lithe mustangs as only Cossacks and Mexicans can. In the center of the whirl were Gentleman Jeff Leffingwell and Turk Fadden wound in ropes like two wasps in the spider's silk.

The Kid smiled. He chuckled softly as he looked down on the scene. Then he went back to his chair with his back to the door and finished the cigarette.

He made another, lighted it. The room was filling with the sharp scent of the tobacco. The smoke was a mist here, or a pale blue-brown wreath there. The Kid put out his hand and grasped the bight of one of those loops of thick smoke. He drew his hand away and marked where it had been, smiling.

Something whispered behind him. The flame leaped in the throat of the chimney.

"Come in, Tonio," said the Kid.

He had heard no opening of the door, but now there was the sound of many footsteps. He leaned back in his chair until his shoulders were comfortable against the round of it. Before him strode three men. Another, he knew by the lightnings that were quivering coldly up and down his spine, stood just behind his chair.

They were the type of men he wanted. They were dressed as if for a festival in gold-braided jackets with great colored silken scarfs around their lean hips. They were armed to the teeth. They were young. They had the eyes of men who do not dare to be afraid, because danger is always present and if fear once opens the door it will never leave.

The central figure was the tallest. His clothes were a trifle more gay, also.

"You are what, gringo?" asked this fellow, sneering as he delivered the insult, but speaking perfectly good English.

"I'm the man who has come for you, greaser," said the Kid.

"Ah," said the Mexican, his lips twitching. "You know me? You lie! You never have laid eyes on me before!"

"I know you," said the Kid, "by the color of your hair and the color of your eyes."

Tonio Rubriz blinked his slaty-blue eyes. He squinted at the Kid.

"Do you think I'm a fool?" he asked.

"Nevertheless," said the Kid, "some one has made a fool of you."

Rubriz lifted his glance to meet the eyes of the man behind the chair. Yet he seemed to hesitate before giving an order.

"You may talk a little," said Rubriz. "Before the end, perhaps I shall have something to say about fools who ride into Ormosa and ask the devil to appear."

He laughed, and his companions laughed with him. The Kid admired the flashing of their fine, dark eyes and the white shining of their teeth.

The Kid smiled also.

He tilted back still farther in his chair, as though in excess of comfort of body and spirit. He clasped his hands behind his head, thereby disarming himself, and rested the soles of his boots against the edge of the table to sustain his balance.

"There are a lot of things that I have to say to you, Tonio," said the Kid. "They'll all be said, you can be sure, but it will take a little time, and your spirit will have to be altered, first."

"Altered? Ah?" said Rubriz.

He lifted his brows. His features might be American enough, but his smile was Mexican. No other race knows how to pull back the lips in a perfect smile without a trace of mirth in it.

"When will you alter me, my friend?" said Tonio Rubriz.

"Now," said the Kid, and straightening his legs violently, he hurled the table, the tray, and the lantern straight at the three. The lantern struck one of them in the face, filled eyes and nose and throat with hot oil, and started him yelling and gasping. The table floored the other two in the darkness while the Kid, hurled backwards by the same impetus that had knocked the table headlong, crashed against the man who had been standing behind him.

He grappled that man with one arm. They hurtled

across the floor and struck the wall. A gun must have been in the fellow's hand for it exploded beside the very ear of Montana, filling his brain with thunder.

With the barrel of a Colt, the Kid struck for the head of the shadow that writhed with him on the floor. The steel clanked on the stone pavement. He struck again. The body kicked out and lay still.

The Kid arose like a crouching cat.

One man was running blindly through the darkness, shouting that he was choked. The other pair had disengaged themselves from the fall of the table. The Kid could see them while he himself remained unseen, for the dull sheen of street light came vaguely through the window and gave them a background.

One of them was taller than the other. The instant he was sure of that he fired, aiming between knee and thigh. The shorter of the pair dropped.

The Kid sprang to the side. A gun was fired twice. The bullets splashed against the heavy rock face of the wall. Then Montana leaped in and struck for the gun hand of the marksman. Steel met steel with a crash that benumbed the arm. The other revolver clattered across the floor.

The Kid shoved the cold muzzle of his Colt under the chin of that form which he hoped might be Tonio Rubriz.

"Back up through the door," said the Kid. "Don't try for your other gun or I'll lift the roof off your head."

The form of darkness cursed in soft Mexican, like a spitting cat, but it backed through the door. The Kid

slammed it behind them. There was a key on the outside of it and he turned the key. Some one in the room
began to shoot at the closed door.

Down the hall streamed a very faint light from an
open door. Montana saw that it was actually Tonio
Rubriz who stood before him.

"This is better, Tonio," said he. "In a little while
we'll be able to talk."

Rubriz was moaning in an ecstasy of shame.

These things had happened in very few seconds.
Now footfalls hurried up from the patio below.

"Walk straight before me down the corridor," said
Montana. "I shall be behind you with a gun in my coat
pocket ready to break your back. Walk straight
through."

"God has forgotten me," said Tonio Rubriz, and
walked on.

Chapter Twenty

THERE WERE A dozen in the throng that came up the
stairs and spilled into the hallway. They were all those
wild mountain men, with shaggy faces and active
eyes. They fell back to either side against the wall and
let Rubriz pass as though he were a prince royal.

So Tonio led the way into the patio. Above them
they heard beating against the locked door. They heard
wild voices calling out.

"What did you do with the two Americans?" asked
the Kid.

"They are on the way from the town," said Tonio, choking out the words.

In the patio light the Kid could see his face clearly and knew that he was on the point of dying of rage and miserable humiliation.

That was exactly as it should be.

In the street, there was a closely packed congregation of villagers gathered against the opposite wall of the highway, looking up at the darkened window out of which the shouts were pouring. Here and there stood a number of good horses, their reins thrown.

"Get on the best horse," said the Kid.

Rubriz mounted. The Kid leaped into the saddle on an adjoining horse. "Take after the two Americans," he directed.

Tonio Rubriz led the way at a lope out of the town. Behind them arose an astonished chorus of voices. It was still rising like a wail into the air as the Kid issued with his captive from the town lights into the cold quiet of the starlight beyond.

"Will they follow us?" asked the Kid.

"Follow me?" said Tonio Rubriz, in a burst of agony and of pride. "Never! They will never dare to follow me. They still think that I'm a man, though a filthy gringo, a—"

"Hush," said the Kid.

Before them he saw a rider who was coming slowly towards the town, a man tall enough to make his horse seem small.

"Hai, Lavery!" he called.

"Hai!" called the voice of Richard Lavery in return. "Montana?"

They drew together, with Montana saying: "Here's the man you want, Lavery. He's just been cursing the gringos. You can tell him what he is himself. Watch yourself. He's not armed, but he's all wildcat."

They sat their horses in silence. Montana could see his captive turned his head slowly to look at one of his companions and then at the other. Out of the town behind them the tumult rose in a crescendo, like a siren. The Kid could see that picture of running men, of horses being saddled and mounted.

Richard Lavery scratched a match; Montana knocked it out of his hand.

"Don't insult him, Lavery," he directed. "He's the real nugget, eye-color and all; he's the real Lavery. But don't stare at him. There's enough Mexican in him still to make him cut your throat for that. Here. If you're tongue-tied, I'll do some talking."

He turned in the saddle.

"Listen to me," he said. "Tonio—Rubriz—whatever you call yourself—the fact is that old Mateo never put a drop of blood in your veins. You're gringo, friend. That's why a pair of gringos came for you."

He heard the quick, hard-drawn breathing of the other.

"Señor," came the reply, "you are a very brave man, a very cunning man. You have taken me out of Ormosa like a runaway dog. I am worth a ransom to you, I suppose, and my father will pay. But if you insult me again, señor, I swear to God that I shall try for your throat in spite of your guns!"

"D'you hear him, Lavery?" asked Montana. "There's never been a bit between the teeth of this mustang. I've changed my mind. Light another match and hold it in front of your face."

He added, to the captive: "Now, Tonio, here's a great moment. You've read things like this in rotten romances. Light the match, Lavery."

Richard Lavery obediently lighted the match and held it in front of his stern face.

"You're seeing your father, Tonio," said Montana. "Not pretty, but all man and a yard wide. Mateo Rubriz stole his son twenty years ago because of a grudge. This is Richard Lavery. His ranch is big enough for you to have heard about it."

The light of the match died out. Tonio had said nothing. As the light failed, the darkness seemed to rush in closely around them unbroken by the rays of the stars.

"Your mother's alive," said the Kid, carelessly. "She has a pair of eyes that match yours, Tonio. And she'll want to look on your shoulder to see if there's a birth-mark on you—a pair of splotches, one bigger than the other, like a dot inside a half moon."

"My father," said Tonio, "is Mateo Rubriz!"

"A capable sort of a crook," said Montana. "And he raised you in his profession. There's a double edge to that knife, Tonio. He robs Lavery of a son and then he turns that son into a Mexican gunman. Pretty, isn't it?

150

He turns a gringo into a Mexican and the Mexican hunts down the gringo kind. What could be neater than that?"

"Mother of God!" said Tonio. "Why do I know that this is not a lie?"

"Because you're a logical fellow," said the Kid, "and you know that Texas ranchers are a hard-boiled lot. They don't throw away their property into Mexican hands if they know what they're about. It has to be proved."

"Señor Lavery," said Tonio, "I have heard of your name. I think there is truth in your face. Tell me—was there such a mark as he says on the body of your son?"

"There was," said Lavery.

The arms of Tonio flung up in a dark gesture against the stars.

"Mercy of God!" he cried out. "The sign is on my body, too."

He began to strike a hand against his face, groaning.

"Steady, old son," said the Kid. "It's a hard thing to be born twice into one life. But lock this idea inside your head. Your name is Richard Lavery the Second. You're as much a gringo as I am. And Mateo Rubriz has done Mexican murder on twenty years of your life. We've got to ride on to catch up with the two other gringos that you and your friends raised the devil with this evening. They belong to the party, in a sort of left-handed way. Lavery, go on beside him. I'll ride ahead."

He spurred down the trail.

He found the pair hardly a mile ahead. They made no effort to get away as he rode up, for their hands were tied behind them, their clothes had mostly been stripped from their backs, and they plodded along like slaves haltered together, surrendering to despair. The voice of the Kid, however, wakened them like good wine. A touch of a knife made them free.

"I'm gunna get me a greaser," said Turk Fadden, stifled with rage, as soon as his hands were free. "Gimme a gun, Montana. I'm gunna go back into that hell-hole and get me a greaser. I'm gunna get me the tallest greaser that I seen there. I'm gunna get me the gaudy—that done the ordering—the one that laughed himself pretty near to death!"

"Go get him, boy," said the Kid. "That's young Dick Lavery."

"Young Dick hell," said Leffingwell. "I'm going to wear his scalp! Look at us! They stripped us naked as rats, almost. The dirty—"

"Dick Lavery is the head of the crew," said the Kid. "And he's coming up the road with his dear father, just now, feeling a little sick at the stomach because he's been turned into a damned gringo. Now, Leffingwell, you can tell Tonio Rubriz, alias Dick Lavery, the whole yarn about how you helped to dig him out of the Mexican darkness. See what a hit that makes with him."

The Leffingwell sense of humor had not been educated to such a point that he could appreciate the gist of this remark, and when Tonio came up with Richard

152

Lavery, by the light of a golden half moon that had risen in the east, Leffingwell actually stood in the road and orated to that newfound soul in pain.

Nobly Leffingwell included Turk Fadden, dropping his hand once or twice on the shoulder of his compeer. Fadden grinned and edged nearer, into the story.

The effect on the real Dick Lavery was a total conviction. The pointing finger and the raised voice of Leffingwell were hardly necessary. There was the mark on the shoulder for a proof, and the certainty that these three men had not ventured into danger for a mere nothing. But Tonio gripped the pommel of his saddle with both hands and hunched his head down between his shoulders in an agony. "Hey," said Turk Fadden, "I dunno that I foller this. We turn you into a millionaire and you act like we'd struck the colic into you!"

"Shut up," said Leffingwell. "It's the birth pains that are twisting him. How can the greaser die out of a man and the gringo come into him in five minutes without tearing him up a little?"

"Both of you be still," commanded the Kid.

He looked at Richard Lavery, the upper part of whose face was black-masked by the shadow of the brim of his hat, but on the lower part of it there was an unalterable smile.

Whatever he had said to Tonio on the road, he was silent now, watching the grief of his son with the unconcern of one who knows that the passions of childhood die soon. In all that followed, Richard

Lavery offered not a single word of suggestion. He seemed contented that Montana should direct everything, and the Kid was grateful for that silence when he knew that a hundred times the older man must have had to set his teeth to keep from speech.

"We've got to move on," he said. "If Mateo Rubriz organizes a hunt for you, as he's sure to do, before long—well, we have only three horses to carry five men, and we'll be traveling slowly. What's the quickest way of getting horses, Lavery?"

The use of that name made the other jerk up his head again. But he merely said: "I've got to go back. I've got to see Mateo Rubriz."

"You want to see him," said the Kid, "and ask him to account for that birthmark and your blue eyes and your age, which is exactly that of Lavery's stolen boy. You want to corner him and make him confess. Well, partner, I'll tell you how he'll confess. He'll put a bullet through your head!"

"I have to see his face," said Dick Lavery. "I have been a Mexican all my life and proud of my country. Now you want to turn me all at once into a Yankee, made of iron and ice-water. I am the son of Mateo Rubriz. We have ridden together and fought side by side how many times. But you snatch me away from him and turn me into the son of a Yankee rancher! I must see Mateo Rubriz before I go. If the father dies out of his face and leaves him a stranger—then—well, I shall ride back with you."

"When the father dies out of his face," said the Kid,

"you'll die the same instant. Talking won't budge you, Lavery. A gun will have to do the trick, then, and I have one. You're in our hands and you'll have to march with us. Leffingwell, climb aboard this horse. You and Turk Fadden take turns. I'll walk. Mind you, Lavery—if you won't go peacefully, you'll go in ropes!"

Chapter Twenty-one

THEY WENT NORTH, until, in an hour, they were hopelessly entangled in a sea of mountains, split by many great ravines. Lavery, of course, could have guided them, but Lavery was silent as a stone, so the Kid decided to wait until daylight before laying a course. If Mateo Rubriz, as was likely, soon started a furious hunt for the missing Tonio, his messengers would not be likely to thread a way to the place where the four were hiding. And in the daylight they would be able to plot the avenue of their escape. So in a corner of a ravine, between a thicket and the high rock wall of the gulch, the Kid camped his party. They bedded themselves down hastily, unsaddled the horses.

The moon, cruising over the eastern mountains, was diving through a continual wash of little clouds that never could quite obscure that sailing prow. By this light the Kid observed an odd scene between the Laverys, father and son. The elder man had kept apart, never troubling his son, while Tonio sat on a rock with his chin in his hand and looked with the deep vacancy of thought. At last the rancher went over and stood behind him. That was one of the queer parts of the talk, that he stood behind his son and seemed trying to make his words part of Tonio's fancy.

He said, quietly: "We all fight against change. Everything that is new is hateful. Besides, you've been taught to despise your blood and your people. The best way is not to make a struggle of it. You'll be as free as a hawk, if you wish. You won't be held down to a life on the ranch. You'll never have to see any of us until you want to. I'll only tell you one thing. You have a mother, Dick. And the day she lost you always seems only yesterday to her."

When he ended, Tonio looked up at the moon suddenly.

"Señor Lavery, you have a daughter?" said he.

The Kid could make nothing of that answer. Lavery said, "Yes," and Tonio went back to his meditations. He said not a word more.

Montana was taking no chances. He tied his left arm to the right arm of Tonio. He used a bit of twine and he tied it with hard knots.

"We'll sleep, boys," said the Kid. "We need to lay up sleep in our systems the way a camel needs to lay up fat in its hump."

He set the example, and though he had slept long and soundly that day, he lay awake only a few moments staring at the big breast and the outthrust chin of the cliff above him, and thinking of the dangerous leagues that lay between them and that ranch in the Bend.

He wakened out of a deep sleep, with the sense that something had been taken from him. The guns were still with him. Leffingwell and Turk Fadden were snoring in a soft harmony. But in the distance there was a light, regular clicking sound, such as the armed hoofs of a horse will make when it passes over rocks.

Then he was aware of Richard Lavery standing over him, pointing in the direction of that departing sound.

"He's gone!" said the rancher.

The words came vaguely into the mind of Montana. He had to draw himself out of the nebulous world of sleep for a great distance before he knew what was about him.

Then he remembered Dick Lavery and was aware that the man was gone. The intricate knots in which the Kid had reposed such trust had been unraveled without giving the twine so much as a single twitch; for the least jerk, the passing of the merest shadow, would have been enough to rouse Montana.

He leaped up to his feet. The horse he had ridden remained lying down where it was tethered but Tonio's horse was gone. Tonio had gone back to "look Mateo Rubriz in the face"!

The Kid started saddling his mustang. Lavery did the same with the other horse. Montana called to Leffingwell: "Wake up, Jeff. The bird's flown. He's gone back to play with fire and he's going to burn his hands to the bone, this time. I'm after him. Wait here for a day. If I don't come then, I'll never come."

"Wait here? Alone?" cried Turk Fadden. The

volume of the echoes which he had raised frightened him and made him hush his voice to a whisper. "My God! the greasers will bunt us alive if they catch us! Don't leave us, or—"

He ran forward, clutching. The Kid struck away his hand and put the horse in motion.

"You'll take your chances," called the Kid, "and I take mine."

He looked back. Turk Fadden was shaking a fist after him, and cursing. And Leffingwell stood tall and silent, wrapping his body in his skinny arms.

Down the ravine the Kid fled as fast as that mustang could gallop, and it went like the wind. When he came to the mouth of the gulch he saw, far before him, the silhouette of a rider forcing his horse over a high divide. It was merely a glimpse before the picture dropped out of view.

That was how the Kid was guided across that savagely broken country. He had merely a flash of his quarry time and again. From a height, he saw, in the dark of a valley beneath him, a patch of lights. That might be Ormosa, he judged.

Richard Lavery had followed all that distance, riding very well, never speaking.

They came to a gorge up which Tonio had disappeared, and in the middle of the gorge the narrow valley split into two ravines.

"Take the right-hand cañon!" shouted Montana to Lavery. "If you come near him, shout your name, or else he's likely to shoot. Keep shouting if you sight him.

He's all at sea and he's likely to do the wrong thing. If you catch up with him, fire three shots to let me know!"

Then he rode on up the left-hand gorge and saw Lavery disappear to the right. Every step of the journey had increased Montana's respect for the rancher. He liked a man who could do things, obey instructions, keep the mouth shut. Lavery had all of these virtues.

The moon rode high, the shadows of the trees were stunted patches on the ground; every rock was whitened in this light. It was a ghostly place, but the voice that challenged the Kid was abrupt and human and Mexican enough.

"Who goes?"

The Kid did not stop his horse, though his heart leaped in him.

"Pedro?" he asked, carelessly.

"No," said the voice of the hidden man. "Halt!"

The Kid drew on the reins, but slowed the walk of the horse instead of halting it.

"You fool," he said, turning a little towards the spot from which the voice had issued, "didn't Tonio tell you I was coming?"

"Tonio?" said the other. "Who are you? I don't know you. Halt, or I'll shoot!"

"Oh, shoot and be done with it!" said the Kid.

He let the mustang go on at the same slow, unhurrying walk.

"Then take it through the head!" said the angry voice of that sentinel.

But the bullet did not follow.

"Tomorrow I'll make you sweat for not knowing me," said the Kid. "But Tonio needs me now!"

He passed into a denseness of shadow. He heard the Mexican cursing by the fluid name of many a saint, but the rifle did not explode, the voice went out in the darkness, and as the Kid began to breathe again he saw the gorge opening before him into a broader basin of grassland, spotted with many trees, and a house in the middle, built low, but with a squat tower at one corner of it.

Like a familiar face of danger, the Kid observed it and felt in the marrow of his bones that here he had reached the goal of his search.

Several horses were scattered over the grass, hobbled, and still grazing in spite of the lateness of the hour. Probably they had been hard ridden of late and therefore needed to make up time with their foraging.

He took the mustang to a dense clump of trees, tethered it, and approached the house on foot. Moving from tree to tree, he circled it. There were lights only in one corner, as though a single room were being occupied. To the rear was a shed which obviously had been added after the house was long built. It was merely a flimsy structure of logs and poles with a thatched roof. Probably part of the horses were kept under this shelter.

It seemed the obvious point for forcing an entrance, so he went to it like a stalking cat, swift but silent.

The door of the shed was open. He could hear the

animals inside stamping their hoofs and grinding their fodder. The rank smell of sweating horseflesh came out to him.

All was utter blackness, but he entered, moving cautiously down the back wall, brushing against saddles and tangles of reins. The chains of a silver bit tinkled like a ghostly bell as he went by.

He saw an eye of light, now, piercing a corner of the darkness and throwing a patch on the opposite wall. He went towards it, brushing against one of the horses, which instantly began to bawl like a pitching mustang. The whole line of tethered horses jumped and kicked and snorted in sympathy.

Through the hole by which the light had passage the Kid heard a strenuous voice ring out, commanding men to examine the horse-shed at once because there was some one in it, surely.

The Kid would have fled but he dared not move through the dimness past the driving heels of those horses. A mustang is not a mountain lion, but it can see almost as well in the dark and it is just as dangerous.

Footfalls came stamping with the jingling of spurs and the voices of the men, but all the Kid could do was to step behind one of the saddles which hung down by a stirrup from the wall, its big Mexican skirts almost touching the ground. It was a very imperfect shield for him. He pushed up the upper flap of the saddle, but even so it screened hardly half his face. He pulled the blanket off the peg and dropped it down over his boots. Yet part of his trousers must be visible.

Lights were coming. They swung past the shed, visible through the cracks and holes in the logs. Now two lanterns were at the entrance, held by men who turned the light and their inquiring revolvers here and there. The mustangs were still seething and writhing in their panic.

"It's that gray devil of a Pancho," said one of the men. "A rat ran under his feet and he's gone wild."

In fact, at the end of the line the horse against which the Kid had brushed was a shining little gray bronco, still fidgeting.

"I'll teach him. He'll be going to school all his life till I cut his heart out with my spurs, some day," said another voice.

A Mexican came, sliding the bail of a lantern up his left arm and handling a quirt with the other hand. As he shouted, the horses jumped aside and pressed against one another and the manger. So he came within reach of the gray and began to cut it with the whip.

He was not a yard away from the Kid, who could see the savage gleam of pleasure in the eyes of the Mexican as he wielded the quirt. The gray mustang squealed under the lash. It reared and tried to break the rope of the halter. Then it attempted to climb into the manger. Last of all, it jumped back and pumped its heels at the head of its master. The Mexican stepped back a little or his head would have been cut from his shoulders by the flash of those hoofs. All the more angrily he used the whip like a striking snake that moved in exact rhythm with the kicking of the gray, leaving marks as of red paint glistening on the flanks and haunch of the mustang.

The horse gave up. It crowded against the end wall and submitted, head down, its whole body wincing. The Mexican stepped in and gave three mighty blows with the full force of his arm, shouting out wordlessly with a savage triumph at every stroke.

The Kid handled a gun and forgot his own peril. A deathless desire to kill that Mexican warmed his soul.

But the flogging had ended. The other men, looking on from the entrance, were laughing and applauding. That was the way, they said, to teach a devil of a bronco manners.

He of the whip leaned, suddenly, picked the saddle blanket from the ground where it covered the feet of the Kid, and threw it over the peg, thereby veiling the head and shoulders of Montana. It seemed to the Kid that there was a sudden moment of hush, as though the man of the whip had made a silencing gesture to the rest of the group. Perhaps he was at this moment pointing out the exposed boots of the Kid and drawing a gun?

But in a moment the lights retreated, flickered down the outside of the shed, and left the place in perfect darkness.

Chapter Twenty-two

THERE WAS NO danger that the gray mustang would make further trouble. It stood like a lamb while the Kid stole past between it and the wall. He climbed the manger, on which he stood with his face at the level of that eye of light that broke through the 'dobe wall. Several bricks had been dislodged, so that through the aperture the Kid could see nearly every part of the room beyond. It was half kitchen and half living room, the sort of a chamber that the heart of a peon delights in. On some iron cranes at the end of the room various black pots were swung over the open fire. The pungency of stewing peppers was in the air, with whole swirls of wood smoke and tobacco smoke that made the scene like a glimpse through a fog. One man tended the pots over the fire. Half a dozen more sat about a long table, one with a bandage pulled around his head. Up and down, up and down across the room paced Tonio, yet he was not the man who filled the eye of the Kid. It was Mateo Rubriz who occupied his mind.

Tradition and legend said that Mateo Rubriz always wore a little red skull-cap. This fellow had on such a cap but he hardly needed that identifying stroke. He was a big, heavy chunk of a man who wore plenty of stomach; yet he looked able to run up the side of the wall. He had the jaw of a brute and the nose of a master; there were humor and the knowledge of life and men in his bright little eyes. He was the only one of the lot who was not aflash with Mexican finery of gold and silver. His face was that of a peon; so were his clothes. He had a rag of red silk tied around his throat—which men said was hideously scarred—and he was wearing a shirt of cheap white cotton, very soiled, and with the sleeves rolled up to his elbows. His forearms were big. Under the skin there was not a scruple of fat to hide the quivering of muscles and tendons as he shuffled cards and laid them out in precise rows for his game of "patience." The hands tell the man, and these hands were almost delicate, tapering down from small, round wrists. The moment the Kid had seen this man the rest of the room became dim, like a stage-setting around a great actor. Montana looked nowhere except from the hands to the face of Mateo Rubriz.

"Tonio," said Mateo Rubriz—"Tonio, I want you to talk to me."

Tonio continued to pace across the room, up and down, up and down. He said nothing.

All the other men grew hushed, glancing at the elder Rubriz and then at Tonio; there were awe and a rather savage expectancy in their faces.

"Rodolfo has had his little say," said Mateo Rubriz. "He told me how my son and three of my men went into a room where one gringo was sitting. One gringo!"

Rubriz held up a card, considered it with a frown, laid it back on the deck gently. The pack looked like a block of solid wood in the careful, firm grip of his fingers.

"Rodolfo told me when he came back with his broken head. Luis is half blind. Pedrillo has a broken leg. We know how my son was taken out of that room by the gringo, but we don't know what happened afterwards. Talk to me, Tonio."

Tonio continued to walk up and down, up and down. Now and then his pacing slowed and he turned a brilliant, savage eye over the group at the table.

Mateo Rubriz picked up a bottle and poured red wine into a silver cup. The edge of the cup and its two handles were set with what seemed enamel, at the first glance, but it was too brilliant for that. It was jewel work in topaz, emerald, and ruby. Rubriz examined the dainty pattern of this work.

"Come, Tonio," he said. "You think you have been shamed. But I tell you this, my lad: we are never on the real top of the mountain. It is only the devil that makes us think we are on high. Just when we begin to loll on the throne, along comes some man with enough hunger in his belly to sharpen his wits and dumps us out on the ground. Like the lees of the wine. He throws us out in the dust and the chickens come and scratch around, but even the chickens can find no more than the stain of us."

He laughed.

"I should have been a priest," he said. "I can think of such things to say, by God! You'll see when you come to die, some of you, what a comforter I can be if

I have a few moments to waste on you. Come, Tonio. Drink this wine with me, my son!"

He held up the cup to show its beauty in the light. He drank a little and smacked his lips loudly. He was like a father tempting a small child.

"He's drunk something beside wine, perhaps!" said one of the men, chuckling.

Rubriz whipped out a knife and flung it at the throat of the speaker. The man winced aside; the knife stuck in the door, singing like a wasp. A big revolver had followed the knife into the hand of Rubriz, but still he held up the wine-cup and had not spilled a drop from it.

"Get out of the room, all of you," said Mateo. "When a Rubriz talks to a Rubriz it is fitting that a flock of mongrels should hang about to lick up the tidbits. But now I am tired of you. Get out of my sight!"

They got up without a word, looking at Mateo, backing towards the door as though they feared he would follow them with bullets. His face had changed, in fact. His cheeks had been like brown russet apples with a stain of bright red in them. Now there was a gray spot to take the place of the red.

One man fumbled behind his back, found the knob of the door, opened it, and leaped back into the safe darkness beyond. The others followed.

"Close the door, Tonio," said Mateo Rubriz.

Tonio closed the door and stood for a moment with his hands against it.

"Now walk, if you want," said Rubriz. He leaned back in his chair, rested his elbow on his paunch, and began to sip the wine. "There is nothing so wonderful as walking, Tonio, to take the soreness out of the mind and out of the muscles. See a wolf how it paces and paces all day and every day behind the bars of the cage. It has met man, the master. It keeps pacing and pacing, trying to think. So you, Tonio, you have met man, the master. Eh? And your mind is sick. Your stomach is sick, too. All the life you ever have tasted is turning in your stomach, making you sick, eh? Keep on walking but talk to me a little, now and then."

He kept on sipping the wine between phrases, and his head would turn a trifle from side to side as he followed the pacing of Tonio up and down the floor again.

"You have grown too fat in the wits," said Mateo Rubriz. "That is all. Seven times in my life I have been about to die. It was always because I had begun to think that I was God. Once I received the stroke of a whip across my face. Do you see? Here!"

He drew a slanting line across his face from the left temple to the chin.

"That is where the whip of a gringo struck me, Tonio. At the time I had to stand still and receive the blow. There were a hundred of them standing about, waiting for the greaser to stir. So I had to take the blow and with my silence, as you might say, thank him for it! Why did I have to take the whip-stroke? Because I had been a fool, and you have been a fool or you would not be eating out your heart now after a man had mastered you. Come, sit down and drink some of this wine with me. There is not only wine but there is also understanding in this cup. You see, I know. It is not so much the shame. That one could stand. But shame at the hands of a gringo, eh? That is why the scar of the whip is less on my face than on my soul. Oh, Tonio, I have lain awake a thousands nights and eaten my hands, remembering. A gringo! A gringo! But by sunset tomorrow I shall have *your* gringo tied between stakes. I shall flay him a little at a time and let dogs eat the hide. You shall watch. No, you shall handle the skinning-knife! Do you hear me, Tonio? Sit down, my son!"

Tonio came to the table and faced Rubriz.

"The shame can go," he said. "Yes, there was shame. In Ormosa, too! Well, I have to forget that."

"No, you'll never forget it. Why should you forget it, Tonio?"

"Because I have something else to think about."

"It is good to think," said Mateo Rubriz, "but drinking is better still. Therefore, drink with me, Tonio. Here—from the same cup."

"Look at me," said Tonio.

"I look, my lad," said Mateo, "with a father's love, with a father's dear love. I see my poor son humiliated and bent by a misfortune. I swear to him that with all the blood in my body I shall pay and pay until I have wiped out that shame and made him laugh with joy. Is that enough, Tonio?"

"Enough and a thousand times more, if you are my father," said Tonio.

Rubriz bounded to his feet. The Kid could see that those feet were bare and that the trousers had been furled as high as the knee to free the hairy legs.

"Death of my life!" murmured Rubriz. He went around the table at a run, stretching a hand before him. Tonio endured his coming. "The gringo has been speaking to you," said Rubriz, crowding close. "What did he say? Ah, God! the smoke and the fire in my brain! What do *you* say? *If* I am your father?"

He was facing the Kid. His features were so swollen and red with blood that the Kid could see a thin white mark drawn from the left temple to the chin.

Tonio stood back a little.

"Wait a minute. Let me breathe. Give me a little room," he was saying. "You know that I've loved you. There has been nothing to me like Mateo Rubriz. You've given me everything. I remember when I asked for a pony and you rode two hundred miles to steal the gray stallion and brought it back to me. If I wanted one peso you gave me a hundred. You taught me to ride and to shoot and to be—a Rubriz! And every day of my life since I can remember I've been ready to cut my throat and pour out my blood for you. Is it true?"

"My dear son—my dear Tonio!" cried Rubriz. "Say whatever you wish. Strike me in the face! Nothing can touch our love for one another! What are words? The wounds we have taken side by side speak a stronger language."

"I remember another thing," said Tonio, looking

desperately at Rubriz. "The hate for the gringos. And the time you beat me. The only time! You beat me with your hands. You remember the day?"

"I remember," groaned Mateo Rubriz. "I curse the hands that struck you. I cursed them then and begged you to forgive me and wept. I'll weep again, Tonio. I'll beg you again on my knees to forgive me!"

Instead of answering directly, Tonio said: "It was because I had been spending time secretly learning English; and I surprised you that day by showing that I could speak it."

Rubriz flew into a passion. "If all the gringos had only one throat, and one tongue in that throat, I would tear out the tongue first before I slashed the throat. Do you understand? I would wipe from the earth the language of the men who called me 'dog'!" he shouted.

Tonio was a sickly gray-green as he went on: "But you can speak English, and why should it be such dangerous poison for me to speak it also? But from the first I was not to know anything of America. Never! Now I think that I understand. Listen to me! There is a man named Lavery who has a ranch in the Bend north of the Rio Grande."

Rubriz caught in a breath and folded his arms suddenly over it.

"He had a four-year-old son who was stolen twenty years ago. The boy had blue eyes and black hair and on his left shoulder a double birthmark. I am twenty-four years old; I wear that identical birthmark; my hair is black and my eyes are blue. Therefore, my name is Lavery!"

"May the name die and rot on the earth!" yelled Rubriz.

An outbreak of many voices from the front of the house stopped Rubriz when it seemed as though he were about to rush at Tonio. What he heard made him spring to the door and throw it open. Over the threshold at once men crowded, pushing Richard Lavery before them.

Chapter Twenty-three

THE MEN WHO brought in Lavery were babbling his name excitedly. Rubriz stood for a moment with his arms stiffened at his sides, in an ecstasy.

The Kid stood on tiptoe and discovered that he could sight his revolver through the break in the wall. He was glad of that because the entrance of Lavery meant murder; and when the killing began the hand of Montana would have to be in it.

Then he saw Rubriz doff the red skull-cap and back up in front of Lavery, making a deep bow with every step.

"Hai, brothers!" he cried. "You have brought a great guest to a humble house. You have brought me a lord of the land. Let him be seated. Give him my chair. Be seated, señor. Be at your ease. My wine-cup, some one. And wine. You lazy dogs, do you know in whose presence you stand? It is the great Señor Lavery and he knows how to handle Mexican dogs. He quirts them across the face. Look! I bear the mark! That is how I have learned how to serve him."

Lavery had been brought to the place where Rubriz had been seated. Now he was thrust into the chair and his arms lashed to the sides of it.

"Wine for him, instantly!" shouted Rubriz.

One of the Mexicans took the filled wine-cup, grasped Lavery by the hair of the head, and, jerking the head back to an angle, tilted the cup at his lips. The wine spilled over Lavery's breast in a double stream, red as blood. The crowd shouted with joy.

Lavery said nothing. He kept his eyes fixed on Tonio, who sat at the table with his face buried in his hands.

The direction of that glance and the position of Tonio seemed to reach the mind of Rubriz at the same moment. He replaced the cap on his head and waved towards the door.

"Out with you all!" he commanded. They scattered back before him. As they went through the door he advanced, waving them off. "A good night's work!" he cried after them. "The wineskins will have to bleed for this. The sheep and the goats will have to die for it. We shall have a three-day feast, my children. Away with you! Let me hear you singing!"

He closed the door after them and came straight back to Tonio. He put his hand on the shoulder of the lad.

"Look up, Tonio," said he.

The head of Tonio was slowly lifted.

"Look!" said Rubriz. "That is the hand that swung the whip. This is the mark that it left. I stood before him. The blood ran down my face over my body as the wine had run over his. Something more than wine shall run over him. Eh, Tonio? Look at me. This is the mark—here! Give me your hand. You feel the seam of the scar? Tell me, Tonio, if he were the king of the world would you claim his blood?"

The head of Tonio turned, slowly, towards Lavery.

He said in Mexican, "Padre, all these years have been a lie." And then in English, "That man is my father!"

Rubriz screamed out, as though a knife had been stuck in him. He went backwards step by step after the manner of the old swaggering tragedians. Tonio stood up.

"Tonio! Tonio!" yelled Rubriz. "Take the words back and spit them on the floor!"

"Say nothing, do nothing, Dick," said Lavery with wonderful calmness. "A young life is better than an old one. Let the beast have me, but save yourself for your mother."

"Tonio!" cried Rubriz. "Speak to me! Look at me!"

Tonio pulled out a long, blue-barreled Colt. He turned on Rubriz, saying. "Keep back from me—señor!"

"Señor?" echoed Rubriz, in a terrible voice. "Señor?"

And he ran straight in at Tonio.

Montana saw the gun drop level and the bead drawn. He looked to hear the deep voice of it booming and then to see the body of Rubriz crash to the floor and skid with the speed of his running. But at the last moment the gun wavered in the grasp of Tonio. He could not pull the trigger. Then the rush of Rubriz struck him headlong to the floor.

Mateo had him by the throat, shaking him up and down and back and forth with a tremendous grasp. The face of Tonio distended like that of a drowned man. Tonio fainted. Montana, taking aim with a sure hand, saw that all danger to Tonio was gone in that instant. Mateo Rubriz, snatching up the heavy body as though it were an image stuffed with straw, cradled Tonio in his arms as a nurse cradles an infant. And as Tonio recovered, groaning, fumbling at his bruised throat, Rubriz placed him in a chair, steadied him with one hand, placed the silver cup of wine at his lips, and made him drink.

"There," said Rubriz, putting down the cup, crouching on his heels before Tonio, "there, Tonio! It is better, eh? God wither my hands that fell on you. God kill the devil that leaped up out of my brain. Tonio, see your poor father. See Mateo's broken heart that is bleeding before you. Speak kindly to me, Tonio. Remember how we lay wounded in the rain before San Jacinto? Remember how we tried to suck water out of the mud? How we chewed the water out of our clothes? There is more pain in me now than then. My body was burning and dying, then. Now it is my soul. Forgive me! Here is my own knife. Take it. Here is my breast. Here is my throat. Make yourself safe from me forever. Kill me, Tonio, but forgive me and love me."

The knife fell from the nerveless hand of Tonio and made a tingling sound against the floor. Out of wild eyes he stared at Rubriz.

"But it is true," said Tonio. "And after all, I am a gringo! A gringo!"

"No!" shouted Rubriz, "You talk like a fool. You *are* a fool. Are you not my son? What is blood? The dogs and the cattle have blood. But my soul is breathed into you. I took you to hate you, but the glorious God sent love into me. When you cried in the night, I drove the nurse from the room. I put my hands on you and the love of God flowed into my hands out of your body. You smiled at me and went to sleep holding my finger. Look, Tonio—this finger! Ha! Look at it. I would wriggle it a little. Still you gripped it while you slept. You frowned and held onto it. My heart laughed while I watched you. That was how I made you my son. I made you Mexican. They are a nation of warriors. I made you my child. But now the marks of my fingers are on your throat! Beat me, curse me, but forgive me, Tonio."

He flung up his powerful arms.

"Blood of Christ, blood of Christ," groaned Mateo, "enter his soul and make it merciful. All I have stolen from churches I swear to replace. For silver I shall give gold. I shall kiss the feet of the priests. San Juan of Capistrano, I confess. I fall on my face. Intercede for me!"

Tonio, lurching to the side, stretched his arms out over the table and bowed his face on them.

There was time, now, for Montana to give a little heed to Richard Lavery, and what he saw was a picture worth remembering, for the rancher wore a stern and aloof expression as though, in fact, he were displeased by the violent intimacies of this scene which he was watching and as though he wished to give the impression that he was not observing it too closely.

He would not even pay any regard to his son, but staring towards the smoke and the shuddering flames of the fire on the open hearth, he kept his head high. His face was stone.

Montana was struck with an incredulous amazement. During twenty years this man had yearned for a son in his house, and now he failed to give so much as a glance to Tonio. In all his days, Montana had never before felt so worthless. Yonder fellow Lavery, he knew, was of the stuff that builds empires, and he, Montana, was a worthless creature, a pest upon the face of the land.

He looked back with actual relief towards Mateo Rubriz, that robber and manslayer.

Rubriz was bending over Tonio, stroking the long black hair that fell forward. "The foul air makes you faint!" cried Rubriz. "The filthy cook lets the place grow stinking with smoke."

He ran to a window and flung open the shutters. The entering wind billowed through the mist. Rubriz returned to Tonio and, kneeling beside him, put an arm about his shoulders.

He said: "As for that other name, damnation take it! That was the man who sat his horse before me, in the street of Bentonville. We had taken a few cattle off the range, I and some friends. The devil haunted us with bad luck. Our horses were shot from under us by the gringos. We were forced to surrender. We were taken into the town. Some of the Americanos wished to hang us. But Richard Lavery said, 'Run the ragged dogs across the river, and put a mark on them before they go!' And with that he struck me with his whip. I saw the whip-lash flying through the air. I could have dodged it. But I wondered if God meant to put such a terrible shame on a Rubriz, so I stood fast, and the lash cut to the bone. I, a Rubriz, stood in the dust of the street and a gringo lashed me like a dog!"

He broke off to point at Lavery.

"That is the man, Tonio! Do you see him?"

The dull eyes of Tonio turned towards his father.

"Do you see that merciless face of stone, my son? Will you look at the harsh and cruel face of that man? That is the gringo face; that is the bloodless gringo heart! Do you say he is your father?"

Lavery, at this, turned his head and looked full at Tonio, but he kept his glance perfectly calm and indifferent. There was not the trace of an appeal in the look.

Rubriz went on in a great passion: "After he had struck me, the hours stopped. Time stifled me. Drink

178

choked my throat. My belly was too small to hold food. I chewed the thought of murder, and it had no taste. But I went by night and took the child out of the cradle. It was very small. It was a bundle of clothes with a mite of flesh and warmth inside them. That was all. It was not you. No, no, Tonio. You I remade. A voice out of the sky told me, before the morning came, that you were meant for me. By a miracle from heaven the doors of my heart were opened and you were placed inside. I have held you there ever since. I hold you there now. I hold you, Tonio! Search in your soul, but you cannot say that you hate me! Answer me! Can you say that you hate me, Tonio?"

"No," said the groaning voice of Tonio, "I cannot hate you, father."

Rubriz held up mute hands of thanksgiving. Tears ran down his sweating face. He shook his head from side to side, his smile a gaping and a distortion.

"Deeds are greater than blood. We have done deeds together, Tonio," he cried in his trembling, huge voice. "When the Rurales chased me down the valley of the pines—do you remember how you came like a god, like an angel, and took me on your horse, and supported me and saved me, and fired back at them?"

"Ha!" said Tonio. "I think of the night at. Medina el Rey when they hemmed me into the patio, and you came."

"In Chihuahua I slept and snored like a drunken fool while they gathered around me. But you broke through them and carried me away."

"No," cried Tonio. "We fought through them together."

"Yes, yes, side by side! My Tonio!"

Tonio leaped to his feet.

"The gringo blood has been drained out of me!" he shouted. "All that is mine is pure Mexican."

"It is true!" thundered Rubriz. "The mercy of God is choking me. I am dying of joy. My heart is bursting. Tonio!"

"One heart and one hand, my father!" cried Tonio.

The Mexican lifted his hands and his wet, shining face slowly.

"San Juan of Capistrano," he said at last, in a broken voice, "all the other saints are as dead as dust. You alone have life and power. Death of my soul, but I shall make your little church in Santa Katalina become great. I shall drive worshipers into it with whips. I shall cover your altar with gold. Your priests shall be as fat as pigs. They shall laugh with joy all day long. Tonio, child, I am weeping. Every tear is a happiness too great for my heart to hold. My eyes had forgotten tears, but the blessed saints and God the mighty send these joys to Mateo Rubriz."

Chapter Twenty-four

THE TEARFUL EMOTION of Rubriz changed the instant he laid eyes on the immobile face of Lavery. He threw out a hand in a grand gesture and exclaimed: "This is a message to you, señor. From the warrior soul of

Mexico to all the Yankees in Dollar Land. Tell them, if you see them again, that to be once a Rubriz is to be a Rubriz forever! Ah, Tonio," he added, "this day will never be forgotten. If only you can tell me how to make you happy!"

"Let them go in peace," said Tonio. "Send them both away, quickly."

"Send them away?" echoed Rubriz. "Throw away a hundred thousand pesos that is as good as in our pockets? More than that! He will sell his whole ranch and pawn his Yankee soul to set his daughter free."

The words struck Montana solidly. He put his teeth together hard and got hold of himself to see that Lavery was rising from his chair.

"They are my own blood," Tonio was saying. "Do you want me to turn my own blood into money?"

Rubriz, staring at him, groaned long and loud as though down a long and dim perspective he were growing aware of things in Tonio's mind that could not be answered. He choked back the words that were working in his throat.

Lavery found his voice to say: "Daughter, Rubriz? Did you speak of my daughter?"

Rubriz rose to his bare tiptoes as he pointed over his head.

"Here in my house! Here in my hands!" he shouted. "One day was yours, gringo, and you enjoyed it with a whip in your hands. This day is mine. You are here—and the girl is up there. Hai! I have you both. I throw you away as I please. You are mine."

181

Lavery seemed to turn brittle and shuddering, body and voice. He looked towards Tonio and said: "Did I ever claim you? You degenerate, bloodless coward!"

"Don't strike him, Tonio," said Rubriz, joyously. "Oh, the gringos have tongues in their throats, too—until they're torn out. Keep your hands away from him till I've thought what to do with him, and if—"

"Be quiet!" said Tonio.

He leaned his hands on the edge of the table and his handsome face was gray. He said to Lavery: "She is perfectly safe. When she came, señor, I could not know—"

"What do you say?" yelled Rubriz. "Are you apologizing to him? Are you—Tonio! Are you—"

"Let them go," said Tonio. "Let them go quickly. Before I go mad, send them both away."

Rubriz looked at Tonio with care. Then he came to him and put an arm around his shoulders, leading him towards the door.

"Leave all things to me, Tonio," he said. "Perhaps not instantly. But very soon I shall send them away. Perhaps this same night. Perhaps that would be the best. Yes, and I begin to see that we had better ask no money for them. No, we shall ask no money. Never fear that Mateo Rubriz will shame you. All shall be as you wish. Go to your bed. Sleep! Sleep! I shall send Oñate to play his violin so that you will sleep deeply. Eh, my boy?"

"The devil take Oñate and keep him!" said Tonio. "I want to be alone!"

182

He went out of the room, while Rubriz held the door open for a moment and looked after him. It was a thoughtful face that Rubriz showed as he turned back into the room again.

He closed the door behind him and rested his shoulder against it. He put his head back and closed his eyes.

Lavery was fighting to speak, but he would not let a word come out until his lips had stopped twitching, or so it seemed. When he spoke, his voice was perfectly calm. He said: "About my daughter, Rubriz. You are quite right. Let me see her. Let me have her safely home. And you shall have money enough to—"

"Money, money, money!" screamed Rubriz on a rising pitch. "The dirty Yankee tongues can talk nothing but money. The filthy Yankee throats can swallow nothing but money. Bah! Bah! Miguel and Mario! Hai!"

The door was jerked open almost at once.

"Take this man. Wrap him in ropes like a bale. One of you sit by him and shine a lantern in his face. If he escapes, I tie you both together and lay you in the sand, naked, and let the sun cook you. Take him and get out! He is your life. Remember. If he slips through your fingers, it is your life that is gone."

They took Lavery out of the room, Rubriz calling after them: "Send me Roberto. Send the old robber to me."

After that Rubriz settled down in his chair, his head falling against the back of it so that he seemed to be studying the ceiling. But his eyes were closed.

It seemed to Montana that perhaps the simplest solution for all of these entanglements, these Gordian knots, was to crash a bullet through the brain of Rubriz, now, and try to escape with the rest during the insane confusion that followed. At least, Tonio would then be the head of the outfit and nothing important was so apt to go wrong under his management. But when Montana drew his bead it happened that he saw a grayness in the hair of Rubriz. And then the eyes of the man were closed. That, for some reason, made it impossible for the Kid to fire.

He could call himself a fool, but he could not flick the hammer of his gun. Even the killing of a beast can be like murder.

The door opened. There entered a hardy fellow of fifty years with bare feet whispering over the floor. He was dressed even more scantily than Rubriz, without the red at the neck and on the head; but there was importance in his face. It was a square face with the skin fitted so tightly that there were high lights on the cheek bones and on the chin. His hair was gray, his eyebrows were gray, his lashes were so gray that when he looked down he seemed like an eyeless mask.

He went over to the chair and Rubriz and stood silently beside it.

"Berto?" said Rubriz, without opening his eyes.

"Yes," said Roberto.

"Heat some wine," said Rubriz.

Old Roberto went to the hearth, poured red wine

into a pan, and put the pan on the coals. From a shelf he got spices and stirred these into the wine. He sat on his heels and kept on stirring until fumes began to rise from the pan. After a while he brought the wine back and poured some into the great cup and put it in the hand of Rubriz, who lifted his head and seemed to have barely strength for drinking.

Afterwards he groaned and lay back in the chair and held out the cup.

"Drink the rest, Berto," he said. After speaking his mouth remained open. His lips sagged so that he looked like a dead man, with his closed eyes.

"I drink tequila, not hot slop," said Berto, gently.

"You are wrong," said Rubriz. "The belly is bigger than the brain and it needs to be comforted. My belly is old and cold, Berto, and it needs hot wine."

He kept groaning deep in his throat as he talked.

"My brain is old, too," said Rubriz. "It is tired. I have to think too much. I have to think for Tonio and Berto and all the rest. My brain is tired, Berto."

Berto tasted the wine, made a sour face, and put the cup on the table. He looked down at the floor. Both he and his master were eyeless men, for the moment.

"And you are old, too," said Rubriz. "How old are you, Berto?"

"I? Forty," said Berto. "No, God forgive me! Forty-one years old."

Rubriz made a blind gesture.

"Give me your hand," he said.

Berto took the hand and held it.

"God will forgive you for lying," said Rubriz, "because you lie well. You are fifty years old, Roberto. But—I forgive the lie because I love the liar. We are old men together, Berto, eh? These youngsters know nothing. They have not heard enough bullets to know the song of them. But we, having heard them often, know the music. Are we tired of it?"

"No, señor," said Berto.

Rubriz was suddenly awake, laughing silently.

"Old devil, old hungry rat!" he said. "Hai, Berto! You are my brother. The rest are nothing, and you are my brother. Eh?"

"Yes, señor," said Berto.

"But you are old, and even God cannot help that."

"No, señor," said Berto.

"You are so old," said Rubriz, "that a woman painted on a church wall is as much to you as a girl that nothing but the wind has ever put hand on. You are that old, poor Berto."

"No, señor," said Berto.

"No?" asked Rubriz, sharply.

"No, señor," said Berto.

"Ah-ha?" murmured Rubriz. "That is the way of it, then? Am I right? Is that the way of it?"

"Yes, señor," said Berto.

"Then listen to me. Do you know that there is a woman in the house, a gringo girl? Young, beautiful!"

"Yes, señor. Young, but gringo."

Rubriz laughed. "You could not waste your time with her, eh? Is that the truth?"

"Time?" said Berto.

He lifted his two hands and held them out as though something were running away through the fingers. "Well, there is time to use and time to waste," said Berto.

"She could be earned," said Rubriz. "She has a father, Berto. It would be very well for me if her father died—far away in the hills—far away, no one knows where. If he were to die, it would comfort me more than the hot wine comforts my belly."

Berto scratched his chin.

"If he were squeezed, he would run gold faster than blood," said Berto.

Rubriz roared out, suddenly, "You gray old mangy dog, are you to do my thinking for me?"

"No, señor," said Berto.

He began to dig at the floor with his bare toes and smile down at his foot.

"Take them both away," said Rubriz, making a sudden gesture. "Take the man and cut his throat. Take the girl wherever you please and never let her come back."

"Yes, señor," said Berto.

"What?" shouted Rubriz. "Is this the way you thank me?"

Roberto ran the red tip of his tongue over his lips.

"I thank you, señor," said he.

"Here is some money to pay the way," said Rubriz.

He took out a leather wallet whose mouth was drawn together with a buckskin thong. He tossed it into the air and it fell on the table with a heavy, jangling sound.

Berto picked it up and worked at the knot, saying, "How much shall I take?"

"Oh, Berto, Berto, Berto!" said Rubriz. "Of all my men, I can trust you only. For you, only, blood is as water. And yet you are growing old and your brain weakens. You fool, are we not brothers?"

He sat up, fingering the arms of his chair.

Berto weighed the purse in his hand, moistened his lips again, and smiled once more.

"Thank you, señor," said he.

"Get out of my sight," said Rubriz. "Mind you, not a soul must know. Not a whisper must be sounded. If the ghost of the echo of a word of this comes to the ears of Tonio—do you hear me?"

"Yes, señor."

"Ah, Berto," said Rubriz, "when I look at your gray old face and think how we have trusted one another, and never in vain, and what throats we have cut, and what gold we have taken, I love you, by God! more dearly than my own blood. Wait. I must go down with you to speak to the men who are guarding Lavery. You understand? You are supposed to be taking the man and the girl towards the Rio Grande to claim the reward. And if, on the way, among the mountains, strange brigands fall on you and take them out of your hands—how can that be helped?"

"It cannot be helped, señor," said Berto. He kept on smiling.

Rubriz had risen when a small tide of voices came

rushing from the front of the house. The door was swung open. On the threshold Montana saw his Rurale, the shorter companion of yonder tall fellow who had had the scarred face. They are faithful to their trails, those Rurales!

This fellow was speaking so that the little greasy black line of his mustaches bristled and stood up.

"Be calm, Señor Rubriz," said he. "I have come as your friend, for I follow only one trail at a time. This time it is a gringo that I want."

Chapter Twenty-five

THERE HAD SEEMED to be one figure, only, dominating the world, the moment before. Now to Montana it seemed that the little bulldog of a Rurale was the more formidable fellow of the two. He had neither the brains, the strength, nor the criminal acuteness of Rubriz, but he was patient as the sea.

Rubriz wanted an explanation. As his lion's voice stopped roaring, a big Mexican with a skin almost black began to pour out his story of how the solitary rider had passed through the entrance to the valley, saying that he was expected, and how could it be dreamed that this was the very gringo who had first captured Tonio and—

Rubriz stopped that speech. He dropped the butt of a revolver into the face of the outpost with a force that hurled the unlucky devil through the doorway; his body landed with a loose, jouncing shock on the floor of the hall. Certainly his face would never be the same.

Rubriz jumped over the fallen man, yelling orders, curses. The valley was to be searched, and every inch of the house. There was nothing in the world that Mateo Rubriz wanted, he said, except to put his hands upon this gringo!

As that storm poured raging out of the house, Montana got from the stable like a wildcat out of a bear's den when the bear enters. As he came into the open, he heard the rattle of voices, the thudding of running feet, and he knew perfectly well that that little valley would be searched with a fine comb.

He jumped up, caught a projecting beam that thrust out at the edge of the roof of the horse-shed, swung himself like a pendulum, and managed to lay out his body flat on the roof.

A dormer window with a dullness of shaded light in it stuck out of that roof. He went for the window and found it open. That was enough for him. In ten seconds the searchers would be scanning that same roof and they had rifle bullets to touch whatever their eyes saw. He snaked his way through the window and stood up in front of Ruth Lavery.

She was not pretty, just then. She had a scream frozen on her face. Her eyes were frozen wide open, like her mouth, and the whites showed all around. Her two hands were up, shoulder high, with rigid fingers extended.

"Steady, steady!" said Montana. "Thaw out and sit down."

She thawed out and sat down. Rather, she slumped and seemed to hit the chair more or less by accident.

"The air's so full of wasps," said the Kid, "that I just ducked in here to get out of the way of trouble. D'you mind?"

"Oh, Dick," said the girl. "Oh, Dick, Dick! *What* has happened?"

He looked around the room first. If it came to hiding, the place was as bare as a tomb. There was a little iron skeleton of a bedstead and a tiny washstand with a huge pitcher of water standing beside it. There was no paint on the 'dobe walls. The floor was of planks roughed off with an ax. The place looked like a cave, except for the ceiling. This was held up in the center by a big post that rose from the center of the floor, and the large rafters all met in the center on top of this post. The rafters made the ceiling look like a spider's web. The Kid looked on the scene with a curious, detached feeling. He had stared at other places where he expected to die and he always felt the same way. This time the feeling was very vivid. He could hear the stairs groaning under a burden of many feet. He could see the door open. He, from a corner, would pump some lead into the dark forms that swarmed outside, but they would spill into the room, nevertheless. Men did not hold back with a Rubriz to lead or to drive them. They would get him. As he lay on the floor, the bullets would hit him somewhere around the shoulders and range back through his vitals. When a bullet strikes you in the body the ache of it freezes you numb from head to foot. There isn't much pain at first.

He turned towards the girl.

"Pull yourself together," he said. "You've got stuff, so make yourself all one piece. You're going to get a few shocks."

He went over to her. She put up a hand towards him, like a child, palm up. She seemed to wonder why he was. there; she seemed to think that so long as he *was* there everything would be all right. So he took his words like chunks of lead pipe and hit her with them. It wasn't exactly out of cruelty but because he wanted to see how much steel there was in her and how it would take a beating.

"I'm not Dick Lavery. I had the birthmark tattooed on my shoulder. I came to your place to make a clean-up. Then I weakened. I'd seen the real Dick Lavery down here in greaser-land. I started out to get him. Your old man tagged along. Your old man is down in the cellar of this house. I'm up here, and your brother is somewhere in between. He's the *hombre* they call Tonio Rubriz."

In the sea there are translucent things. You can pay admission to see them in big glass tanks, where the Kid had seen them. You can look right through them at the blue stain of the sea water, and inside the transparent bodies are dark whorls and dim circlings of life. That was the way the Kid looked through Ruth Lavery now. The life in her came up through the darkness of fear. She stood up and stared into his face.

"All right," she said. "I understand. What about the real Dick?"

"He's still Tonio. He knows that you're his sister and Lavery's his father, but he prefers to be a Rubriz. There was a scene. It was like a play. It was just like a play."

He sat down, started to make a cigarette, then remembered himself and dropped the makings into his pocket. Outside, hoofbeats were thumping here and there in a fine staccato. Voices went back and forth at the speed of running horses, changing pitch like church bells when you ride quickly by them on a Sunday morning. They keep ringing out higher and higher as you come towards them, making a bigger and a bigger promise, but just as you go by the bell-clappers seem to hit lead and the sound goes flat. "Boob, bumbbell; boob, dumbbell," they always seemed to say to the Kid. That was the way these voices of the man-hunters rang on his ears and they spoke the same message to him.

"Tonio," he explained, "makes a bargain with Mateo to let you and Lavery go free. Mateo agrees and then gets an *old hombre* called Roberto, that looks like a gila monster, to take you and your father away and cause you to disappear in the high hills. That's where we all sit just now."

After a moment she said: "Shall I put this lamp out? Would that be better for you, if they come to search? Shall I put it out and pretend to be in bed?"

"After all this yowling you wouldn't be in bed. You

193

might be sitting in the dark, though. Put out the lamp."

She leaned over it. He saw her face for a moment as she puckered her brows against the light and pursed her lips. Then the lamp puffed out.

The darkness washed right across the room and seemed to rebound from his mind as from a wall, because in his thought he could still see her.

With the darkness came an increase of the noises, not so much from outside the house as within it, where timbers creaked and voices were stirring.

"Hai! Hai! Hai!" some rider was yelling as he swept towards the house. "This is the horse, and therefore the man cannot be far!"

A good, round chorus of approval greeted that discovery.

"Your horse?" said the voice of the girl, who was standing at the shoulder of the Kid. The nearness of it surprised him.

"Listen," said the Kid.

"Yes," she answered.

"I wanta tell you something."

"I'm listening. What is it—Montana?"

"About you and your mother, I wanted to tell you—"

The darkness ate up his voice. Then he said, "Oh, well—"

"All right," she said. "You don't have to say anything. Where's your hand, Montana?"

He held it out. She found it quickly. The moonlight came into the room at a steep slant through the window. He could see the blackness of her against it.

194

"Except for us, you wouldn't be down here, snagged and done for," she said.

"Quit that, will you?" said he.

"All right, I'll quit it," she said. "Isn't there any way? Are you surely lost, Montana?"

"It's all in the cards. This time I didn't fill. That's all."

"If you laid out there on the rafters above the center post, they wouldn't see you, perhaps. Lamplight and lantern-light throw a lot of shadows. And people only see what they expect to see. They woudn't expect you to be foolish enough to try to hide up there."

"No, they wouldn't," said the Kid. He laughed. "You know why?"

"Because you've got a reputation down here," said the girl.

"That's the reason," said the Kid, with the same whispering laughter. "I've got some reputation down here."

"Montana, I want to tell you something."

"Go on," said the Kid.

"I want to tell you—well—I want to say—"

"Go ahead," said the Kid. "You say anything you feel like saying. We're all going to be a long time dumb."

"I can't say it," she answered.

"That's all right, too," said the Kid. "Everything's all right. Listen to me. You're all right, too."

"If you say it, it's true," said the girl.

"You're scared," said the Kid. "You're only a girl and you're scared."

"I'm not," said she.

"You are," said the Kid. "You're scared, and your voice had the webbles in it. But you're only a girl, and that makes it all right. I wanted to tell you something."

"I'm not scared," said Ruth Lavery. "You haven't any right to think that—"

"Hush up, will you?" said Montana. "I want to tell you something. You won't think I'm a sentimental sap?"

He heard her draw her breath twice.

"No," she said.

"I hate a sentimental thug that gets yellow and talks rot when the pinch comes. You know, the kind that makes speeches. All I wanted to say was your mother is O.K."

She was silent. He waited for her to say something, then he went on: "She's the most beautiful woman I ever saw. If you pull through this greasy mess it would do me a bit of good if you told her that. Say I said it about her, will you? She's the most beautiful woman I ever saw. Listen. Quit it, will you?"

"I'm not doing anything," said the girl.

"You're crying," said Montana. "A few shakes and shudders are all right, because you're only a girl. But crying is out. Understand?"

"Yes," she said.

A thundering river of noise came into the house.

"They'll be up here in a minute," said the Kid. "You back off into that corner. So long, Ruth. Good luck to you."

Chapter Twenty-six

THE KID STEPPED back against the wall, for he had decided that he would die on his feet, and when he dropped he would be shooting as he fell. That was better than taking it lying down.

The girl came and stood beside him. She wore some kind of a perfume that smelled clean. All the room was gray and her face was gray, too, but he could see the glint of her eyes.

"Go over there and duck into that corner," he commanded. "Step lively."

"I'll stay here," said Ruth Lavery, "unless you get up there on the rafters."

"You want me to make a fool of myself?" he asked. Then he knew that there was no use arguing. It's never any use arguing with a woman. He jumped, caught a rafter, and swung himself up. He lay flat out, just above the center post. Something almost intangible but vaguely sticky broke over his face. Something ran rapidly up his cheek, over his head, down his neck. That would be the spider from the web. He shuddered. Snakes were all right, but he hated spiders.

Footfalls climbed the stair; a hand beat on the door.

"Come in," said the girl.

They had the door open before she spoke and then they came in, three lanterns swinging in various hands. Rubriz was not there. A big young bull of a

Mexican seemed to have charge. He walked up to the girl and said, "Where is the gringo?"

"I don't know," she said. "I'm alone here."

"Search!" he commanded.

There was no place to search. They walked around in circles. Every man of them looked under the bed or behind it. Two of them actually moved the little washstand. Others peered out the window. And all the while the Kid lay flat out on the rafters which were much too narrow to really shelter his body. He saw them looking up at the ceiling, but the girl seemed to be right—they saw nothing because they expected to see nothing there.

The leader said, "Why are you in here without a light?"

"There was a lot of noise and shouting," said the girl. "I was afraid and blew out the light."

"Why should you blow out the light if you were afraid?" he asked. Then he turned around without waiting for the answer. "Gringo women are bigger fools than the men," he said. "Can you find nothing?"

Some one came up the stairs in three light, springing strides and stood panting inside the doorway. It was Tonio. His glance flickered from side to side like a bright sword-blade.

"Get out!" said Tonio.

"He isn't here, Tonio," began the leader, "and—"

Tonio was almost as big as Montana. He got hold of the burly Mexican with a wrestling grip and threw him out the door. The man went staggering and cursing and crashing all the way to the bottom of the stairs. The rest of the gang dodged quickly past Tonio and went out; he took a lantern out of the hand of one of them, and closed the door.

It was bad business, manhandling a Mexican as Tonio had done, but it was more than fear of the consequences that made Tonio lean against the wall, breathing hard. The hand that held the lantern pressed against his breast. The lifting of his chest kept the lantern swinging a little and creaking on its bail. He peered at the girl.

"All of those—" said Tonio, making a gesture. "I'm sorry. As soon as I heard them, I came up here. Tell me a thing. Did one of them touch you?"

"No," she said.

The Kid, like a hawk in the sky, watched them. He saw Ruth Lavery making a small step at a time towards her brother.

"Did any of 'em say anything to you?" he demanded, harshly.

"Nothing that mattered," said she.

"I thank God!" said Tonio.

She got as far as the table and stood there. Tonio got hold of the knob of the door, jerked it open, and started to flee. Then he stopped himself. He came back into the room, saying: "You are going to be safe. You will be taken care of. There is nothing for you to worry about."

"I don't worry about myself," said the girl. "I'm

thinking of the man who came down here to help find you, Dick. His life is in terrible danger now."

The Kid set his teeth, and grinned. He liked the way she dropped that name into the middle of the sentence, casually. "She's as bright as a knife," said the Kid to himself.

"As for him," said Tonio, "a fighting man takes fighting chances. And—" The other thing that had been in her words seemed to strike him as an aftermath. "You know who I am?" he groaned. "Who told you that?"

"Montana," she answered.

"Has he been here, then?"

"Yes. He's here now. Montana, come down."

The Kid was stunned. It seemed a perfect betrayal, but at least he had the drop.

He said out of his upper shadows, "Don't move a hand, Tonio."

Tonio looked up with a strange indifference. "I have been shamed by you once before," he said. "Now nothing matters."

The Kid slipped over the side of the rafter, hung by one hand at arm's length, and dropped softly to the floor.

"Why don't you put the gun away, Montana?" asked Ruth Lavery. "This is my brother. Do you think you have anything to fear from him?"

"I've told you already that he belongs to Rubriz," said the Kid. "Tonio, walk to the table, put the lantern on it, turn your back to me, and hold up your hand."

"Dick, stay where you are!" commanded the girl.

She walked straight up to Montana and took hold of the Colt.

"You're doing the wrong thing," she said. The Kid had his teeth hard set, and the muscles at the base of his jaw jumped in and out and in and out. He said nothing because he was too angry for speech. He was so angry that he hardly cared how soon a bullet hit him. Then he looked over the brightness of her hair and saw that Tonio had not moved to pull out a gun. He was simply hanging his head.

Well, the girl had been right before and perhaps she was right again.

"You were wrong, Montana," said the girl, "but of course you couldn't tell that Dick simply needed time to think things over. You couldn't tell, because you're not a Lavery."

She went over to Tonio and put her arm through his and smiled up into his face.

"He couldn't understand you, dear," she said, "but of course *I* understand."

Tonio lifted up his head an inch at a time and looked wildly about him.

"God teach me what to do!" he gasped.

"He will," said the girl.

The Kid went over to the window and looked out into the moonlight. The voices and the trampling had poured out of the house again. A pair of riders went by, their horses flashing like watered silk.

"I'll get out of here," said the Kid, "if you can take care of her, Tonio."

"Are you going to let him go out there and face the guns, Dick?" asked the girl.

The Kid bent over to slide through the window.

"Señor!" breathed Tonio. "Wait! Wait!"

The Kid stood up and turned around. The girl had been right again. She seemed to be always right. Tonio came to him. He took hold of the arm of Montana with one hand and the arm of the girl with the other.

"You don't have to speak, Dick," said the girl. "I know how terrible the pain must be. It's like being born again, but this time you'll become your true self."

"He has shamed me and beaten me," said Tonio. "Tell me—is he a good man?"

It was a very simple question, but the Kid did not feel like laughing.

"Can't you tell what he is, Dick?" asked Ruth Lavery.

Tonio stared at her. "You," he said, "are brave and true and beautiful and gentle."

"He came here to take you back to us and to your right life," she told Tonio. "Do you think he's a hired man, Dick?"

She kept dropping that name into each sentence, and every time it struck the ear of Tonio he shuddered with emotion. Now he said: "My father and mother gave me one life, but Mateo Rubriz has saved my life and given it to me again a dozen times. I am a Mexican. His way is my way!"

"It's not," answered Montana. "You made him promise to send your sister and father safely home.

Instead, he's turned them over to a fellow who's to take them away and cut their throats in the mountains so that they'll never again try to pull you away from him, Tonio."

Tonio cried out, too loudly, "If you say that—"

"Hush!" said Montana. "I'm not lying. What the devil do you mean to me? Nothing! I get nothing but kicks out of this job. But I heard the whole thing after you left the room. Your father called in old Roberto. He's to take charge."

"Two men—" began Tonio.

"Oh, go down into the cellar room and take a look," said Montana, with a weary carelessness. "You'll find Roberto in charge by this time."

"To murder them—both?" asked Tonio, under his breath.

"Because he loves you, Tonio," said the Kid. "You're only a borrowed son, but you seem to be the only son he has. Would he let a pair of little murders stand between him and you? Not a bit of it. If your mother were here, he'd knock her over the head along with the other two."

Tonio whacked the face of Montana with the flat of his left hand and pulled a gun with his right. "You gringo snake!" he said.

The Kid had not even tried to touch a weapon. "You'll pick up some different manners after you've lived awhile among your own people, Tonio," said he.

Tonio still leaned forward for a moment on the verge of murder. Then the voice of the girl got into his mind as she said: "Dick, Dick—" over and over. He got hold of himself with a wrenching effort.

"I am an ingrate and a dog no matter with whom I stay," said Tonio. "Wait here. If Roberto really is in the cellar room guarding the señor—my father—"

He got himself out of the room in a hurry. Montana ventured on a cigarette because he felt that he had to have one. The girl sat down and cried. She stopped her sobs and began to draw in long, audible breaths.

"It's over! " she said to Montana. "He's ours. We've won!"

"I'm glad you've stopped blubbering," said the Kid. "You wangled this job pretty well—for me. It's all over now except getting ourselves out of the hands of Rubriz. Maybe you think that that's going to be a joke?"

"What do I care?" asked Ruth Lavery. She threw up both her hands in a senseless gesture of happiness and abandon. "If we die, he'll die with us and he'll die a Lavery!"

Chapter Twenty-seven

WHEN TONIO STRODE through the hall, Mateo Rubriz, who was walking up and down in front of the open door of the house, saw him and called him out. Only two of his men were at hand, waiting beside their horses for orders.

Rubriz, in the height of good spirits, waved to the right and to the left.

"I've sent them all off yonder," said Rubriz. "They're searching the edges of the valley and the hills. The gringo cannot run far on foot and our lads will find him as surely as owls find mice on moonlight nights. Have no fear, Tonio! And pray the good God that there will still be a little life in him when he is brought to you, my son! You can repay him, then, for any wrong that he has done to you, eh? But that is a sort of pleasure that you have never learned to enjoy, Tonio. And what a pity! Men are strong, Tonio, but pain is still stronger. Men are made of steel, but pain is a fire that melts the steel like wax. Oh, I have handled men who were heroes and turned them into little crying children. When you are older you may learn the touch!"

Tonio said nothing. He turned to go back into the house.

"Stay here with me," said Rubriz. "Why do you wish to go? Stay here with me, and presently you will hear the noise of guns which will prove that they have him. There! Hai! Hai! Do you hear it?"

Rubriz ran a few steps out into the moonlight to listen, for in the distance, out of the west, came a rattling of shots.

Whatever they were shooting at, they had not located Montana. Tonio grunted and twitched his lips. Then he went back to the cellar door, opened it, and saw the dull glow of lantern-light coming up the stairs.

"Who is there?" called the voice of Roberto.

Tonio put out both hands and braced himself against

the walls, for the moment he was sure of that voice he was also sure that Montana had told him the truth. Roberto, he knew, was the special instrument for executing the wrath of Rubriz. Roberto was the old and true companion who loved cruelty for its own sake and valued the life of a man no more than he valued the life of a rabbit.

So Tonio braced himself with trembling arms and thought of the past, and saw the face not of Roberto but of Rubriz, a picture with a thousand moods, and most of them savage. It was the sort of thing that Rubriz would do. Violence was the only thing that he truly understood. Since the gringos were trying to steal away his son, he would simply remove from this world the gringos who were making the attempt.

"Who's there? Answer!" called the voice of Roberto, sharply.

"Tonio," he answered, and went down into the moist, cold, moldy atmosphere of the cellar.

The wine-bottles were ranged on either side of the big, low-ceilinged room. Against the outer wall sat Richard Lavery with his hands manacled before him. Old Roberto, with a sawed-off shotgun in his hands, stood up to meet the intruder.

"What do you want, Tonio?" he asked.

"I want to see the gringo," said Tonio.

"Well, stay there and you can see him well enough," answered Roberto.

"Does he belong to you? Are you afraid to let me touch him?" asked Tonio.

"No matter what I'm afraid of," said the Mexican. "Stay where you are!"

He was the only one of the band who did not bow to the will of Tonio in all things. More than once Tonio had complained to Rubriz of the surly ways and the independent habits of Roberto, but Rubriz would merely say: "You can't teach an old dog new tricks. Never come up on the blind side of Roberto or his teeth will be in you—and once he has a hold he knows how to keep it!"

Roberto was the favored retainer, the most trusted of all the men. Now he stood his ground resolutely.

Tonio looked gravely past the guard to the calm, steady eyes of his father. That was the way the man would meet death in some dark pass among the hills, calmly, looking straight into the moment of his fate.

"Well," said Tonio, "you will have your way. You *always* have your way, Roberto."

"An old head holds more than a young head," answered Roberto. "What do you want here?"

"Something out of the gringo's pocket."

"What is it?"

"A golden pencil," said Tonio.

"A golden pencil?" Roberto smiled at the youth in contempt. "Well, you shall have this," he answered. "In his coat pocket would it be?"

Lavery had lifted his brows a little quizzically as he heard the remark of his son. And now Roberto turned and leaned over the prisoner.

Tonio made one stealthy stride forward and leaped.

He made no sound, not even as his foot left the ground, but something like the bright shadow of danger must have rushed over the subconscious brain of Roberto, for he twitched suddenly around. That was why he received the butt of the revolver on his forehead instead of the back of his skull.

The sound of the blow was a sharp spat. Roberto's knees sagged. He made an effort to throw his shotgun to the level, but Tonio jerked the weapon away from him. Roberto opened his mouth as though to speak. There was a troubled look in his eyes. And all the while he kept sinking little by little. Presently one great shudder seemed to shake the last stiff strength out of his limbs and he fell on his face.

Tonio trussed him foot and hand and gagged him. He got the key from his pocket, also, and with it unlocked the handcuffs that held Lavery.

As he fitted it into the lock he explained, rapidly: "Señor Montana is upstairs with your daughter. The most of the men are away hunting for him along the edges of the valley. The four of us must get to horse and ride very hard. Are you ready, señor?"

The spring lock clicked, the iron opened, and Richard Lavery rose to his feet. Perhaps no man ever had more to induce him to break into a flood of words. What he had heard and seen in the last few seconds had been enough to show him that his son belonged to him in something more than blood. But he could not talk. He could only nod. He knew that his face was as a stone and that Tonio was deeply disappointed because not one syllable of trust or affection could part the lips of the "gringo."

A nod, and then he had to let it go at that.

Well, talking is woman's work, after all. If by the grace of God, fortune, and hard fighting he could ever get his son back to the ranch beyond the Rio Grande, his wife would be able to talk to Dick. She would have plenty of the necessary words.

Nevertheless, Lavery sighed a little as he saw the eyes of his son harden a little.

"Here," said Tonio, as they stood at the door that opened from the cellar steps into the hall of the house, "is the way to the horse-shed. You'll find the horse of—your daughter —in there. And three bay mares that belong to me. They'll carry us well. Go back there and saddle as fast as you can. I don't think that you'll be interrupted. I'll go up and get the others. Have you a gun? No—take this!"

He pushed a revolver into the hand of Lavery, who took it in silence, made a gesture of assent, and instantly glided off to perform his task. Tonio looked after him for only an instant; then he bounded up the steps to the room which held the girl and Montana. They were with him instantly, hushed and swift-footed as they followed him down the steps.

As they turned into the hall, Montana saw the burly shoulders of Rubriz swinging past the open door, but Rubriz at the moment had blinded himself with song.

The three reached the horse-shed where Lavery already had saddled two mustangs. The Kid flipped the saddle over the back of the black mare and drew up the cinches until the little horse groaned. Then at the door of the shed they mounted, turning their eyes silently on one another, for it was the last time that they might see these faces. Tonio had helped Ruth Lavery into the saddle.

Every moment was an electric pulse of danger, but he lingered for an instant, staring up at her in the moonlight. Perhaps in that instant his mind was walking out of the long past and coming fully into the new existence. He took one of her hands and pressed it against his face; then he swung into the saddle.

He took command of the party, saying, "Walk the horses after mine. When we get to that group of trees I shall spur for the entrance of the valley. It will need shooting to break through there. The señorita will ride behind. Montana and I will go first. Now!"

Even then he was unable to call her by name, the Kid not-iced. For his own part, suddenly, Montana felt that every risk in this adventure already had been repaid as he looked at the three Laverys. They were all the good steel, easy to bend and hard to break. Whatever Tonio had done, his past had not stained the bright metal of his soul; it could be scoured away.

The Kid felt suddenly like a cheap and rather dirty crook.

In the meantime he was walking his mustang with the rest, and looking down a little uneasily at the narrowness of his horse across the shoulders. A horse has to have strong and sloping shoulders to carry weight, and Montana made a big burden. However, no one knows a mustang until it has been well tried. He tried the grip of his knees on the horse and fitted himself into the saddle; he kept easing his weight by rising a little in the stirrups, for his doubt of the horse was great. Yet it was one of those bays which Tonio approved.

They were close to the trees when they heard, from the house behind them, a hoarse voice calling, stifled behind the walls.

That would be Roberto.

"Ride!" called Tonio, and shot his horse into a racing gallop at once.

The Kid was under way hardly an instant later. He had a glimpse of the front of the house through the moonhaze, the lighted window gleaming like tarnished gold. He saw three men run into the building.

Then he took note that the girl rode very well, confidently, balancing the mare with a good pull of the reins. Her father was erect as though he would not compromise his dignity by leaning forward to cut the wind. Tonio was like an Indian, flattening along the back of the mustang, getting the utmost out of it. The Kid knew riding and he knew that this was the best.

They were at full speed, the ground seeming to lift before them and rush up towards their faces, when a wild voice cried from far away: "Tonio! Tonio! Tonio!"

Well, it was an hour too late for that voice to call Tonio back; it was twenty years too late, in one sense.

211

But every time the voice called, Tonio winced closer to his horse.

Then from the left other voices were shouting. They were seen. The whole force of the men of Rubriz—and that little squat bulldog of a Rurale—would come pouring in pursuit, now.

They entered the trees at the mouth of the valley with a rushing sound, like a wind and rattling thunder. A horseman jumped his mustang out of a thicket, yelling: "Who goes? Halt or—"

It would be hard to ask Tonio to shoot one of his late friends. The Kid knocked that Mexican out of the saddle with a forty-five-caliber chunk of lead and then they swept out into the next ravine.

Chapter Twenty-eight

THE KID LOOKED up at the San Carlos Mountains. They had seemed, until this moment, a great entanglement, a hostile mystery because they were unknown. But now as he listened to the muttering of hoofs behind and heard the voices of the pursuers singing out to one another, faintly, the great dark labyrinth of the mountains looked down on Montana like the faces of old friends in a time of need.

But he was worried. Tonio, keeping in the lead, guided them as one who knew what he was about, and undoubtedly they had four good horses under them. On the other hand, all of the Rubriz horses were sure to be excellent and all of his savages knew their mustangs as a cat knows its claws. Above all this, the majority of them were as lean as hunting-dogs, whereas the two Laverys and the Kid were all solid burdens.

Tonio seemed to understand the difficulty, too, because he kept to a racing gait for a full half hour, doubling and twisting among the cañons until it was plain that he was trying to lose the pursuit in the first burst of running. After that he pulled up in the throat of a narrow gulch and they listened to the panting of their mustangs and the distant hammering of hoofs that streamed across the air, drew slowly nearer, and then suddenly poured at them in a river of sound as the hunters turned straight into the gorge where they were waiting.

The first trick had gone to Rubriz and his men. Tonio, with a groan, straightened out his pony for another burst of sprinting. It could not last, however. They knew it. So did Rubriz's men who were howling like so many devils as they came up the hot trail. If only there had been no moon they might have hoped!

Tonio twitched his running horse to the side of Montana.

"You and I stop and block the way," shouted Tonio.

The Kid looked at him. There were twenty men riding for Rubriz and there were no fools or children in the hand-picked lot.

"Right!" called Montana.

Tonio got beside his father. Montana could not hear what was said. He did not need to hear, for he could see Lavery shake his head and actually pull on the reins. So the Kid came up on Lavery's off side, and yelled at him: "You fool, are you going to argue? Are you going to throw all of us away? Are you going to let that girl run loose again through Mexico? Ride on—and be damned to you!"

Lavery's proud, rigid head turned by small jerks until he was staring at the Kid. Then he bowed forward a little and increased the speed of the horse.

The girl understood. Something about the way she sat the saddle told the Kid that she understood.

Up the cañon came the yammering of the Mexicans. When Mexicans or Indians begin to scream like women it means that they are ready to run amok; that was how Rubriz's crew had begun to screech as Tonio held out his hand and gripped that of his father. Then he swung over to the girl and tilted out of his saddle. It was very good, gallant riding at that speed and over that broken ground. Anyway, he got his arm around her and the Kid saw her face tilt up to kiss her brother.

She could have that picture to remember the rest of her days. The news would kill old Mrs. Lavery, of course. But the girl would live, all right, and so would her father. The old Lavery steel would just be hammered a little harder, polished a little brighter. Now and then, years later, they would look at one another and see that picture again of the moonlit gorge and the big cactus hanging out from the walls like deformed creatures of the sea, and Tonio with his hat off, and the wind in his handsome face as he laughed to re-assure the girl, and kissed her good-by.

"Oh, well!" said the Kid.

He pulled up his horse with such weight that it sat down in cow-pony fashion and skidded to a halt. Montana took that horse by a foreleg, as he dismounted, and tumbled it flat on its side. He sat on its head behind a rock. Tonio was doing something off to the right. The Kid paid no heed to him. He had a good Winchester in his hands, and certain shadowy forms were sweeping out of the black throat of the ravine.

He began to shoot, and he was shooting to kill, his upper lip twitching and snarling, the hate in him guiding the bullets.

He hit something. He knew that by a difference in the yelling down there in the black confusion of shadows. Then all grew still. The horses no longer were raising the echoes with their hoofbeats. The Mexicans no longer yelled.

The voice of Tonio cut in from the side: "Rubriz is there. He'll have men high up in the rocks on either side of us, before long. They'll pick us off. Listen to me, brother!"

"I listen," said the Kid, searching the gloom of the cañon with savage eyes.

"Tear up your coat. Tie cloth around the hoofs of your horse. Quickly! Quickly!"

The Kid understood. A fever of speed was in his hands as he muffled the little iron-hard hoofs of that mustang, but Tonio was already up and waiting for him when he finished. They went away, walking, leading the horses in the thick of the slanting shadows, close to the wall of the gulch. Now and then they had to come out into the clear, cold, deadly light of the moon. It seemed that the ravine would never bend out of the straight. And the horses dragged back against the reins like stubborn mules, refusing to hurry their steps.

The wrapping came off the left forehoof of the Kid's horse. Every time that hoof struck it seemed to find a rock and made a clang like a hammer stroke. But they dared not pause to rewrap the hoof.

The silence grew heavier. Then there was a forking ravine to the right. They dodged into it. They mounted. They went on at a dog trot, that one naked hoof striking out noises as loud as a bell. They could breathe now.

Then another hoof and another hoof joined the beating.

Had Rubriz's men, far behind them, discovered that the pair had slipped away?

They threw away the last caution and galloped the horses hard.

"We can't overtake your father and sister—not if they've ridden the way they ought to ride," said the Kid. "We have to cut back and pick up those two rats, Leffingwell and the other. After all, we can't leave them out here in the mountains."

Tonio made a single gesture of assent.

They got off the rocks onto some ground that muffled the noise of the hoofs. Then, far away, they heard the dim clangor of the pursuit begin.

They twisted through half a dozen windings, from ravine to ravine, halted, and listened.

That far-off river of sound grew fainter and fainter. It dissolved in the moonshine, so to speak, was born again on the air, died once more.

They took their time, from that point forward, riding in Indian file with Tonio in the lead, never speaking. In fact, they needed to save their horses as much as possible. They had dodged Rubriz in the first act, but the game was not ended until they were safely across the Rio Grande. Good horses and lots of them were what they needed.

As for Lavery and the girl, they had a fairly good chance of getting clear because it was not on their trail that Rubriz would labor his hardest. He wanted Tonio. Probably he wanted Tonio alive or dead—better dead, Rubriz would feel, than left to the hands of the Laverys, to forget his Mexican soul.

Then suddenly the Kid found that they had come down into the valley where he had left Fadden and Leffingwell. Now he saw them.

Leffingwell stood out in the moonlight with a gun gripped in his hand. Turk Fadden was a vague shape in the shadow behind him. And when, from a distance, Leffingwell recognized the two riders, he uttered a cry of joy and relief that welled up from the bottom pit of his soul.

It was easy to see that the pair were almost maudlin

with joy, now that their companions had returned. Turk Fadden kept laughing as though he were drunk, and Leffingwell rubbed his hands together and opened his ugly mouth to speak, and then could only clear his throat and make a humming sound of satisfaction. It had been a death-watch, Leffingwell said, finally. He listened to the brief explanation the Kid gave of what had happened.

"All I want," said Leffingwell, "is to get out of this damned country. The money be hanged!"

The Kid kept watching Tonio. He looked older, more fragile; and several times it was possible to find in his face a striking likeness to Mrs. Lavery. The sight of that resemblance made the Kid scowl with a strange resentment and disgust.

Now that the four were together in the cañon, the eastern wall of which was brilliant with the moon, Dick Lavery said: "Señor Leffingwell, Señor Fadden, my countrymen and friends, I shall find a way to reward you and to thank you, if I live. But life is what we have to fight for, now. My father—"

He paused here, his voice pinching out. Then he went on: "Mateo Rubriz has friends all through these mountains. Once we break through the rim of them and get into the opener levels to the north, we'll be much safer. But now we must turn our time into miles or we shall die. If he catches us he'll find a way to kill every inch of us with a separate death. Montana," he said to the Kid, "if we can get through the pass between those two mountains, there in the northeast, before morning, we'll be two-thirds of the way to the Rio Grande, so far as the danger goes!"

The Kid surrendered all direction to him, instantly, and they started marching towards the distant pass, which seemed to deepen as they approached it. They were terribly handicapped through having too few horses, of course, but in a small plain not half an hour from the start, Tonio remedied this by roping a pair of range horses which he and the Kid rode bareback, with a turn of rope around the lower jaw instead of a bridle. Leffingwell and Fadden had the saddles. After that, they made better time through the mountains.

The moonlight began to grow paler, now. And as the moon herself became dim as a tuft of white cloud, all the stars went out and rosy floodlights were turned up behind the eastern mountains. The day grew constantly clearer. It was the time which mountaineers know and love beyond all else, when neither a blazing sun nor the low-set diamond-work of stars limits the sky but for a few minutes it opens and there is visible in it eternity beyond eternity of the clearest green-blue. Even Turk Fadden turned up his face during these moments, and squinted, as though down a gun barrel.

Said Dick Lavery: "There are the signal smokes. Do you see? Look there in the south!"

High in the horizon they saw a long streak of smoke rising like a chalk mark against the pink and the blue, an exclamation point with three white dots beneath the long stroke. As it dissolved, another long column rose

219

to take its place and again there were the three neat, round puffs beneath it. To the west, also, and to the east, rose other columns of smoke, of different design. That to the west was so distant that the Kid could barely descry it.

"What does it mean?" said Turk Fadden, gaping.

"It means that we must ride our horses until we kill them, friend," said Tonio. The effect of his mixed training appeared in him as a rather charming but archaic gravity of speech and of courtesy of deportment. "Those are all men who would be glad to die for my—for Mateo Rubriz. There are plenty of them. They will use up horseflesh in this search as though they were burning stubble fields. They'll come as swift and as hungry as eagles. Why not? Rubriz will make the man rich for life who places us in his hands."

"Ah," said Leffingwell, thoughtfully. "Will he?"

The Kid hardly heard that murmured word, for all four of the horses were now in motion, galloping furiously towards the pass. The gallop turned into a laborious loping, and the lope to a dog trot, and the dog trot to a walk, as they scaled the sharpening angle of the ascent. They lifted above timber line to make it; the sun was streaming into their faces when they reached the floor of the pass and found it as level as though the icy spade of a glacier had struck away and polished the rocks. It was a red granite. It shone like glass on its eastern faces and it was painted black with shadow on the western sides of the rocks. The white snow began not far up the slopes.

Pointing into the floor of the pass there were a number of ravines, great and small. It was out of one of these that they heard a rumbling that dissolved into the crackling noises of hoofbeats. They sent their own horses on at full speed. Then a stream of half a dozen riders spilled out from behind a shoulder of the ravine, screeching like Indians when they saw the quarry.

The Kid observed the head of Tonio turned with disdain towards the six riders. It was apparent that he was not used to running from so small a group. But, looking back towards his companions, Tonio summed up Fadden and Leffingwell with a glance and shook his head. They had to ride for their lives, not fight for them.

Down the pass they sped with this good prognostication—that the mounts of the six pursuers seemed totally spent. They turned a bend in the pass. Not rock, but earth was under the hoofs of the mustangs, now, and a descending slope. They gained impetus suddenly.

Behind them came the six, spilling out around the bend, all giving tongue together until it was a single wail of rage and despair that arose. The Kid, looking back, saw the Mexicans stop their horses and fling themselves down on the ground to open rifle fire.

"Scatter! Scatter!" shouted Tonio, swinging his horse to the side. They fanned out in a looser group.

The first rifles were speaking as the four rushed their mustangs down the slope, Leffingwell bouncing in the saddle, flopping his elbows like wings at his sides, and Fadden sitting low, like a true jockey.

One moment, the Kid saw him in place. The next instant the riderless horse was running out in front. There was Turk Fadden to the rear, struggling to his knees. The Kid, groaning, pulled in on the reins.

Another bullet struck Fadden. He dropped limp and dead and the Kid loosed his horse gladly on the downslope.

They swung behind a providential barrier of tall rocks. The firing died away behind them. Swiftly a pleasant valley opened and the horses loped steadily along the easy going.

"Who were that lot?" asked the Kid, ranging his horse beside Tonio.

"Hermozo and his Indians," said Tonio, his lips straightened as though in pain.

Leffingwell rode up, shouting with glee: "We've beaten them again. We'll always beat 'em. I feel the good luck in my bones."

"What of Fadden?" asked the Kid, bluntly.

"Turk Fadden was always a fool. He was cheap. Now his share goes to me, and that's where it belonged from the start. Three can make better time than four, after all!"

That was the epitaph of Turk Fadden.

"True," said Tonio. "Three can make better time than four, but not when one of the three is only half a man."

He was reining his horse with his left hand. Now he

turned on the bare back of the mustang and the Kid saw a stream of crimson that flowed freely from the shoulder of the jacket and turned the sleeve and the hand beneath it red!

Chapter Twenty-nine

THIN STREAMS OF snow water crossed the little valley, here and there. At the first of these they halted. Leffingwell was helpless with groanings and cursings while the Kid cut away the sleeve of Tonio's Mexican jacket and then the shirt beneath it. He ripped away his own shirt to make the bandage, working rapidly.

Leffingwell argued, with many wide gestures: "Look, now! We can't get away with it. We're beat. Those damned Indians shot too straight and they've beaten us. Have some sense and see that the only thing we can do is to try to turn him back to Rubriz. That's the only way that we'll ever make anything out of him."

Said Tonio. "He's right. There's no good trying to pull me along with you. Besides, I'll be all right. They won't hurt me. Mateo Rubriz won't try to put a knife in me!"

The Kid looked sharply up into the face of Tonio.

"They were shooting to kill; they were shooting at you; and you know it," said he.

The eyes of Tonio widened a little and turned towards the distance.

"I'll be all right," said he. "It was only an accident, of course. I'm one of them, no matter what I've done."

"If Rubriz can't have you living, the gringos shall only have you dead. That's his idea," stated the Kid. "I know something about the Mexican—"

He stopped himself, for he saw a shudder run through Tonio.

Now the Kid finished strapping the arm across the chest. They remounted, Tonio taking one of the saddled horses and Leffingwell the other. The Kid was at home like an Indian on a bare back. And still no danger came in sight of them though it might flower from behind any of a thousand rocks, at any time.

They sloped out of the valley into a spreading desert. Their horses were very tired. Constant spurring was needed lo keep them to a trot. And as the heat of the day increased, flung up into their faces from the surface of the ground and raining like a shower of flames upon their backs and shoulders, the Kid saw that Tonio was setting his teeth to endure.

They reached a small ranch house. A few horses grazed in a field near by. The Kid made Tonio stretch out on the floor of the house. Leffingwell he trusted to get plenty of food from the frightened Mexican woman. The Kid, in the meantime, caught up the three best horses, found an extra saddle, and prepared for the next march.

They paid for what they had taken, liberally. The Kid would have spent his own stock of money, but

Tonio insisted. He said to the Kid: "I have been given a good many things, but all the money I have with me I worked for—in one way or another!"

He made a grotesque face.

They rode on. Tonio, whom the Kid watched with a tigerish eye, was pale, but there was plenty of set in his jaw and plenty of wear in his nerve. That much was patent. No one could tell how long he would last, however; and it was a long way to the yellow waters of the Rio Grande!

The pallor of Lavery turned to a flush, by the middle of the afternoon. In the evening he ate little of the provisions they had taken at the Mexican house. He talked still less.

He merely said to the Kid: "Richard Lavery—my father —you know him?"

"He's a hard man," said the Kid, "but he's a right man and a white man."

Tonio made no answer. He was lost in thought.

Afterwards he went to sleep and began to mumble to himself.

"That bird has a fever. He's going to be a dead one," said Leffingwell. The Kid answered with a glance, not with words. The last red smoke of the sunset was in the west. A hunting owl began to call over the desert. The tall cactus stood up like frozen snakes to look at the three men and their dry camp.

"What are the chances?" asked Leffingwell.

"The chances are one Leffingwell and myself against Rubriz and that scar-faced Rurale," said the

Kid. "You sleep with that in your belly and try not to get heartburn."

Tonio continued to mutter in his sleep during the first half of the night. The Kid wakened again and again and heard him. But when the gray of the morning began and they started, Tonio seemed well enough.

They reached another house and another chance to get fresh horses, food, and hot water for the dressing of the wound of Tonio, while the morning was still young. By stopping at houses they were blazing their trail but the needs of the wounded man compelled them. Three grim-faced Mexicans watched them sullenly. One of those fellows was sure to follow their trail after they left.

But there was no deed of that spy-work. The Kid was still at work on the shoulder of Tonio when Leffingwell strode in with an exclamation of fear.

"There's a dust-cloud coming and no wind behind it. Come out here and look."

The Kid stepped to the door in time to see the head of that cloud lift. Underneath appeared the small forms of many riders, journeying steadily.

It was Rubriz. As they got to horse and fled, Tonio swore he could recognize the leader of the hunt by the slant with which he sat the saddle. And no one but Rubriz, he declared, knew how to keep tired horses to such speed. But the fresh mustangs that carried the fugitives stretched out a distance that dropped Rubriz and his men behind some low hills, by sunset.

They had traveled very fast and very far. The Kid felt they could make the Rio Grande by one more day of such riding.

They found some alkaline water and camped. Tonio refused food.

"You'd better eat," said the Kid. "You'll need strength."

"I can't eat," said Tonio.

The Kid lighted a match and held the light to the eyes of the wounded man. Those eyes were covered by a yellow-and-red film. The pupils shrank to points before the flare of the match. The face of Tonio was burning hot, hot as fresh sunburn. His hand was dry. His pulse raced with a quick, broken rhythm. As he lay flat on his back, the Kid leaned over him and studied the beat of that heart with his ear pressed to the breast. He was no doctor, the Kid, but he could tell the proper life-step of a heart from this confused muttering.

He opened the bandages and washed the wound again. The whole shoulder was swollen. At his touch, pus ran out from the mouth of the bullet hole. Plainly the wound was infected and the infection was the root of the fever.

When he had finished redressing the wound the Kid sat down and hugged his knees. Tonio fell asleep. There was a quaver of weakness in his moaning and he moaned with every breath he drew. It was like the complaining murmur of a small child that has been sick for a long time.

Leffingwell hunched himself close to the Kid.

"You see how it is," he whispered. "There's no chance at all. He's a goner. If we stop here, Rubriz will swallow all three of us. If we try to take him on the fever will kill him, anyway. He'll drop out of the saddle before tomorrow night."

The Kid looked up at the stars, dim and yellow behind the thick veil of the dusty desert air.

"We've done enough for our money," said Leffingwell. "*You've* done enough. You've tried to get the real Dick Lavery. It can't be done. There's only one thing left."

"What's that?" asked the Kid, dreamily.

He made a cigarette and lighted it.

"The one thing," said Leffingwell, "is to go straight back to Rubriz with a flag of truce and give him Tonio."

The Kid smoked leisurely. He was tasting the alkali dust but he was tasting the smoke, too. It increased his thirst, which he dared not slake with more of that acrid water.

"You've made a fine try at doing the right thing," said Leffingwell. "But it's no good. Put this fellow out of pain. And then you and me will go winging back to God's country."

"Listen to me," said the Kid.

"Yeah, I'm listening," said Leffingwell. "Any idea you have I'd always listen to."

"Before I started on this ride I thought I might not be able to play the game straight. I understand what's

228

pulling at you, Leffingwell. I understand the pull in every crook because I'm a crook myself. But let me tell you something: I go through with Tonio or else I go out. You do what you want with yourself."

Leffingwell made a sound like a kicked dog, though he kept that cry hardly bigger than a whisper. The strength of his reaction lifted him half to his feet.

"You leave me alone to try to—" he began.

He was silent. The Kid went on smoking.

"There's another thing," said the Kid. "If we manage to go through with this, I'll make sure that Tonio gives you a reward for that first bright idea of yours. But if you lift a finger to spoil this game the way I want to play it, I'm going to kill you, Leffingwell. I'll kill you the way nobody ever was killed before. I'll dig your heart out with my hands and unravel the strings of it. You understand?"

Leffingwell did not risk an answer.

The Kid went to Tonio, wet a cloth, and laid it over his face. Tonio grunted with the relief of that coolness, as he wakened.

"Where's there a town, near here?" said the Kid.

"What!" screeched Leffingwell, all his nerves getting into his voice. "What d'you mean? Town? Are you crazy enough to go into a town, with Rubriz and his gang probably there before you?"

"Leffingwell—" said the Kid. He paused. Leffingwell was silent, except for groaning. The Kid went on, "Tonio, do you know of a town?"

"West of the hills, only about four miles," said

Tonio. "You wouldn't risk going into a town, would you?"

"Well," said the Kid, "I'll see you later."

"Señor," said Tonio, "you never have told me your name."

"My name is the first quick fit," said the Kid. "They call me anything—from Montana Kid to the Mexico Kid. And here south of the Rio Grande most of them call me the Kid—just that."

"El Keed?" said Tonio, drawling out the word in Mexican. "Ah—now I understand—everything. Señor, you are not going into a town for my sake. If I am to die, I am to die. There is nothing else to do about it!"

"All right," said the Kid. "I'll see you later."

He stood up. Leffingwell hurried beside him through the darkness towards the hobbled horses.

"If you leave me alone out here with that Tonio moaning and hysterical and Rubriz sneaking up on me through the night I'll go crazy, I tell you. I'll have to clear out."

The Kid flopped a saddle heavily onto the back of a horse. He drew up the cinches. He put his knee into the ribs of the mustang and tightened the cinches again, while the wind went out of the bronco in a gasp.

"You'll stay here, Leffingwell," said the Kid. "Right here, taking care of Tonio like a female nurse. If you don't, I'll manage to find you even if you turn yourself into a gopher and dig a hole in the ground a mile

230

deep. So long, Leffingwell. You're going to be a man in spite of yourself."

He jogged the horse away. The alkali water sloshed in the belly of the mustang. It grunted in weary complaint at every step. The sand swished around the moving hoofs while the Kid rounded the edge of the low hills and far away saw the trembling lights of a town.

Chapter Thirty

WHERE TWO HUMMOCKS of ground guarded a shallow hollow between them, the Kid dismounted, threw the reins, and started ahead on foot. The town lights were near. They seemed to grow broaded but dimmer, turning from white to yellow.

Presently a rush of dogs flooded out of the long street of the village. Their clamoring roared between the houses like thundering water down a cañon, but the sounds spread out to a comparative thinness when there were no longer walls to reflect the barking. These dogs, as they flashed through the bars of light, were a collection of mongrels that resembled coyotes. They all swept up to the Kid as though they would leap at his throat or cut him down by the legs. They raised their noise to a hideous crescendo, but the Kid walked on without a word. They snuffed at his heels and at the traces which he left behind him but he paid them no heed.

After a moment most of them turned their attention

to other things, such as sitting down to scratch at fleas. One of these sat in the very path of the Kid. He kicked it ruthlessly out of the way. Its screech of pain set all the others fleeing, yipping. One would have thought that wolves were running behind them.

The Kid grinned and came on more slowly. Welcome silence was about him as he stood at the head of the street.

He saw the brightness pouring from what must be the chief drinking-place. Through that light passed the figures of the villagers, wisps of smoke floating often over their shoulders, their cotton clothes glistening. Children played in the street, the dust rising in thin golden clouds across the shafts of lamplight; and in the doorways sat women. They were sewing or rubbing out corn to make the wet meal for tortillas. And they visited one another without changing place, merely lifting their voices.

One of them at last stood up from a nearby threshold and went slowly up the street. The Kid glided out of shadow and across that doorstep. Inside, a few red coals on the hearth gave him sufficient light to guess at the interior. In a corner he found what he wanted. For clothes were hanging on the wall near a rolled-up, straw-filled tick. He got a tattered straw hat with an enormous brim, a cotton shirt and cotton trousers, a pair of battered huaraches that might fit his feet. That loot he gathered into his arms. Inside the hovel a baby began to cry, striking a few tentative notes and then blaring forth with full strength.

The Kid slipped out as he had come, turned the corner of the house, and presently in the outer darkness he was stripping off his clothes. He donned the villager's costume, rolled his own clothes about his boots, laid them away behind a rock, and stood up to consider. There was one great disadvantage, considering what he had to do; his clothes now fitted so close to the skin that he could not conceal a gun. He would have to go barehanded into whatever danger lay before him.

But having contemplated that necessity, he shrugged his shoulders, pulled the wide straw hat over the back of his head, and made a half-circle that brought him into the town from the western instead of the eastern end. He went straight towards the flare of light. His unshaven face would probably be dark enough and his sun-blackened throat and hands ought to pass as Mexican. For his language he had no fear. He was so familiar with the tongue that it colored even the processes of his mind. There was one weak point and that was the color of his feet, which were as white as those of any Teuton. Perhaps that color would be unsuspected under the layer of dust that he accumulated by walking through the middle of the street.

It was his hope that he would not have to enter the fonda to make his inquiry.

"Friend—" he said, to the first man he overtook.

The villager paused and then recoiled.

"My father and sister are with the donkey, three

miles east," said the Kid. "My father is sick. Where shall I find a doctor?"

"Ah, who knows?" said the villager.

He drew back still farther.

"Is there a doctor in the town?" asked the Kid.

"If God is willing, perhaps," said the man.

The Kid wasted no more time; he knew the type. Near the flare of lights he saw a pair of youths chattering, laughing, their teeth flashing.

"I am trying to find a doctor, friends," said the Kid.

"A doctor today and a priest tomorrow," said one of the pair. They both laughed heartily.

"Can you tell me where to find a doctor?" asked the Kid.

"Yes. In his house," said the second of these banterers.

"Well, where is his house?" asked the Kid.

"The doctor's house is on the doctor's land," was the answer.

The Kid sighed and so managed to breathe out most of the savage impulse which had burned up in him, but again he knew that to persist in inquiry at this point would be futile.

He had to face the worst. So he went straight through the open doors that allowed the light to blaze forth into the street. It was the sort of a place that one might expect to find—restaurant, drinking-tavern and store all combined. At the little tables sat groups of the villagers, drinking, smoking, playing cards, or merely chattering with voices that ran up and down the scale in music. The proprietor was a negroid type with thick lips, a head that diminished rapidly towards the top, and a matting of curly hair.

The Kid groaned, as though with relief, when he entered the place. He stamped on the floor and beat his hands against his trousers to get the dust off. It flew out in a cloud.

"Hai!" shouted a pair of angry men who sat close by and had been covered by the flying dust. They stood up and bawled at the Kid. "If you are a dog, shake your hide in the street!"

The Kid turned towards them and put his fists on his hips. He gave his shoulders a swagger from side to side. It was impossible to avoid attention by slinking in quietly. It seemed best, therefore, to make himself a center of attraction.

"If you are my master, kick me out the door!" he roared.

He held his pose just long enough to be impressive and not long enough to draw a knife thrust.

He went to the drink-counter. The thick lips of the proprietor compelled him to smile his way through life, but his eyes were yellowish and dead as the eyes of a catfish.

"Tequila," said the Kid. "And frijoles. Tortillas. I might as well eat while I'm here. My mouth is big enough to eat on one side and talk on the other. Where is there a doctor? Is there a doctor in this town?"

The patron called to the woman who presided over the cookery and the fumes that filled the end of the room: "Frijoles. Tortillas. Quickly, quickly! Sit here, señor!"

He pointed to a table. The Kid sat down, hooked his heels around the legs of it and drew it between his knees. He dropped his elbows on the sides of the table. Everyone was looking. The Mexican does not glance. He stares like an infant, thinking slowly and beholding much. The proprietor brought a glass of tequila, looking like green-tainted water. The Kid tossed it off, closed his eyes, and let it burn its way into his stomach. He kept his eyes closed.

"You are traveling," said the patron.

The Kid said nothing. He kept his eyes closed.

"It is hard to travel without a pack," said the proprietor. His voice sounded more distant, so that it was plain he had looked away towards the others in the room, as though to assure them that he would be their spokesman and winnow all the grain of news out of this stranger.

"Ugh! " grunted the Kid, opening his eyes.

He smacked his lips loudly. *That* is tequila," he said. "Is there a doctor in the town?"

"God be kind to the man who needs a doctor," said the patron, wagging his head.

Some of the men were continuing their card games, slowly, two-thirds of their attention focused on the stranger.

"What is your home town?" asked the patron.

"The Americanos," said the Kid, "may the itch settle between their shoulder-blades and the flies eat them and the sand blow into the sores. Is there an Ameri-cano here?"

He stood up and looked about him. He was a stranger but yet he was now greeted by a few smiles. He had struck on a theme that was pleasant to all.

"Why should not a man carry a little can of black stuff that looks like tar over the Rio Grande?" said the Kid. "What harm can there be in a pint of it?"

"Opium!" said the patron. "Ah-ha! Opium!"

He made a loud clicking sound with his tongue. He invited the crowd to understand, winking at them and at the men who were gathering in the doorway to see a stranger.

The Kid sat down again, scowling.

"Should a man be beaten to death by Americanos for a nothing?" he demanded, holding out his hands to the opinion of the world.

"Did they beat you?" asked the patron, eagerly, his eyes searching for bumps and welts.

"My father is still sick. Perhaps he is dying. Is there a doctor in the town?"

"It is better to die in our Mexico than in a gringo jail," said the patron. "You are lucky not to be in the jail."

"May the teeth fall out of their heads and the itch blind their eyes," said the Kid. "Is there a doctor in this town?"

The woman came bringing the food. It was she who gave the Kid his first answer to the question.

"Ignacio, run to the doctor. Bring him back with you."

Ignacio backed towards the door, staring at the Kid. Then he disappeared, darting through the crowd.

The Kid began to eat. The tortillas became scoops in his dexterous fingers and he felt some of the attention melting out of the air. Hoofbeats began to sound with a drumming noise down the street and the crowd spilled out through the doorway again to see what fresh strangers were coming in. Even the patron went to stare. The horsemen stopped in front of the tavern. Their stirrups leathers creaked as they dismounted. A thick cloud of dust rolled across the doorway and through that dust advanced the powerful form of Mateo Rubriz.

Chapter Thirty-one

AT THE KITCHEN end of the room there was a passage by which a fugitive might escape, but Montana knew that would be futile. Running would draw gunfire and some of those sleek-faced young tigers who were following Rubriz would probably be able to run him down, at that.

So the Kid made himself busier than ever with his beans and tortillas.

There were a dozen men with Rubriz, far more than there was room for in the place. So they made places by beginning to jerk the chairs from beneath those who were already installed. These villagers, though they looked like a formidable lot, made no protest. Even the negroid patron did not raise his face. As for the Kid, he was glad enough to go with the rest. It was exactly what he wanted. But as he abandoned his chair and started towards the door, a voice yelled, close to him: "The Americano!" and he saw the face of that man into whose face the oil of the lantern had been dashed in the tavern at Ormosa.

There were men of Rubriz thronging all through the room. If he tried to escape he would certainly be shot. If he tried to resist he would be overwhelmed. But he followed the second thought that flashed through his brain. The man of Ormosa he clipped on the chin so that the fellow staggered like a drunkard and put a bullet through the ceiling. And out of the same man's belt he snatched the hunting-knife. He caught up a chair in his left hand, up-ended it, and springing back against the service bar, he crouched there like an animal trainer about to receive the attack of wild beasts. There was a steel-blue glitter of guns before him, yet the Kid flung himself heartily into the part which he had chosen. He stamped alternately with either foot to keep the beat of the rhythm as he thundered out.

"Now learn what a man of Chihuahua can do. Hai! You coyotes! You eaters of stinking goat meat! Come to me! Learn what Juan Fernandez can do!"

The others stood about him undeterminedly. Rubriz had begun to laugh. And when the man of Ormosa, recovering, silently leveled his revolver, Rubriz struck his hand down.

"That is the man! That is the Americano!" said the fellow, in a loud protest.

"The gringos don't take to knives; they have guns, Rafael," said Rubriz. "Here, you, what is your name?"

"It is my own name," said the Kid, savagely.

"You are Juan Fernandez, eh?" said Rubriz. "Here— the rest of you start feeding. Find what's in the place. Pay for everything. Remember that we are far north. Pay for everything, break nothing. Do you think we have time to waste? But you, then—you are Juan Fernandez?"

"My name is what it may be," said the Kid.

"You've just given your name, friend," said Rubriz, grinning. "And Chihuahua is your town?"

"Chihuahua is as good a town as any," said the Kid.

"What of Ormosa?" said Rubriz. He sat sidling in a chair and rested his hands on his knees. "Do you know Ormosa?"

"Why not?" said the Kid.

"You're a very crafty fellow," said Rubriz. "Nobody shall be able to pull information out of you, eh? Where is Ormosa, then?"

"Ormosa is in its own place," said the Kid. He looked straight into the bright, twinkling eyes of Rubriz.

"I tell you that is the man, that is the Americano!" exclaimed the man of Ormosa, leaping up from his place at a table.

"You lie!" shouted the Kid. "Call me a dog, but not a gringo! You lie! You are the son of a liar; your children will be crooked in the tongue, also. Your mother and your grandmother were liars!"

The Mexican ripped out an entangled oath. Rubriz put him back in his chair with a word and said to the patron, "Who is this?"

The negroid answered: "This is a man who says that he was going over the Rio Grande with his father, and they had some opium with them, a pint can of it. And when they were crossing the river the gringos caught them and beat the poor old man. They are traveling with a donkey and the old man is sick from the beating, still, and this fellow has come into town to get the doctor and my son Ignacio has gone to call the doctor. That is simply all, señor."

"Listen to me," said Rubriz. "Have you ever heard of Mateo Rubriz?"

The Kid started. He drew himself up straight and squinted at the other.

"One hears of names and names," said the Kid. "Mateo Rubriz is a name, too."

Rubriz laughed loudly. He rolled himself from side to side and smote his knees.

"Here's a man who won't be fooled," said Rubriz. "Do you hear him? Nobody from Chihuahua ever had a quicker wit than that. It would be hard, to cheat him in a horse-trade, eh? So Mateo Rubriz is a name, eh?"

The Kid glowered at him.

"You laugh," said he. "But leave your men here and come out alone with me. I'll tell you something then that is worth a little money."

"Do you want to fight me?" said Rubriz, grinning more broadly than ever. They were *all* grinning, for that matter. Only the man of Ormosa kept squinting at the Kid with his head on one side, as though doubt and suspicion were continually tormenting him. "Do you want to fight me?" repeated Rubriz.

"He who asks for a fight will be content with a beating," said the Kid, scowling more blackly than ever.

"Listen to him!" said Rubriz, chuckling. "He's a wise man, I tell you—this American of yours is a wise man, Rafael. Do you hear his wisdom?"

"He talks like a country priest," said Rafael. "Well, he looked like the American, at first. He was about of the same face. But the American was bigger by twenty pounds, now that I think of it."

"Now that you think of it," said Rubriz, "but before your second thought came he might have been a dead man, or—"

"You!" shouted the Kid, pointing his knife at Rafael. "You—you are the one for me! You, with the gringo knife—look, friends, if the knife is not a gringo knife?—and your gringo gun—and the hat on your head is gringo, also—aha! Listen to me! *You* are the Americano! Take a knife and come to me and I'll prove that your blood is gringo water, too! Do you hear me, you coward?"

"A match!" shouted several voices, delighted.

Rafael rose slowly from his chair.

"Give me a knife," he said. "I have heard enough of his words. I'll show you how *this* Americano can use a knife."

"Sit down, Rafael," commanded Rubriz. "Now, Juan Fernandez, you have offered to fight two of us. Fighting is a thing you like."

"Well," said the Kid, "it's a poor dog that won't fight for his own collar, and so I say it is a poor man that won't fight for his name."

"True again," said Rubriz. "A man could write a book of these sayings, in time. But speaking of names, I am sorry that you do not know Mateo Rubriz."

"You are looking for him, perhaps?" said the Kid. "Well, señor, I know what I know. That is all!"

"And what do you know?" said Rubriz.

"I have known men who have seen this Mateo Rubriz," said the Kid, importantly.

"What do they say of him?" asked Rubriz.

The Kid shrugged his shoulders.

"Well," he said, "he is a man who has done many things, and yet, believe me or not, he is not very much taller than I am, nor a great deal heavier."

A whoop of joy came from the followers of the bandit. Rubriz himself nodded his head as one who contemplates a picture in the mind.

"He is not very much taller?" echoed Rubriz.

"He is not," said the Kid. "These other people laugh and I tell you that he who laughs today howls tomorrow! A cousin of my own wife's sister told me in the great plaza at Chihuahua, standing under the trees on Good Friday last, that he saw with his own eyes Mateo Rubriz and that the man is not much taller than I am."

There was more laughter; even Rafael joined in it. The Kid stood triumphant, however.

"Now, then," said Rubriz, "what if I tell you that Mateo Rubriz lacks at least three inches of your height?"

"You would be a fool to tell me that," said the Kid.

Rubriz stood up.

"Look at me," he said.

"I look at you, señor," said the Kid.

"Am I a fool?" asked Rubriz.

"You are as God has made you," said the Kid.

"I am Mateo Rubriz."

The Kid put back his head and laughed until the place rang again. But there came an exclamation from the patron of the place, a muttering cry that said: "God protect us! It *is* Mateo Rubriz!"

"Madre de Dios!" groaned the Kid, and from his hands the chair and the knife crashed to the floor.

He crossed himself. He stared. His mouth fell open. And all those followers of Rubriz laughed until the tears ran from their eyes. Rafael himself was most forward in that laughter.

"You are afraid, friend," said Rubriz, "but you have wits enough to know that Mateo Rubriz is a father and a brother to all good fellows. Tell me—what is your business?"

"In the name of God, señor," said the Kid, "I am a very poor man!"

"I believe it," said Rubriz, smiling. "I believe it, Juan Fernandez. That is your name?"

"Yes, señor," said the Kid.

"And you are from Chihuahua?"

"Yes, señor. God forgive me!"

"And who is your father?"

"Tomaso Fernandez, the shoemaker, señor. He is a known man in Chihuahua. Even gringos have stopped and admired the brown boot with the red and yellow embroidery at the top of it; that boot stands always in his window and he made it with his own hands!"

"Very well," said Rubriz. "And if that's your father's business, what is yours?"

"By the will of Saint Christopher," said the Kid, "I have steered my way through the world sighting between the ears of a mule, señor. But now, señor, it is the will of God that I have no more than a donkey and a sick father to load on its back."

"And what if Mateo Rubriz said to you; 'Juan Fernandez, you look to me like a strong, brave fellow. Follow me and be my man!'"

The Kid jumped his heels together with an audible thud.

"In the name of God, señor," said the Kid. "You are pleased to laugh at poor Juan Fernandez."

"No, Juan. I'm not laughing. Will you follow me?"

The Kid leaped into the air with a shout and shook his fist at the ceiling.

"Am I a fool?" he answered. "Shall I turn my back on fortune? Señor, you will find that I can—"

"Take the doctor to your father," said Rubriz. "Let him tie up the old man's sores. Bring your father like a good son into this town. And then we will talk again.

Here is a fee for the doctor and something to buy liquor for yourself!"

He threw a piece of money, which the Kid caught from the air. It was gold!

With staring eyes, he beheld it, sniffed at it, and tried it with his teeth.

A roar of laughter seemed to call him to himself.

"Pardon, señor," said the Kid, "but the saint of this day shall be *my* saint hereafter. I shall change my name to his name. Señor, I go and I shall come again. I shall hope to know you better and I shall hope that you come to know me."

He backed towards the door and, reaching it, he turned and cried with an imperious voice: "Where is the doctor? Show me the doctor! The man who wastes my time is wasting the time of Mateo Rubriz! Where is the doctor?"

Chapter Thirty-two

THE DOCTOR WAS already there in the crowd, a thin young man with great glasses that made his face look like that of an old and starving cat. He climbed onto a shambling horse that had a medicine-kit strapped behind the saddle and told the Kid to show him the way to the sick man, so the Kid struck out at an easy dog trot, a veritable Indian's run which took him rapidly down the street to the end of the village.

Gradually he turned to the south.

"Now, friend," said the doctor, presently, "I thought that the sick man lay east of the town?"

The Kid took the bridle reins close to the bit.

"Friend," said he, "let me tell you something. Have no fear. Do as I wish you to do and there shall be no harm for you tonight. But ask questions and doubt the way and you come to trouble."

The poor young doctor, with a groan of fear, clutched at the revolver which hung in the saddle holster. The hand of the Kid was already on the gun.

"You are as safe," said the Kid, "as a baby in the arms of its mother, unless you yell out or try to get away. Besides, there will be ten fees for you in one at the end of this trail. Ride straight on!"

He guided the doctor around the back of the village, found his clothes and guns, donned them, and continued to the point where the mustang had been left.

So the Kid came in due time, just before the rising of the moon, to the camp. He called out, as he drew nearer to the obscure shadows. The voice of Leffingwell, choked with mingled fear and relief, answered him.

In two minutes they were at the side of Tonio, and the doctor was at work with trembling hands. But to do the thing which he understood steadied him presently. He laid the wound open. The Kid, over a low fire which was sunk in a hollow of the ground, heated water in a canteen. For an hour the doctor worked, paring and probing the inflamed flesh.

Tonio, recalled to his full wits by the height of the torment, lay rigid and looked at the dull stars above him.

When a neat bandage was finally placed over the wound the doctor said: "He must be taken to a cool place and kept quiet and tended with care. The infection is strong and deep. It may cost him his arm. It might easily cost him his life."

Leffingwell muttered: "Ah, and I've known it. I told you a day ago that the job was hopeless. I told you that it was finished. But, after all—"

"Leffingwell," said the Kid, "this is a thing for Tonio to decide. Let me tell you something. I've been in that village, yonder, talking with Rubriz. He's grown thin in this manhunt. By the look of his eyes he has not slept since he started. If he is this close to us now, he may be closer still tomorrow. But as for deciding what is to be done with Tonio, Tonio has the only voice."

The voice of Tonio began on a quavering note of weak complaint. He stopped speaking, steadied himself, and started again in his normal tone. He said: "Friend, there is nothing that I wish, now, except to die among my own people. If I come into the hands of Rubriz again there will be no life. It will be war between us. And then hate, and then the end for me, quickly. If I lose my arm, if I lose my life, it is my loss and I accept the chance. Only for you, I see that it is a very foolish thing to hang me around your neck and then try to escape from Mateo Rubriz. You never can do it. I know him and I know his men. Horses that would stagger and stop under you they will keep at a gallop. They will go without water or food like buzzards in the sky. For my own sake, I wish nothing except to go on. For your sake, I wish nothing except to be left here. The doctor is a kind man. He'll take me safely into the village because he knows that Rubriz will reward him."

"Ay," said Leffingwell. "Rubriz will load him with more gold than a mule could carry!"

The Kid answered: "The thing's settled. We have to rest ourselves and our horses for a few more hours. Then we'll go forward again. Doctor, you'll stay with us till the start? Can you give him something that will reduce the fever?"

"I can," said the doctor. "But Mateo Rubriz—"

His voice shook away to nothing.

"Then stay with us," said the Kid.

He hobbled the horses, stretched himself on the ground, and muttered: "Mind you, Doctor, if you try to steal away from us, I'll follow; and this moon gives enough light for straight shooting."

After that he slept; and the knowledge that the next day might be a time of frightful effort and danger only made his sleep the sounder.

When he wakened, the moon had covered a great arc of the sky. He sat up. The doctor was cross-legged on the ground beside his patient, fanning Tonio's face. The horses were lying down.

"Where is my other friend, Doctor?" asked the Kid.

"An hour, two hours ago, he went away," said the doctor.

"Two hours ago?" exclaimed the Kid, leaping up.

He stared over the plain. One of the horses stood up. Here and there human forms seemed to be moving towards him but a second glance always resolved them into cactus.

"Rubriz and the mule-load of gold!" groaned the Kid.

"Do you think he has gone to tell Mateo Rubriz where you are to be found?" asked the doctor.

"He has," said the Kid. "And it's time to start! Two hours ago? Did you say two hours?"

"Yes," said the doctor.

"Then take your horse and go back to the town. Tell me again about my sick friend. Do you think it may cost him his arm or his life if he travels again today?"

The glasses of the doctor turned like the eyes of an owl towards the Kid. He hesitated before answering: "He is brave, señor, and brave men do not die easily. There is less heat in the arm. His fever has fallen. And God may help you."

The Kid poured money into his hands.

"This is too much," said the doctor.

"It will help you to remember tonight," said the Kid. "If Tonio gets well—if we live to the end of our journey—you'll have still more money than that from us. *Adios*!"

The doctor was bewildered by his good fortune. He stuffed the money into his pockets and climbed on his old horse. He wanted to give the travelers his blessing but when he thought of Mateo Rubriz his devotion to truth made him compromise. He merely said, in a heartfelt voice, "God help you!" and jogged away into the night.

The Kid was already at work. Leffingwell had not ventured to take one of the horses, perhaps because he feared that the mustang would make too much noise in starting. But in two hours, even on foot, Leffingwell must have reached the town, he must have found Rubriz, he must have told his news; and before this Rubriz and all his men were sweeping through the moonlight on that trail.

When the horses were saddled and the camp broke, the Kid assisted Tonio into a saddle. Tonio said nothing. His lips were pinched into a straight line. Already he was beginning to need his power of will. He sat in the saddle with his head bowed, holding onto the pommel with his left hand.

Briefly, the Kid started to tell him that Leffingwell had deserted them and turned traitor. But Tonio cut him short.

"I heard you talk with the doctor," he said.

That was all. The throbbing of his wound had kept him awake, no doubt, and he had listened to everything without uttering a word. He was the true son of Richard Lavery, after all. The Kid set his teeth, swung into the saddle, and put his horse into a lope.

The mustang that bore Tonio followed, and Tonio lurched heavily, weakly back against the cantle, before righting himself. A mist of dust rose behind them and hung in the air. The Kid, looking back, knew that that mist would be faintly visible for half an hour, before the last of it settled in the windless air. And all the while Rubriz was rushing towards them from the town!

By the stars the Kid set the course. The desert was before him like a sea, without a landmark. He looked towards Tonio and saw him riding erect with his eyes closed and his nostrils flaring a little.

They were still a long voyage from safety. A long day for even a strong man and expert rider!

The best way to get mileage out of horse flesh is at a full trot. But only soft dog trot or lope could the Kid venture on because the movement of the trot would be intolerable to Tonio, he knew.

The hours rolled behind them. Still there was no sign of the pursuit coming up. Dark shapes on the horizon turned into hills, bald and naked except in a few places where pines were growing.

The night ended; the day began with a slow staining of the horizon all around so that it was hard to tell in which direction lay the east. The whole round of the world was smoking and flaming as though a universal fire were marching towards the travelers. And now the Kid saw that it was not only the pallor of the moonlight that had made Dick Lavery seem so haggard and white. As his cheeks grew hollow and his eyes were enlarged by shadows, more and more his mother appeared in his face. But he kept on riding. How he had endured all through the night was a miracle, now that the Kid could see him in the reality of the day.

There was something else to notice in the dawning of this day—the signal fires which were once more painted against the horizon. They were not so milky white as when they had been seen through the crystal air of the mountains; the desert distances made them purple below and against the sky they were a fading gray. East, south, west, and northwest those signal columns climbed up from the ground, melted away, and were renewed.

Said the Kid: "Tonio, can you tell me what those signal smokes mean? Can they have been sent up by friends of Mateo Rubriz?"

Tonio turned his head. His eyes burned but they had no meaning in them. He stared at the Kid and said nothing. The Kid looked back at him with a very critical squint of the eyes. He did not pursue his questioning, for he saw that the mind of Tonio was no longer moored to any sense of reality. The fever had finally made his wit a drifting derelict. This was the moment when the Kid definitely gave up all hope.

The advice of Leffingwell actually returned to him. If a man should kill a horse with a broken leg, why should not a poor, foredoomed fellow like Dick Lavery be put out of misery so that his companion might have a chance to draw clear? In the cool, grim mind of the Kid every thought was registered calmly, and then put away.

The sun rose. The heat instantly became intense. While the rose of the dawn was still in the rays they had power to burn the face, and when the sun climbed above the purple belt of the desert mist it seemed at a stride to reach the strength of midday. Tonio began to slump lower and lower in the saddle. Now and again, he pulled himself strongly upright.

The Kid waited for him to slump sidewise to the ground, but like a runner that staggers but will not fall, Tonio kept in his place. He was delirious. Sometimes he broke out with laughter. For hours he muttered to himself.

Twice, as they went through the hills, through the desert beyond, through more hills later on, the Kid found water. Each time he stretched Tonio in the shadow of a horse and drenched him with the water after they had drunk and the Kid had filled their canteens. And each time Tonio begged to be left where he lay. The Kid had to lift him like a thousand-jointed burden and force him again into the saddle.

Hope began to come up in the Kid. Not many miles away, beyond these hills and across the flat that succeeded them, ran the yellow tides of the Rio Grande. The mountains of the Bend were already bluer than the sky in the distance, and among them was the Lavery ranch, the Lavery men, Richard Lavery himself like a mind of iron, his wife with the life of faith coming back into her eyes and the blood of life flowing again in her body. The girl was there, also. Well, if he managed to reach the ranch house on this journey he would pause only as a bird pauses in flight.

In the midafternoon Montana looked back from a high place among those last bleak hills and saw the dust-cloud that crawled over the plain behind him. He watched until a gust of wind stripped the mist away and showed the riders—a dozen of them.

But they were so far back that a fierce hope came up in the breast of the Kid. They had a chance to make a final bid for freedom. If their horses were tired so were the horses of Rubriz. The question was Tonio. Could he make the final effort? No one could tell. He wavered in the saddle, but he had strength to set his teeth and until that strength was gone he was not beaten.

So the Kid drove the horses on through the last of the hills, down the last gap between them, towards the desert beyond.

They were out of the lips of the pass when the Kid saw the danger. Far before him appeared a rider, coming up from a low swale. The man was a good mile distant. He came straight at the fugitives, firing a rifle over his head with one hand, like a pistol. The reports were thin and dull, like noises on the other side of a thick wall.

The reason for that signaling became clear. Behind the rider, the Kid saw another horseman, and another, and to the right yet others. They were closing in on the mouth of the pass!

So the Kid drew rein. He understood why Rubriz had not pressed the hunt more closely from the rear.

He had simply waited until his smoke-writing in the sky had extended a living barrier to the north of the fugitives. Now he could close in from the rear to find and destroy them.

Chapter Thirty-three

THE KID TURNED his horse. He had to take that of Tonio by the reins and lead it, for Tonio insisted on trying to pull the mustang about again in order to continue the march to the north. They entered that patch of badlands in silence. The strength ran suddenly out of Tonio. The Kid had to grasp his shoulder to keep him in the saddle.

In such a time one thinks of miracles, but the Kid knew that no miracle of intervention could save them. They were squarely cornered.

He knew how the hunt would go. While the main body of the men of Rubriz kept to a fairly central valley that wound through the hills, a few of the sharpest of eye would ride the ridges, here and there. It should be quick work. There were not many outcroppings of rock to interrupt the gaze or offer covert. The trees were more scant than hair on an Indian's face. Very soon two men and three horses would be found.

Suppose that he turned and rode back to surrender?

But men continue to struggle after the ship and the boats have sunk; they swim although nothing can save them from drowning. So the Kid went on.

He entered a broad, low-sided valley paved with rock, wind-polished rock that turned to flame under this sun. They passed, in the middle of this valley, a singular, sharp-sided depression, five or six feet deep, a dozen feet long. What had made it one could not imagine. It seemed to have been drilled out for some insane purpose. Perhaps it was caused by a movement of the folding rocks; perhaps it was simply a softer stratum of stone which the rains of winter had gradually dissolved.

They passed it. As the Kid turned and looked back it was gone from view again!

At once he stopped the horses. He had to dismount with care. When he was on the ground, the loose weight of Tonio fell helplessly towards him. He drew that burden over his shoulder. The head of Tonio hung down; his voice muttered ceaselessly. With one arm, the Kid steadied the weight; in the other hand he carried three filled canteens by their straps.

The mustangs went on. That which the Kid had been riding was a stubborn little bay with a lump of a head and an eye as red as a starved wolf's. That mustang kept steadily plodding on and the other two beaten nags followed. So the Kid turned and carried Tonio back until he found the crack among the rocks. He was almost on top of it before it opened again under his eyes.

Into it he lowered Tonio, and himself followed.

It was an oven. Under the western wall of it extended a foot or two of shadow. In this shadow he stretched out Tonio, but the rock even there was so heated that the skin of the hand prickled at the touch of it. The air was dead. It was thick as soup and hot as soup. The Kid had to keep his lungs laboring to get enough oxygen out of it, and in thirty seconds his shirt was black with sweat.

And Tonio?

He lay with his mouth open, gasping slowly. His face turned gray. Rivulets of sweat formed and coursed in the small lines which these last two days had carved in the skin. He was dying.

The Kid wadded the hat of Tonio into a pillow. He took his own hat as a fan and began to work it rapidly. He uncorked a canteen. Every moment or so he poured a few drops into the open mouth of Tonio. Now and then he moistened the white lips. And still Tonio was dying.

The Kid looked up into the pale blue of the sky as a man to whom only one sort of help can be of avail, but all he saw was the drifting form of a buzzard. He strained his eyes. Far to the south was another speck, still fainter, and yet farther away something that might be a third.

He looked down. The mouth of Tonio was still open, but it no longer worked to get more air. There was no perceptible motion of the lungs. The eyes were not shut tight, as before, but partially open, and glazed as though by some infinitely secret thought.

"God help me!" whispered the Kid.

He flattened himself on the rocks. The heat of them

burned through the cloth and scalded his knees; the sun poured like boiling water over his back. With his ear pressed to the breast of Tonio, he listened. He thought he heard a raging pulse of sound. It was only the surge in his own veins. Then, faint and far but growing like the noise of a distant tread approaching, he made out the dull, the feeble, the broken rhythm of the heartbeat.

The Kid got up to his knees. He scattered water on the face of Tonio, opened the sweat-soaked shirt at the breast, forced the draught from the fanning hat down under the cloth until it trembled and billowed out above the belly. The sick man groaned, opened his eyes wide, and shut them again. His mouth began to close and open as he fought for life again. His head turned regularly from side to side. One could have counted out seconds and minutes by the motion of it.

It was strange that the Kid prayed not for Tonio, but for himself, muttering: "God help me! God help me!"

But he had found ways to work over Tonio, to cool him, to make his breathing easier. He was holding the end of a thread that attached the life of Tonio to the earth.

Once he was afraid that his own grip would be broken when a sweeping darkness brushed across his mind. After that, an ache began to pound in the base of his brain. He ventured to give himself one good swallow of water; after that the ache subsided and disappeared.

Now he heard voices for the first time. The sun was westering. The whole floor of the little chasm was covered by shadow, though the air seemed hotter than ever. The rising of that shadow, as a matter of fact, had begun to seem to the Kid like the rising of water that would soon choke them. Then he heard the voices and the brisk clicking of the iron-shod hoofs of horses over those iron rocks.

The Kid took out both guns and laid them in his lap. With his left hand he continued to fan Tonio; with his right hand he fondled one of the Colts. When they came close, it would be a pity of his life if he could not get two of them, to pay for Tonio and himself. Three, perhaps. That would make one for boot and the devil would surely feel a special joy in welcoming the men of Rubriz.

The voices, no longer dissolved by distance, began to speak words he could understand. One was a Mexican telling a story of a certain girl he had known in Mexico City in the golden days after a raid had filled the pockets of this bandit. The laughter that appreciated the tale was the laughter of Leffingwell! It seemed to the Kid, as he listened, that he recognized the hand of fate and some tokens of an eternal justice.

Shadows moved across the rim of sunlight on the eastern wall of the little chasm. The shadows halted.

"We can take a look at that hole in the ground," said the Mexican.

"Nobody could be in that. El Keed wouldn't put himself in there for any fool to find," said Leffingwell.

"Well, I'll take a look," said the other.

The Kid stood up with a gun in each hand. It was Leffingwell and that Rafael who had faced him in Ormosa. They yelled out with one voice, pulling at their reins. The horses swung about.

The Kid fired at the Mexican—and missed! He would not believe his hand or his gun; they could not have failed him.

The Mexican, crouching low, turned with a poised gun. The Kid shot him through the back and as he sloughed out of the saddle the Kid shot Leffingwell, twice. Leffingwell fell, also. His foot caught in the stirrup. He dragged, bounding on the rocks. The mustang stepped on the body, fell, rose again, and ran off freed from the encumbrance. Both horses were racing wildly for the head of the valley.

The Kid jumped from the hiding-place. No other riders were in sight, so he could make sure that the pair were dead. He ran to them, and found that the back of the Mexican was broken. Leffingwell was shot through the lungs. A bloody froth kept bubbling and breaking on his lips. He writhed. The words he tried to speak would not come but he pointed towards the gun in the Kid's hand to beg for the bullet that would end his torment.

The Kid smiled and went back to Tonio in the hole among the rocks.

Chapter Thirty-four

NO ONE CAME for a long time. The pool of shadow filled the hole to the brim and still Tonio was alive. It would be sunset before long.

Then something brushed through the air above them and the Kid saw a buzzard skimming so low that he could mark the naked head of the carrion-eater and the big, transparent feathers at the tips of the wings. Those feathers looked old and frayed as though the wind had worn them away.

There was another and another of those signs of death in the air. It was strange that their circling had not drawn the attention of Rubriz and his men before this.

Before the Kid had finished wondering, he heard many men and horses, horses at the gallop. Well, they must be spurring deep to get a gallop out of their horses at the end of such a day as this! He sprayed a little more water over the face of Tonio and continued the fanning.

A voice broke on him, rousing all his soul. It was like the roaring of a great wave against the shore after the murmurs of a day of calm, for it was the voice of Mateo Rubriz, thundering. He was telling his men to scatter and ride like fiends. For only fiends could catch a fiend like El Keed. Of all the pursuers El Keed would have wished to kill Leffingwell and Rafael above the rest and these were the ones who here lay dead!

The Kid heard the rushing of hoofs. He stopped fanning Tonio and sat again with the two guns in his hands, waiting. Hoofbeats rushed close, as though the riders would plunge straight into the trap, but in every case the sounds went by. Perhaps they could not imagine, these fierce riders, that the slayer they looked for might be content to lie like a worm at the bottom of a hole.

The noise ended as a summer storm ends. The Kid stood up and peered forth at the sunset colors rimming the hills all around. By that light he made out the silhouettes of departing horses, and over two saddles were draped lifeless, clumsy bodies. The Kid smiled again.

The wind was rising. It fanned his face. It even reached into and stirred the heavy, warm air of the pit in which he crouched again beside Tonio. By the afterglow he studied the face of his companion and listened to the ceaseless whispering flow of the words.

After a time he stood up again. The hills were black; the valley was like a pool of standing water, and the sky was freckled with stars. He leaned and called, "Tonio!"

He had no hope to get anything but a delirious answer. To his amazement he heard a startled voice exclaim: "Yes, yes! Here I am."

The Kid took him beneath the shoulders and sat him up.

"We're going," said the Kid.

"Where?" asked Tonio.

"Away."

"Where are we?"

"Trapped. But we're going away."

He lifted Tonio up, clambered to his side, and supported him to his feet.

"Can you walk a little?" he asked.

"I don't know," said Tonio. "Yes."

"Put your arm over my shoulder. Take a good hold. That's it. You'll go better after you've practiced."

It was true. They got on across the flat of the valley. When they struck the first upslope Tonio stumbled and went down, suddenly. He landed with a flat whack against the ground. The Kid raised him. Tonio staggered, but held his feet. They went on again, more slowly. Tonio's breathing was a series of gasps.

He fell again. The Kid straightened him once more, put an arm around his body, and supported him more strongly until they came to the low top of a hill and looked out over the plain beyond. Then he paused and made Tonio sit down.

"Where are we?" asked Tonio, again.

"We've been lying in these hills all afternoon. You've been delirious and I don't suppose you remember suffocating. We rode through the hills and I hope that we could get on to the Rio Grande. But as we came through the men of Rubriz were there before us. We had to turn back. There was no place to hide except a hole in the rock right out in the middle of a valley. We've been there, cooking, for hours. Rubriz hunted, but he didn't find us. I got you started again after dark. I thought you and I might be able to stagger

264

through and get away. But you can see for yourself."

He pointed. There seemed to be no dust in the desert air on this cursed night. The stars were like a thousand little moons and even the sick man was able to say, "I see them riding up and down and up and down, out there in the open."

"Rubriz knows that there's only one road for us and that's the road to the north," said the Kid. "So he's opened out his string of men and he's parading them till the day comes again. After that, he'll come back in here and search till he finds us. I thought we might be able to get through. If it were a darker night maybe we would have a ghost of a chance—but not this way?"

"Not if you're hitched to me. But you might get through by yourself," said Tonio.

"I'll stay with you, I guess," said the Kid.

Silence met him. Montana rolled a cigarette.

"Smoke?" he asked.

"No," said Tonio.

The Kid lighted his cigarette and puffed at it. Finally Tonio said: "What makes you do it? I'm nothing to you."

"I don't mind telling you," said the Kid. "We're dead men. We're no better than ghosts sitting here and looking at the world with no meaning hitched to us. So I'll tell you. You have a sister. That's the whole of it."

Tonio began to nod before saying: "It's a queer thing. When you say that, it makes a picture of her jump into my head. I can see her."

"That's the kind she is," said the Kid.

"And her mother? My mother?" said Lavery.

"She'd be enough all by herself," said the Kid. "Your mother would be enough to make a man—"

"I understand," said Tonio. "Listen to me. This job you're doing on me is going to miss. I'm not worth it. But because we're both no better than dead, I'll tell you something. If I were in your boots I'd try to do the same thing that you are doing."

"I knew you would," said Montana. "Otherwise, I would have said good-by to you a long time ago."

They sat there without speaking. The moon pushed a triangular heap of fire up in the east and then rolled up in its turn, incredibly huge.

"By that light they might see us," said the Kid.

"What of it?" answered Tonio.

"That's right. What of it?" said Montana.

The moon dwindled in size, grew to an intense white fire and pulled into itself all the light from the stars around it.

"They've seen us. They're getting together to mob us," said Tonio.

The riders were pooling together in the flat of the desert almost straight before them. They streamed in from either side and gathered there, little black, wavering shapes.

"How does it go with you?" asked the Kid.

"I'm all right. I'm cool as water all over, except the shoulder. That's hot enough."

"When you fell down the second time, coming up the hill, you landed on that shoulder, didn't you?"

"Yes," said Tonio.

The Kid pointed.

"They're not seeing us," said he. "They're making coffee!"

The dim yellow flare of firelight began at the center of that increasing group. In fact, now that the moon was up, there was no longer a need to move up and down to keep such a strict guard. For the clear light silvered the desert far away and laid a black shadow beside every shrub, every stone.

"You're staying here," said the Kid. "I have an idea."

"I'll do what you say," said Tonio.

"Work down a little towards the bottom of the hill. I'm going to make a try; it's one chance in ten, or twenty, or thirty."

"Good-by," said Tonio.

He held out his hand. The Kid took it with a long grip, for the upturned face of Tonio, in the moonlight, looked more than ever like the features of his mother. They seemed almost of an age, now.

"So long," said the Kid, and went rapidly down the slope.

Chapter Thirty-five

THERE WERE SOMETHING under a score of men in the war party of Mateo Rubriz which now was gathered for breakfast by moonlight, but there were nearly two score horses. Like traveling Indians, they carried extra riding-stock along. All of these animals, thrown into a loose herd to graze if they would, were under the guard of a single rider and it was the weakness of this watch that had brought the Kid down from the hilltop.

When he reached the flat he moved, sometimes like a snake and sometimes like a crawling beast, from rock to shrub until he was close to the horses. He could hear the rattling voices of the Mexicans on the side. He could see them in larger and larger silhouette against the pale desert beyond and the paler sky as they stood about the fire.

The padding of hoofs, the creaking of saddle leather, flattened the Kid in the sand; he saw the herdsman jog past to head in a little troop of mustangs that was wandering a bit too far afield. The Kid went on, carefully, but using all the speed he could, for he knew that the breakfast with which Rubriz was putting heart in his men would not last long.

The slender legs of the horses were about him as they moved here and there biting off the desert grasses as close as grazing sheep. Then he heard the thunder of the voice of Mateo, exclaiming: "Alphonso, Alphonso! Bring them in!"

The Kid stood up.

"Hai, Alphonso!" he said, "catch me a horse and I'll help you run them."

"The devil!" exclaimed Alphonso, who was quite near. "How did you get in among them and I not see you? Are you Rodriguez?"

"The moon's in your eyes," said the Kid.

"Rodriguez—he's inches smaller. Catch me a horse, Alphonso."

"All right," said Alphonso. "Only, it seems to me—"

The Kid was walking straight towards him, and as he came closer Alphonso suddenly yelled. "Juan Fernandez—El Keed!"

He was a fighting-man, this Alphonso. He went for his guns instead of trying to ride off. Before those heavy revolvers would come out of the holsters the Kid had rapped him over the head with the long barrel of a Colt and stepped into the empty saddle.

A roar of voices went up from the camp as they heard the warning shout of Alphonso. It was the hope of the Kid, as he waved his hat and yelled, that the herd would stampede away from the Mexicans but He who knows the way of the winds still cannot guess the way of a horse. The herd began to swirl; then it bolted in exactly the wrong direction, straight towards the fire!

There was nothing for the Kid to do but follow it. If he were detached for a moment from that sweeping mass of horses the best riflemen in Mexico would soon riddle him with bullets. He felt the mustang beneath him take the bit in its teeth; he felt the surge of hysterical fear in the horse and flattened himself along the back of the bronco.

Over the rushing of the hoofs and the frightened squealing and grunting of the horses he heard Mateo shouting to stop that stampede by shooting at anything and everything.

The rifles began, that instant. It was not very good shooting because the marksmen had to get out of the way of the rushing horses before they settled to their work. But a horse in front of the Kid went down in a dusty somersault. The Kid leaped his stolen mustang over the obstacle and cleared it safely.

Ahead, he saw a mustang naked of saddle struck by a bullet. It rose on its hind legs, whirled like a dancer, and went down. Yet the herd would not stop.

The Kid's own mount stumbled suddenly, wavered—and went down. The Kid had shaken the stirrups from his feet. He struck the ground rolling, and came to his feet with his arms thrown high above his head, yelling.

The apparition springing from the ground made the unsaddled mustang that was flying toward him plant all four hoofs and try to dodge. The Kid snatched a hand-hold on the tossing mane and whipped himself onto the rounded, slippery back.

The whole herd was past him. He was alone, exposed to the fire of all of Rubriz's men, and on a bronco that pitched and fought and squealed with agony and fear as the remorseless spurs of the Kid gripped its flanks.

Bullets filled all the air around them.

Then, with a distinct thud, a shot struck the mustang. It made it forget all thoughts of bucking, that deeper thrust of pain than any spur could give. The little horse straightened out in a furious burst of speed. Another rifle bullet struck it and made it hitch its hind quarters around to the side. But it only flew faster than before. A mound of moon-polished desert rose between the Kid and the guns of the Mexicans. He was safe. The horse that had saved him began to stagger, but already it was running with the rest of the herd so that the Kid could catch a flying pair of reins. When the wounded mustang stopped, the Kid was instantly in a convenient saddle. Now he pushed that herd miles into the moonhaze to the east. It forgot fear in its weariness.

He picked out two animals that seemed to him the strongest of the lot and turned back.

Perhaps the men of Rubriz would linger near the spot where they lost their horses, because a Mexican is helpless as a child, on foot. Or perhaps they were doggedly following the trail of the stolen ponies. Most likely of all, they might have hurried off to find other mounts held by more distant members of the Rubriz party.

At least, as the Kid returned, he saw no sign of the Mexicans. He came straight up the hill, and halfway to the top a form rose from the ground and awaited him, a wavering shadow in the moonlight.

That was Tonio, unsteady as a drunken man, smiling his Mexican smile. "You did it!" was all he said.

The Kid got him into a saddle. He took a double noose of rope and bound Tonio to the pommel.

"All right?" he asked.

"Right!" nodded Tonio, as though he grudged the vital breath spent in that word.

So they went down the hill and voyaged out into the

plain on the last stage of that journey. They could not dodge or change direction. They had to go by the straightest line between two points, as the Kid very well realized when he looked into the dying face of Tonio. So they went on at a soft dog trot, the sand swishing about the hoofs of the horses. The miles moved behind them with a reluctant slowness. That mortal fatigue which comes upon men at the end of a day, when the night will not begin, was in the two. But Montana could call upon a bottomless well of nervous energy and to Tonio there remained only the last worn shreds of his will-power.

But not once did they see shadows coming towards them, or a dust-cloud moving up through the white of the moonlight. Dawn began. It was rosy red when they came to the ford of the Rio Grande and found its yellow waters covered with a false glory of gold. The mountains of the Bend stood up on the farther side, the nearer slopes brown, the farther summits a smoky blue. All was silence except for the faint crinkling sound of the waters against the shore and the groaning oarlocks of a boat that was being rowed upstream through the shallows.

The Mexican sat on his oars, drifting backwards while he watched the pair of them enter the river, the Kid holding Tonio firmly in place. The water came up to the outstretched noses of the horses, but they waded through. Once the current staggered them. That was all. Then they climbed the easy slope beyond and, looking back, they saw the dust-cloud creeping towards them over the wide Mexican plain.

At least the Kid saw it, but the eyes of Tonio were blind with weakness and with pain. He was muttering gibberish all the way up through the pass where the heat of the sun poured down on them again, but they came out of the gorge where the white dashings of the creek drenched the trail and reached the easy levels of the Lavery ranch above.

Tonio himself could not see it. Montana had to mount behind him and support him. His head rolled weakly back. He was still breathing; that was about all.

Montana saw cattle. They were bigger than the Mexican steers he had been looking at during the last few days. They were sleeker and their heads were bigger, more capacious for thought and understanding and—beef! They were American cattle, and he was almost home.

He found himself saying that over and over again, but that was not all the trouble—for there was a general vagueness of mind that troubled him. Now he had risen to the upper level of the valley and he could see the house of Lavery shimmering in the distance. It looked so small and distant that he wondered how he could ever get to it. Moreover, it seemed that the horse was stepping up and down on the same place, a treadmill.

"Don't go and get cock-eyed like a poor sap," said Montana to himself. "You're groggy, that's all."

He saw a cowpuncher ride up on the next knoll and

stare down at him. The man came with a rush and a yell. The Kid could remember his face, but he could not remember his name. The words that cow-waddy yelled had no meaning. They did not fit together. They were simply noise. He was holding out his hands, trying to do things.

"Get out of here!" said the Kid.

The man yelled more things. He laid hands on Tonio. So the Kid cut all argument short by pulling out a long-nosed Colt. That secured action. The man turned his back and fled at the full speed of his horse, spurring the mustang desperately, glancing over his shoulder as though to make out whether or not bullets were flying after him.

Montana rode on, and his horse still was stepping up and down on the same spot, although the house was bigger. It was not any nearer, but it was larger in his eye.

He took Tonio by the hair and lifted the limp head from his shoulder. Tonio's mouth was open. He was drooling. His eyes were partially open, too, and looked like the fishy eyes of the dead.

"That's right," said Montana. "Go on and die on me. Go quit on me. Go on and give up and die, like a louse."

Then he told himself that a dead man would not be drooling at the mouth, like this. And if he could get Tonio to the house he would make him live. It was absurd to think that he could take a living dead man through so many things and then permit him to die.

Life is a flame. Montana would take the flame of life in his bare hands, and pour the welter of it into the body of Tonio faster than time and wounds could burn the life away.

His mustang kept on going, bobbing its head up and down. The house was just as far away as ever, but it was bigger and bigger. People ran out of the bunk house. They ran out of the main house. The cook came on his wooden leg, running as though there were a fire behind him. In spite of his wooden leg he ran so fast that his long hair fluttered. There was a sound of doors banging. Richard Lavery came out. He started running, also. His legs were so long that they looked funny. His head bounced up and down as he ran.

"My God! I'm corked," said Montana. "I'm certainly corked."

More doors banged. And suddenly he was almost beside the house. People were all around him, reaching their hands towards the body he held. He went right on through them.

Lavery came running up, with a wild face. The Kid eased the weight of Tonio into the numbness of one hand and leaned down and took Lavery by the lapels of his coat and shook him till his head wobbled crazily.

"You left her behind!" he said to Lavery. He was sure that he was speaking gently, therefore he could not understand the foghorn screech which was in his ears. "You left her back there in Mexico! You came on through and you left her behind in Mexico for the greasers. You quitter!"

Lavery said something. A booming and roaring sound in the ears of Montana prevented him from hearing what was said, but Lavery was just like all the rest. He kept putting up his hands and plucking at the clothes and at the body of Tonio.

The Kid thought: "They think I'm going to let them get their hands on him. The poor fools! I'm gunna kill some of them pretty pronto. I'm gunna blow daylight through 'em pretty soon!"

They were all standing back; he realized that he had been thinking aloud. A faint voice that must have belonged to Lavery said something about humoring him.

He got off the horse in front of the house, and the weight in his arms turned into lead and brought him to his knees. His knees were made of cork and they would not spring up under him again.

All the crowd began to rush in at him. Crowds were bad business. Mateo Rubriz had a crowd. This was worse than another scene, a million years ago, when he sat in a fonda and told lies to Mateo. Or had that happened to another man whose ghost had told him the story?

They all came rushing in. He got out his Colt again and swung it in a half circle.

"Listen, you dirty, fly-blown buzzards," he said, "this is my partner that was ready to die for me. D'you think you can get him without some shooting?"

Some one began to yell in a very loud voice. That was the foreman. He saw the square, excited face of the foreman.

Then he managed to get to his feet. He tried to go forward, but he only went backward until his shoulders struck the horse. He laughed.

"I'm drunk!" said Montana.

They all stood around him, making uncompleted gestures with their hands. He smiled at them. If one of them touched Tonio he would kill that man first. He would kill one of them before he went down.

The head of Tonio hung down over the bend of his arm. Tonio was dead all over, but a big artery in the base of his throat kept moving a thin blue shadow in and out. That was the last of life tapping at the door, trying to get out.

A voice started inside the house, reached the door, burst wildly out into the open.

He started walking towards the voice because it belonged to some one who was all right. It was perhaps a thousand miles away, that voice, but if he got to it everything would be O.K.

Then he saw that it was not a thousand miles. It was right there before him. It belonged to the girl. She looked terribly afraid and excited. He swung the weight of Tonio over his shoulder, face down. He went on towards the girl.

Voices were barking at her. He put out his hand which held the Colt towards her, and she knew that he was not pointing it at her. She came right on in. He dropped his armed hand on her head and pushed her face back.

"The dirty hound left you in Mexico, but you came on through all by yourself, did you?" said Montana. "Are you all right?"

She said something. He couldn't understand.

"Why don't you talk up?" he demanded.

"I'm all right," said the girl's voice.

"We've gotta get him away from the crowd," said Montana. "Are you all right?"

"I'm all right," she said. "All the rest of them are going away. Father will help you to carry him into the house."

"The stinking rat left you behind in Mexico and you think I'll let him touch Tonio?" asked Montana. "Here, you take his legs. I'll carry his shoulders. Are you all right?"

"I'm all right," she said.

"Are you all right all over?" asked the Kid.

"I'm all right," she said.

"Don't start bawling like a silly little fool! Stop it!" he commanded.

"I'll stop," said the girl.

But she went on crying. She took the legs of Tonio and he took the heavy shoulders. They weighed like lead. They got to the front door. She was still crying.

"Never argue with a woman," thought the Kid, and he heard a husky, croaking voice say the same words at his ear.

They went up some stairs. His knees were cork and

278

they kept breaking down under him. He kept knocking the skin off his shins, but after a while they were in an upper hall. They went through another door. There was a big white bed in the room. It was as big as a five-acre lot. A man who dived into that bed would go to sleep for the rest of his life.

They got Tonio into the bed.

The next thing would be to undress him. He started tearing the clothes away. "Go get some water and towels and things," he said to the girl. "I've got to undress him."

The voice of Lavery said from the doorway. "Montana, please let me come in and help."

"You traitor!" said Montana.

"My God! My God!" said Lavery.

"Get a doctor!" said the Kid.

"They've sent for a doctor, but he can't get here for a long time," said Lavery. "Let me help to—"

"You left the girl in Mexico and Rubriz almost got her in a fonda," said the Kid. "Now you want to get to Tonio and throw him away. I don't know why I don't shoot you. I'm *going* to shoot you!"

"Father!" screamed the girl. But Lavery was no longer standing in the doorway.

The Kid finished ripping the clothes from the body of Tonio. He lay flat on his back. His chest stood up high. You could count the ribs. The pectoral muscles were long, flat strings. The belly sagged away down from the arch of the ribs, and the hip bones stood up like great blunt elbows.

279

"He's a funny-looking bird," said the Kid. He kept watching the faint blue pulse of life in the base of the throat of Tonio. That was the life trying to get out, knocking at the door.

He washed the blood and the dirt off the body. They always wash the blood and the dirt off you when you go to a hospital. They wash you right down to the toes, and the wash-rag tickles between the toes. He was particular about washing Tonio right down to the toes.

Then in a hospital they dress you up clean. There were no clothes to dress Tonio, so he pulled up the sheet over him and then packed the blankets around him.

All around the wound in the shoulder the flesh puffed up, very red, and the red would not wash away.

"He's got to have a doctor," said Montana.

The girl was on her knees at the foot of the bed.

"What's the use of praying?" said Montana.

"I won't pray," said the girl.

"Tell Lavery that I know he's out there in the shadow beyond the door," said Montana. "I'm going to lift his scalp when I get through in here. You tell him that."

"I'll tell him," said the girl.

"Get brandy," said the Kid.

That instant, brandy was thrust into his hand. It was in a tall glass carafe. It was a funny thing that brandy should not be in a metal flask, but he smelled the brandy and wet his lips with it, and it was real brandy.

He lifted the head of Tonio in the cup of his hand and put a little of the brandy between his lips. Tonio coughed and choked. He coughed out a spray of the brandy into the face of Montana. That was all right. If a man's partner spits in his face, that's all right.

He tried again, and made Tonio swallow some brandy.

"Water!" said the faint voice of Tonio.

"Ah, God! Tonio," said the Kid, "I'd give you my blood if that'd help you. But there's no water inside of a hundred miles. There's nothing but sand on earth and buzzards in the sky."

"Here!" said the girl.

It was a glass of clear, cold water. Drops were running down the outside of the glass. The glass was spilling, because the hand of the girl was shaking so.

"Damn you, don't spill that water!" screamed Montana.

He took the glass. His own hand wanted to shake, but he simply laughed at it. If his hand wanted to shake and spill some of that water it was simply funny. That was all it was.

He kept on laughing a little and raised the head of Tonio and gave him the water, and Tonio gulped it with a gurgling sound.

"Take some brandy and water yourself, Montana," said the voice of the girl.

"And let him die for lacking it, eh?" said Montana. "My God! what sort of a woman are you? I thought you were all right. And that's what you want me to do? I'll drink his water, will I?"

He laughed. His mouth hurt him sharply. He licked the blood off his lips.

He moved around to the other side of the bed, where he could watch the open door. He laid his gun on the lap of Tonio and waited. Sometimes shadows moved in the hall; he would shoot the first form that appeared on the threshold.

Then millenniums of hot agony followed. He could not swallow any more. The girl kept holding what seemed to be glasses of cold water in front of him, but he laughed at the illusions. In the desert you come to know what a mirage is.

A coolness came on his forehead. Her hands were laid on it. Her voice was hammering at his weary ears. He opened his mind and heard her saying: "The doctor's come, Montana. Will you let him come in?"

"Thank God if there's a doctor. Let me see him," said Montana.

"Come in, Doctor. Come in slowly. Smile, and come in slowly," said the voice of the girl.

A big brown man stood in the doorway.

"Are you the doctor?" asked the Kid.

"I'm the doctor," said the other.

"You lie," said the Kid. "Rubriz sent you, you greaser dog. You speak English and you think you can fool El Keed, do you?"

"I'm the doctor, Kid," said the big brown man.

"Show me your hands," said Montana.

The stranger held them.

"You think you can kid me that way, do you?" said Montana. "No, show the palms of 'em."

The stranger turned his hands over and Montana

282

thumbed the palms, and they were so soft that his thumb sank deeply into them.

"All right," said Montana. "You're a doctor, all right. Come here and listen to me. You see Tonio, there?"

"I see him," said the doctor.

"Maybe he looks like anybody, to you," said Montana, "but I'll tell you what he is. He's my partner. If you fix him up, I'm going to make you rich. You hear me?"

"I hear you," said the doctor.

"But if you don't get him well, I'm going to break you wide open and take a look at the insides of you," said the Kid. "Understand that?"

"I understand," said the doctor.

"Where's the girl?" asked Montana.

"Here, Montana, here!" said Ruth Lavery.

"She's always bawling like this, but she's all right. She's only a woman. You can't argue with a woman," said the Kid. "The house is full of Rubriz's men. Don't let anybody else come near Tonio. And—tell me if I can take a sleep."

"Yes, for God's sake lie down and sleep!" said the doctor.

"Wake me up if anything happens," said the Kid.

He took his gun.

"I'll wake you up," said the doctor.

The Kid touched the base of Tonio's throat.

"The only life that's left in him is right here," said Montana. "You've gotta make that life spread out. It's like building a bonfire. You start it small and spread it. Understand?"

"I understand," said the doctor.

"I only want five winks," said the Kid.

The floor was a delight. It was cold. When his hand touched it the rest of his body had to follow. He lay down on the floor. His eyes closed. Hands touched him. There was a fragrant smell of cleanness near him.

"He only needs to sleep," said the doctor. His voice boomed like a gong in the ears of Montana. "He—only—needs—sleep."

Chapter Thirty-six

WHEN MONTANA WAKENED there was a buzzing like a telephone wire in the base of his brain. But his throat was damp and cold. In his sleep he had drunk. There was something in a poem about drinking in one's sleep.

He had lain down on a floor; now he was in a bed.

That memory made him leap up from the bed to the floor. His feet were bare on the cold of the boards. He had been undressed and he was wearing pajamas.

"Tonio!" he called.

"Amigo—" said a faint voice.

There was Tonio lying in a great white bed. He himself had just risen from a small cot.

His mind began to spin. A woman got up from beside Tonio's bed and came to him, smiling. He peered at her through a mist of infinite time and saw that it was Mrs. Lavery.

"Ruth!" she said.

Ruth Lavery started up out of an easy chair where she had been sleeping. She came to Montana and gripped his wrists.

"Do you know me?" she asked.

"I know you," he said. "Your father left you—no—no—that was something I dreamed. We're back in the ranch. I remember seeing it off in the distance. The horse kept lifting his feet but not getting forward. I was a little corked. I must have passed out. I'm sorry I passed out."

"You were all right. Now go back to bed," said the girl.

He took in a great breath.

"You'd think that *I* was sick," said Montana. He laughed softly.

"Please go back to bed," said the girl.

She lifted her hands and put them against his shoulders.

"I'll go back to bed if it makes you happy," he said. "What's the matter? Have I done something?"

"No," said Mrs. Lavery. "Let him alone, Ruth. You haven't done anything. Everything's all right. You haven't done anything except bring home my—"

"Hush, mother," said the girl.

"Yes," whispered Mrs. Lavery.

She stood and looked at Montana. Her glance took hold of him like hands and caressed him. Somewhere in the vast distance of the past he had been able to perceive that she was the most beautiful woman in the world. Now he knew what to look for and he saw that it was true.

He went over to the big bed and looked down at

285

Tonio. He was asleep. His face was thin. There was a bluish tinge in his cheeks and his forehead was knotted, hard.

"Don't disturb him, please, Montana," said the girl.

The Kid looked vaguely towards her. He could not get over the feeling that he was needed in the mind of Tonio. He knelt by the bed and laid his hand over the cold hand of Tonio.

The head of Tonio turned towards him. The eyes of Tonio did not open. But the frown smoothed on his forehead. *"Compañero!"* he said.

The Kid heard the girl gasp with astonishment. But it was not strange that women should not be able to understand what was between him and Tonio. They had never sat on the brow of a hill and seen death moving through the moonlight on the desert.

Mrs. Lavery came and leaned a hand on his shoulder. He could see the weakly drooping fingers, bluish white.

The battle for Tonio's life had commenced but not ended. Montana kept the cot that was arranged for him in the same room. There he slept or dozed when he could. Mrs. Lavery and Ruth came when they were allowed, but they had to leave when Tonio started raving. So the Kid was left with the lion's share of the work. In three days the doctor declared that he was reasonably sure that the arm could be saved; but he was not at all sure that the life would remain to Dick Lavery. The long strain of the ride from Ormosa had been too great and from the wound too much of his vitality had drained away.

Sleep would hardly come to Lavery for five minutes at a time. He lay staring at the ceiling, plucking at the edge of the sheet or turning his head restlessly, monotonously, from side to side, with no whit of human understanding in his eyes until the Kid spoke to him. Then, like one who peers through a fog, he strove to understand.

Sometimes Tonio was chattering nonsense and sometimes he was talking almost connectedly. Often he was lost in the madness of the delirium, but again he issued from the sickness far enough to babble at the Kid, going over and over again the incidents of the escape or of the fight at Ormosa.

Gradually, as a field-glass picks one feature out of a distant landscape, so the attention of the Kid narrowed to Tonio, and everything else was cut out of his mind. He knew, vaguely, how Mrs. Lavery came into the room. He knew when Lavery himself entered and put a hand on his shoulder. But the words they said were nothing to the Kid except vague sounds until the rancher told him, on a day, that his wife was confined to bed. She had broken down under the strain. The lips of the Kid pulled back on one side when he heard this.

The comings and goings of Ruth Lavery were brighter moments, however. She was much in the room, slipping about as softly as a ghost. Her presence rarely seemed to trouble the sick man, so she was of use to the Kid. One would have said that she felt no strain at all. She grew neither paler nor thinner. A smile was continually on her lips; she seemed to have entered into a great calm which nothing disturbed. Only, as the fear deepened about them from day to day, her eyes appeared to grow larger and of a deeper blue.

The Kid said to her, on the very first day, "Do you understand Spanish, Ruth?"

"No," she answered.

He was relieved. He had the more reason to feel that relief on the third day, when Tonio recovered for a sudden moment from the delirium and lay with his eyes fixed upon the face of his friend. She was in a far corner of the room; Tonio was totally unaware of her.

He said: "Where are we? Through the hills?"

"Through the hills," said the Kid. "Through with Mexico. Safe on your father's ranch. And you're in bed in his house."

"Hai!" said Tonio, softly. "One day songs will be made about you and what you've done, El Keed! But I'm weak. And you! You've turned into an old man!"

"Have I?"

"Twenty years older, and thinner. Even Mateo Rubriz would be afraid to see you, now."

"All the better for that," said the Kid.

"You have seen her, too?" asked Tonio.

He was speaking Spanish still. It was always Spanish from the moment he was wounded.

"Who?" asked the Kid.

"My sister," said Tonio.

"Yes, I've seen her."

"When you told me that you loved her," said Tonio, "I forgot to ask you if she loved you, also. But only a fool of a woman would be able to know you and not love you."

"She's my friend," said the Kid, nervously aware of the girl in the room. "That's all. Close your eyes, Tonio. Go to sleep. That's the thing for you to do."

"All right," said Tonio, smiling faintly. "How you took me by force and stole me again from Mateo Rubriz, and how you kept me alive in the coffin among the rocks, and how you scattered the horses of Rubriz, and brought me off—Have you told her these things?"

"No," said the Kid. "Be quiet. Talking is bad for you."

"Well, one day I shall talk to her and tell her. And I say this: if the doctors had given me up for dead and the devil had hold of my hand pulling me down into hell, I still would not die till I had told her everything. Therefore call her, so that I can tell her now."

"Tomorrow," said the Kid. "Tomorrow is the time for that. Now it's better that you sleep."

"Well, then," said Tonio, "I am still the child and you are the master. I do as you say."

He closed his eyes and was instantly asleep, the first untroubled sleep in days, while the Kid turned his head and looked anxiously towards the girl. She met his glance with mild, untroubled eyes. Her color had not altered. She could not have understood a word.

Another day went by the Kid, slowly. When he shaved himself that morning the face he saw in the mirror was as Tonio had described it. He looked like the older brother or even the father of that youth who had ridden south into Mexico not long before.

The rancher came to him in the afternoon, saying: "They've spotted Mateo Rubriz at last and there'll be no more trouble about him! He's far south in Mexico. He has given up your trail."

"Good!" said the Kid. "Now I can sleep. I've been feeling his eyes in the small of my back ever since I crossed the Rio Grande."

But the fear had haunted the Kid so long that he could not lose it in a moment. Every strange whisper still made him start a little as darkness fell at the end of that day. He smiled at his nerves and hunched his chair closer to the bed of Tonio.

His patient was definitely better. The delirium had left him during most of the day; he had slept peacefully. He was out of his head again now that the night returned, but his temperature was lower, his hand was moist.

The Kid, having leaned to examine the worn face, straightened suddenly as he heard a soft sound in the room behind him.

He thought it was a matter of nerves, at first, until he was quite sure that it was a sound of breathing. Ruth Lavery had left the room but perhaps she had just returned with her usual ghost-like softness of step. He turned his head and saw behind him, in the middle of the room, Mateo Rubriz, with a sawed-off shotgun in his hands.

Chapter Thirty-seven

RUBRIZ JERKED UP the muzzles of his gun a little. The Kid rose, carefully, and extended his arms above his head. Rubriz beckoned him closer with a movement of his head and again the Kid obeyed.

The barrels of that shotgun were big and he could feel the buckshot that loaded them; with all the flesh about his heart he could feel it. From the bed Tonio exclaimed, suddenly; the gun jumped a little in the grasp of the Mexican and his lips twitched back to show his teeth.

The Kid came forward until the muzzles of the weapon were leaned against his breast. He could see the forefinger of Mateo hooked about both triggers while the free hand of the bandit dipped into the Kid's holsters and took away both revolvers.

Tonio was muttering rapidly.

"Now the door," said Mateo Rubriz, stepping back a little. "Lock the door."

The Kid went to it. A twitch of his hand would fling it open so that he could jump out into the darkness of the hallway, but quicker than the twitch of his hand would be the forefinger of Rubriz. So the Kid locked the door and turned again.

He saw Rubriz smiling at him. Mateo ran the red tip of his tongue over his lips.

"Go back by the bed and sit down," he commanded. "The two of you came out of Mexico together and the two of you can die together, now."

"He has to go with me, eh?" said the Kid.

Mateo smiled again. His eyes were as red as though he had faced blowing sand for days.

Montana went back and stood beside the bed. Rubriz followed and leaned a little to stare at Tonio.

"It won't be so bad, after all," muttered Rubriz. "Already he is turning pale. Already he has the gringo look."

"You're going to blow him out like a light, eh?" said the Kid.

"He is already dead," said Rubriz. "He is a traitor and my part in him is dead. In this gun which I hold there is no murder. There is only buckshot and justice."

"Well," said the Kid, "that's all right. We were both dead back there in the hills; we've had a few days' grace, in the meantime."

"Back there when you killed Rafael and the gringo," said Rubriz, "where were you?"

"There was a place like a good-sized coffin chopped out of the rocks," said the Kid.

"You mean in the middle of the valley—right in the middle of the valley floor?"

"Yes. I thought it might be too close to your nose for your eyes to see it. But Rafael started to search it. That was why I had to kill him. And Leffingwell."

"And you saw me come, afterwards? You were still there?"

"Yes. I saw you and I heard you."

Rubriz smacked his lips.

"Here is the pity of it," said he, "that I should have to kill you like an ox in a stall instead of fighting it out with you, hand to hand, so that I could know whether I am your master or whether I have grown old. Did you ever hear of Pedro Orcaño?"

"He was that terror from Guadalupe. Yes, I've heard of him."

"And of the great Martino?"

"The fellow who started the revolution? Yes."

"I killed them both," said Rubriz. "I have killed a good many others, but they were the best. And yet, by the great San Juan of Capistrano, you are a greater man than they!"

"Thanks," said the Kid.

Rubriz waved his hand.

"I make no compliments, but I am a just man," he said. "For three days I have been lying up yonder in the hills, thinking, thinking. Always one thing—that if you and I had been friends, we could have taken the covering off the world like an orange and eaten it bit by bit. A slice for you, a slice for me! But—how old are you?"

"Twenty-four," said the Kid.

"Ah?" murmured Rubriz. "You look older! I thought you were older. What brought you into this business?"

"Leffingwell," said the Kid. "I had the age and the color of the eyes and hair. He tattooed the birthmark on my left shoulder. I came here and posed as the long-lost son. It all went well enough but these people were too white. I couldn't put the game through. And I remembered seeing Tonio Rubriz go half naked through the streets of Santa Katalina when the Rurales had him."

Rubriz pursed his lips to whistle.

"So I went down to get the real man for the place," finished the Kid.

"And Tonio paid you what?"

The Kid shook his head. "People like you and me, Mateo," said he, "never work for money. Never our best work, at least."

"Good!" said Rubriz. "Very good! The heart is greater than the head. That is true. But now all that good work is gone, eh?"

"I'm sorry about him," said the Kid, pointing towards the bed. "It doesn't matter about me so much."

"No?" said Mateo Rubriz. "Are you such a Christian?" He was sneering.

The Kid answered: "Too many men want my blood, Mateo. You know what that means. I couldn't have lasted very long."

"They have wanted my blood for more than twenty years!" said Mateo Rubriz. "And still I have lived."

"You've lived like a wild beast in the mountains," said the Kid. "That's not the sort of a life I want."

Rubriz began to scowl dangerously.

"And how have *you* lived, señor?"

"Just as I pleased. I've been as high as a governor's right-hand guest. Higher than that, too. I've had to change my name and address a good many times, but I've done what I pleased, slept where I pleased, dined where I pleased, and shaken hands with the sheriff and the federal marshal afterwards."

Rubriz contemplated.

"That is very good," he said. "But you have never been a king."

"No," said the Kid. "Never like you, Mateo."

"No," said Rubriz. "And you have never had a wife and a family?"

"No," said the Kid. "When people like you and me love a woman the best we can do is to leave her."

"Well," said Rubriz, "I can fit most of your ideas under my hide, but not that one."

A footfall came up the hall and a hand tapped. Rubriz made a motion and the Kid went close to the door.

"Yes?" he asked.

"The doctor is here," said the voice of Ruth Lavery.

"Tonio is resting," said the Kid. "He'd better not be disturbed."

"I must see him," said the doctor. "I've come clear out from town with a new preparation. I think I have a chance to break the back of that fever."

"Doctor," said the Kid, "I hope you'll take my word for it, and let him be quiet for—well, for a half-hour. It won't matter then. Will you wait that long?"

He heard the doctor mutter, "This is strange!"

Then the girl said, quietly, "He must have a good reason."

"Yes, of course. But his medical reasons—well, let it go. I'll wait for a half-hour."

They went down the hall again.

"Half an hour," said the Kid to Mateo Rubriz.

The latter squinted his eyes, and nodded. "I heard! A half-hour is a small thing. But in the way you and I can use it, it may be great. We can walk a long distance into the minds of one another in thirty minutes. A half-hour is not a great deal, it is very small, but it may have poison in its tooth, eh?"

"I think it may," said Montana.

"For you and me," said Rubriz, "there ought to be a camp fire shaking its light through the pine trees and the flesh of a kid roasting and some red wine. But all we have is this!"

He shook the shotgun in his hands.

"All right," said the Kid. "By the way, how did you get in?"

"As easily, señor, as wind breathes through the cracks in an old house. More easily than you came into my own house, and carried away—the traitor!"

He glanced towards the bed. His teeth gritted together.

"They told me you were far south in Mexico," said Montana. "So I let myself go to sleep."

"A man who looks very like me is far south," said Rubriz, carelessly.

The shotgun rose in his hands.

"Are you ready?" he asked.

"Ready," said the Kid.

"What is the taste in your throat?" asked Rubriz,

"Like salt," said the Kid.

"And your neck is stiff?"

"No," said the Kid. "I could nod to a friend."

He looked down the double barrels into the grim eyes of Rubriz.

"Now, what's the last thought in your mind?" asked Rubriz.

"Of a woman," said the Kid.

"Of what woman?"

The Kid smiled.

Rubriz lowered the butt of the gun a little.

"You are about to die, señor," he said, "and I tell you first that it is good for the very pit of the belly of Mateo Rubriz to see how easily a brave man can face death with all the color in his face and all the quiet in his mind. And if—"

Tonio broke into a soft laughter. Rubriz glanced suddenly towards him, frowning.

"Now I tell you," said the sick man, "that if your walls were a mile high and a mile deep he would climb over them or burrow under them. He will come! Mateo Rubriz knows that I am here and if you had ten thousand soldiers in Guadalupe he would find a way to come to my help!"

At the end the voice faded to a muttering.

"He thinks of Guadalupe," said Rubriz. "And I tell you, friend, the jail where they kept him was filled with screaming when I came to bring Tonio away. Death of my soul! Do you think what it means to me, tonight, to rub out the work of twenty years? What would he have grown to be, here? A fool of a barnyard fowl! But I lengthened his wings and lightened his heart and made him a hawk! We were two kings, till you came. Now they tell in Mexico how Mateo Rubriz could not keep even his own son—how a gringo came and took him away easily. They shake their heads when they speak of me. There was a time, I say, when the name of Mateo Rubriz made every man look over his shoulder suddenly. But you have changed that!"

"Have I told you lies, Mateo?" asked the Kid.

"You have talked like a brave man who is about to die," said Rubriz.

"Then believe me when I say this: If you kill him you will groan for it the rest of your life."

"Shall I leave him here?" said the Mexican. "Shall I let the gringos stare at him when he goes proudly by and dream that *that* is their blood? In a year he will despise beautiful Mexico and scorn my countrymen and I shall be no more to him than a bad dream. But while he is still half my son he shall die. He *must* die! Tonio would never—"

"I am Tonio Rubriz," said the voice of the sick man, on whose mind the name had made a sudden impression. "I have only one request to make—shoot straight—"

His voice died out.

"He is standing once more against the wall at Mazatlan," muttered Mateo Rubriz, "where they left him for dead and I came in the night and crawled away with Tonio on my back—let him die thinking of that! He is *my* son, now! There is no gringo in his mind!"

He pointed the shotgun. The Kid stood like a stone.

"And take this message for my father," went on Tonio in a faint voice, "that I died honoring him and God."

The gun shook in the hands of Rubriz. He began to rock a little from side to side, moaning, and the Kid saw the big brown toes gripping the rug on the floor. "Tonio!" said Mateo Rubriz. "Open your eyes! It is fit that a brave man should die with his eyes open. Tonio!"

Once more the name roused Tonio. He pushed himself up on his elbow, though his head fell back.

"The blood that runs out of me can't drain all the life away, father," he said. "Go on! My brain is clearer. I see the lights of Mazatlan. Go on! I can't die now that you're with me again. God! God! how cold it is!"

"Now he dies as my son," said Rubriz, "and he passes into heaven with the name of Rubriz on his lips."

He steadied the shotgun. Montana knew there was only one way to brush death away from Tonio. He said: "Poor Rubriz, you have to murder Tonio and the best part of your life all at once."

"Be silent," said Rubriz, "or else you first—"

"Twenty happy years," said Montana, "and you kill them with your own hand. Are you such a fool?"

"He has killed them!" groaned Rubriz. "He has stolen away from me and killed all the days, all the

happy days. He forgets me, despises me, laughs at me, leaves me!"

"If he despised you, Rubriz," said Montana, "why didn't he put a bullet through you before we started out from your valley? Tonio, Lavery, and myself—we could have surprised you as you walked up and down in front of the house. There would have been no pursuit then. But Tonio had not learned to murder the man he loved. You had not taught him that, Rubriz. But you teach him today."

"You talk," said Rubriz, "but I am not a fool. I listen to nothing you say, gringo!"

"Why don't you get done with it?" asked Montana. "You act like an old, weak woman, drunk enough to be ready for murder and woman enough to know it is her son. Pull the trigger, Rubriz. There dies Tonio, and Mateo Rubriz goes back to Mexico greater than ever. But Tonio is dead and those days at Mazatlan and Guadalupe—all the days for twenty years. You murder half your life when you murder him, Rubriz."

"Mother of God," said Rubriz, "how thin he is. Señor, he is dying now! This moment he is dying and his face turns blue."

"True! He is dying," said the Kid.

"Are you standing there like a lump of wood, you fool?" said Rubriz. "Do something! Give him whisky—give him brandy!"

The Kid reached the brandy-flask, saying: "Hold up his head, Rubriz! Quick!"

Mateo Rubriz shifted the shotgun to his left hand and with the right lifted the head of Tonio. He kept the riot gun under the hollow of his arm, ready to fire both barrels into the breast of Montana, who now made Tonio swallow a bit of the brandy. Rubriz lowered the head into the pillow.

"Get a new pillow for him," said Rubriz. "The cover of this one is wet. But that is good when a man with fever sweats. So! His hand is moist. Ah God! how thin he is! The fever will burn him away to an ash. The filthy gringo food has no strength in it and he is starving. If I had him for three days in the high mountains in the sweet, clean air, with roasted partridges and wine—"

"You'll have him there," said the Kid.

"I? Have him again with me?" demanded Rubriz.

"Why, Rubriz," said Montana, "are you a child? Think of what Tonio is—brave, true, and faithful! He will neither want to murder you nor forget you. Now and again he'll ride south into the San Carlos Mountains. They're not so far away. It won't take those mountaineers long to fetch word that Tonio has come to see his father, eh? You will be sitting together or smiling across a camp fire at one another."

"My heart runs away like hot sand through my fingers," said Rubriz. "Could it be so? Yes! I have made him one of us. He is a Mexican. Life is not by the blood, but by the brain. And you—the wisdom of a good saint has been poured into El Keed. I put aside the gun. I put aside blood. I wash the murder off my hand. This is a sacred moment and the air of it purifies the soul. I wash my hands in it!"

"Hush!" said the Kid. "You're waking him again."

"I am the witless son of a mule!" said Rubriz.

He drew back from the bed a little. Montana came to his side and laid a hand on his shoulder. He looked up into the face of the Kid with a sudden flashing of teeth. "Ah, gringo!" he said as he smiled.

"Ah, greaser!" said the Kid, smiling back.

"Do you see? He sleeps!" said Rubriz. "And the blue is gone from his face."

"He sleeps," said the Kid. "The brandy is a good thing. You thought of it in time."

"I have the wisdom in my hands that cures the sick," said Rubriz. "I should have been a doctor. If I were here, in seven days he would sit at the table and drink with me. He sleeps, now. Hush—be quiet! He is smiling. Even in his sleep he knows that Mateo Rubriz is not far away. Is it true?"

"It is true," said the Kid.

"Ah, ah!" murmured Rubriz, shaking his head. "You lie as well as a Mexican. But still it is true that Mateo Rubriz is there in his mind under the lids of his eyes."

A hand rapped at the door.

"It is time, Montana," said the voice of the doctor. And Richard Lavery added, "We'll come in now?"

Rubriz gripped the arm of the Kid so hard that his finger tips gritted against the bone, through the thick, rubbery muscles.

"It is the father," he said, "and I am going out to face him and say one thing to him."

"Suppose they sift some lead into you?" asked Montana.

"You are among your people as I among mine, and not a hand will stir while I am beside you," said Rubriz, confidently. "Speak to them. Now I see why God brought Mateo to this place. It was to see you. Now that I have seen you, I am content."

"Lavery," said the Kid, "I am coming out. Another man is with me. Don't draw a gun, and don't lift a hand. Do you hear me?"

"I hear you," said Richard Lavery. "Whatever you say is as good as done."

"Now we can go out from the room," said the Kid. "If you have to talk to them, say little."

Mateo Rubriz looked at him.

He said, merely, "There are no lies between us!"

"No," said the Kid.

Rubriz went to the door, turned the lock, and set the door wide. The voice of Ransome shouted: "It's Rubriz! By God! he's caught!"

"Stand back from him," ordered the Kid. "Ransome, drop the muzzle of that gun. I'll put a streak of light through the first man that touches him. Steady, Lavery!"

For as Rubriz stepped into the hall he confronted the rancher. Lavery moved slowly backward but Rubriz still faced him, saying: "Once more, señor, you meet the poor greaser you flogged in the street of Bentonville. For that I have had twenty years of the life of your son. Now I leave him with you only because he is too ill to ride. Do you hear me? If you try all the rest of your days, he'll be more mine than yours to the end! On another day he shall come to me or I to him."

He stalked past the pale bewilderment of Richard Lavery, and with the Kid just behind him went down that hall where half a dozen people pushed back to give him way. He walked like a king, lightly, so that his soiled cotton trousers and his bare legs could not detract from his dignity.

They passed from the house. Two cowpunchers were instantly at them, crying out, "Who's that with you, Montana?"

"Stay back from him, boys," said the Kid. "He's a friend of mine called Mateo Rubriz."

The name stopped them like a gun. Mateo Rubriz laughed and walked on with the Kid until the darkness was a cloak gathered about them. Then they paused.

"Here is your gun, Rubriz," said the Kid.

Mateo Rubriz took the shotgun with a careless hand and tucked it under his arm.

"You gave me the name," said Rubriz. "Now give me your hand."

The Kid offered his hand and it was crushed in a grip that numbed his arm to the elbow.

"When I return," said Mateo Rubriz, "I shall tell all that has happened. I shall write it down truthfully. For it is clear that in all of this you have been guided. When our pride grows fat we must be starved until we are lean and active again. San Juan of Capistrano, I see his hand in it for it is a miracle from the first. And San Juan has given me my reward. Tell me if I shall not place six great silver candlesticks before his altar? Or is it batter that you should be my dead enemy or my living friend?"

He released the hand of the Kid, who simply said, "Mateo, we shall see one another again."

"Shall we not?" said Mateo Rubriz. "For two like you and me the whole world is no more than a small bare room. And as for him—as for my boy—my Tonio—"

Here he was compelled to pause.

Then he said: "Tell him all that happened, when his brain is clear. Tell him last of all that you are my friend and he will understand that San Juan of Capistrano has ordered all that happened. Give him also this ring. It has a meaning to him and to me, and tell him that he shall wear it every day of his life. Or else," continued the Mexican, and his voice rose to the familiar deep thunder, suddenly, "I put a curse on him! Will you tell him these things?"

"Everything," said the Kid, "exactly as you've told it to me."

"Ah, then, *adios, amigo mio,*" said Mateo Rubriz. "Now I might tear you and break you with my hands safely, but I would rather rend my own flesh. How God may empty our hearts and in a moment fill them again! Ah, what things I say! It is true that I should have been a priest. Farewell!"

Chapter Thirty-eight

WHEN THE KID returned to the house, he was so tired that the stairs seemed to him an endless mountain lifting in his path. Four of the cowpunchers were in the big room, with their rifles still in their hands. They jumped up when they saw the Kid enter, and looked at them with wild eyes.

Ransome was there.

"Mean-looking *hombre,* that Rubriz, eh?" said the Kid.

"Stewed wildcats with rattlesnake flavoring," said Ransome.

"He's all right, though," said the Kid.

"Sure he is," answered Ransome. "What's a couple or three dozen murders between friends?"

They came to the upper hall and went down it to the room of Dick Lavery. As they turned through the doorway the Kid saw Richard Lavery by the bed and his wife leaning on him and the doctor talking in whispers. There was Ruth, too, who stared at him.

"That's the end of the story," said the Kid. "Rubriz will never trouble you people again."

The Kid went to bed.

He slept the round of the clock, and more. When he wakened, the room spun before his eyes. He stood up. Dick Lavery was asleep and smiling in his sleep. It seemed to the Kid that he was seeing him for the first time in months. There was a great hiatus between this moment and yesterday.

But Lavery was getting well. That was the main thing. The Kid went into the bathroom, stripped, bathed, shaved the black from his face, and dressed again. With every moment, decades of weary age were slipping away from him. In the mirror he saw that his cheeks were sunken and that his eyes squinted as though he were looking straight into the sun. He tried to rub that squint and its corrugations away but they remained as though they were incised in tough India rubber.

When he went back into the next room he saw Ruth Lavery again. "You ought to be in bed. The doctor said you should spend a week in bed!" she exclaimed at him.

"Why should I be dead for a week?" said the Kid. "But I'm hungry. This cayuse needs his grain and hay. You stay here and I'll find the feed-box."

He went down into the kitchen. The Chinaman grinned at him half in joy and half in terror. He went bobbing around with his silken pigtail jumping like a snake behind his shoulders while the Kid sat down at the kitchen table and waited.

He ate a vast meal, accompanied by many cups of black coffee. Then he sat and smoked Bull Durham cigarettes and soiled the purity of that kitchen floor with dabs of gray ashes, here and there. But the Chinaman kept on smiling. He was finding more odds and ends of cake, cookies, berries and cream. The Kid ate them all and drank more coffee and smoked more cigarettes. Gradually, he could feel the knots coming out of his face.

He heard some one singing in the patio.

"Who's that?" asked the Kid.

"The missis," said the Chinaman. He went to the window and looked out, nodding and laughing. "The missis," he repeated.

"That's all right, too," said the Kid.

He left the kitchen and went to the bedroom where Ruth Lavery was reading aloud and her brother lay smiling at her with curiosity and delight. She lowered the book as the Kid came in. Tonio called out to him, faintly, joyously. Without a doubt he had made a remarkable recovery since the night before. The yellow tinge was out of his face and out of his eyes.

"Shall I go out? Do you two want to talk together alone?" she asked.

"Why?" said the Kid. "You're his sister. You may as well hear."

He made his tone impersonal and he looked at her from the calm of distance. But instead of being rebuffed, she merely regarded him with a tender anxiety, a maternal inquiry, as it were.

"You'll want to know what happened," said the Kid to Lavery.

"I've wormed out one thing—that my—that Mateo Rubriz was here!" said Tonio, flushing.

"You were going to call him your father. Well, and why not?" asked the Kid. "He was here. He had come through the guards to put me out of the way and to make sure that the Laverys didn't get hold of you and all his work on you. While he was here you began to rave. When he called you Tonio, you seemed to think that you were back at Mazatlan, facing a firing-squad. Rubriz grew pretty much excited as he listened to you. Then he took it into his head that you were dying. He gave you some brandy. I helped. And he forgot about hating me. We went outside and there he explained that it was the work of San Juan of Capistrano who had reduced his pride and then given him a friend, in me, and that he would see me again. And he gave me this ring for you. You'll wear it every remaining day of your life or he'll put a curse on you!"

He held out a ring set with a big flat-faced emerald, in which was incised a design.

Tonio received the ring in both hands, exclaiming: "But this is his seal and his lucky piece! If he gives me this, he's putting a curse on *himself!*"

"That's all I know," answered the Kid, "I'm going out to take a bit of sun. That's what this lizard needs, is sunshine."

The girl followed him towards the door a few steps.

"You're not angry, are you?" she asked.

"Lord, no!" said the Kid. "But I've slept in the dark and now I'm going to do some sleeping in the sun. That's all."

When he got downstairs, Richard Lavery told him that some one was asking for him, some one who was not a Mexican and who was now getting a "handout" from the cook.

"When you come back, we'll talk," said Lavery. "I have some ideas that will interest you."

"I'll bet they will," said the Kid.

He went out to the dining room of the cowpunchers and there at a corner of the table sat Texas Charlie Cringle with brighter eyes and hair more sun-whitened and a broader grin than ever. Food was heaped before him. The one-legged cook stood in the kitchen door and explained, "He said that he knew you, partner."

"I'd be ashamed to know a worthless, half-baked runt like that," said the Kid. "How are you, Charlie?"

The cook grinned, and allowed the kitchen door to swing shut.

"Hello, Punch!" said the boy, standing up and holding out his hand.

"On the bum again?" asked the Kid, sitting down after the handshake.

"Right away quick," said Texas Charlie Cringle. "I went home and the old man sat up till twelve with me, just like I was a real man. I told him I had some hard cash, and he said he'd invest it for me. So I let him have it. The next day I wanted twenty dollars. He told me that I could do some good honest work if I wanted twenty dollars to spend."

"So you called him a crook and quit?"

"No, I tried to work. I tried three jobs, one right after another."

"Three, eh? How long did you work at 'em?"

"Pretty nearly a week, altogether. But nobody seemed to want to have me around very bad, so I slid out and hit the trail again. Right away you know who I met, Punch?"

"Who?"

"A great old friend of yours. Tom Culver. He told me about the time you had the fight on top of the railroad bridge and had to hang by your hands while the train went by and then climbed up and laughed at each other. He's a card, that Tom Culver."

"Where's he been all this while?"

"He's been in jail while you've been getting yourself famous. That's the only difference. You've certainly gone out and picked up a reputation for yourself, Punch."

"Have I?" said the Kid, dreamily.

"I suppose that old Lavery will give you a coupla thousand acres and a marble house and his oldest daughter, eh?" asked Texas Charlie.

"Do you suppose?" said the Kid.

He yawned. Then he added: "What's a good train out of Bentonville, eh?"

"You mean—you mean—" murmured Texas Charlie. Then he leaned over with a joyous face, exclaiming, "Will you hit the trail with me, Punch?"

"Why not?" said the Kid.

"There's a five-thirty this afternoon. East bound."

"Go and hook it," said the Kid. "Maybe I'll pick it up west of Bentonville."

"Why not go into the town?" asked Texas Charlie.

"Because I hate a crowd," said the Kid.

He got up and stretched himself.

"You look tired," said Texas, "but what you've been doing—it's a wonder you're alive. Going to tell me about it some time?"

"Sure," said the Kid. "I'll shoot off my face, some day, just like every other dirty piker and cheap-skate."

He went out of the room, found a tree near the barn, and lay down under it. The burning sun worked through the branches and freckled his body, his face, his hands, with gold. He slept.

Chapter Thirty-nine

AFTER AN HOUR he wakened again, caught and saddled one of the two horses of Rubriz that he had brought across the Rio Grande, and then took the most hidden and devious trail that wound towards Bentonville.

Once he heard what seemed to him the sound of a horse snorting on the trail not far behind him, and he waited for the animal to come into view. For back in his mind there was a deathless picture of the bulldog Rurale who had the silver-bright scar across his face. He was convinced that before the end of his life he would surely meet with that man again.

But no rider came into view and the Kid went on. He could not afford to waste time hunting down every odd noise that sounded on his trail. He went to the west of Bentonville, to where the railroad grade labored among rapidly rising hills, swinging into great, easy loops. The trail turned into a dim road with a dusty boy coming towards him, thumping a burro from step to step.

The Kid dismounted.

"You like Mexican horses, son?" he asked.

"Do I which?" said the boy, staring at that molded piece of mustang fire.

"This is yours if you can ride it," said the Kid. "It's too slow for me."

The boy said nothing. He simply flared his nostrils, set his teeth, and went up the side of that horse like a buccaneer up the towering stern of a galleon.

It was a brisk battle, but as the whirl of dust began to subside the boy was still in the saddle. The Kid smiled, and disappeared in the direction of the railroad track.

There he found a good, grassy bank and lay down on it. There was a treasure of weariness in him that yearned to be expended at every chance. And he had not long. In half an hour, or less, the train would come laboring by.

He heard a very light crunching sound for no other reason than that his ear was so close to the earth. Instantly he was up, crouching, ready for a leap, the big Colt turning in his hand wherever his eyes went. Then as she parted the shrubs with her hands, he saw the face of Ruth Lavery.

He was so amazed that he forgot to put away the gun

with his next gesture. She came out to him with a matter-of-fact nod.

"Hello!" she said. "Waiting for the train?"

"Yes," said the Kid, darkly, bracing himself.

But not a word of persuasion came from her, not a syllable of argument. She sat down by the place where his body had crushed the grass. He crouched beside her uneasily.

"What are you doing here?" said the Kid.

"I just rode down," she answered.

"Followed me?"

"Yes."

"I heard your horse on the trail," said the Kid, more darkly gloomy. "Where is it?"

"I met a boy on the road and let him have it."

"You did what?"

"He had a pretty good mustang already, but I thought he might be able to use another."

The Kid turned his head sharply and stared. Her blue eyes were quite impersonal. They met his glance easily and then wandered past him towards something in the sky.

"What are you doing here?" he demanded again.

"I'm waiting for the train," she said.

"What—" he began, angrily. Then he checked himself. "It's a joke, eh?" he asked.

"Is it? I don't think so."

"What's the matter with you, Ruth? You mean to say that you're leaving home?"

"Yes."

"Why?"

"Well, guess. Why did *you* leave the ranch?"

"I haven't any part in it," said the Kid. He hunted through his mind for cold, cruel words and used them. "I'd go to sleep on a place like that. It's all right for the Laverys. It's big and all that. But it's a desert island for a fellow like me."

"It's likely to be a desert island for a girl like me, too," said Ruth Lavery.

"Look at me!" he commanded.

She turned her head, smiling faintly, impersonally.

"What crazy sort of nonsense is this?" he asked.

"What sort of crazy nonsense is this?" she corrected, mildly. "Why, you don't think it's nonsense and neither do I. I want to be out where things happen, in the real world. I don't mind the heat, and I don't mind the cold, either. I'm pretty tough."

He snarled at her. "Are you getting romantic?"

"No, I'm just waking up," said she.

"You know what sort of *hombres* are on the road?"

"Yes, fellows like you."

"And tougher still. And I'm not what you think. You've seen me playing Man Friday to the Laverys, but that's only a flash in the pan. That's nothing. That's not me."

"Well, I'd like to see the rest of you," said the girl.

"It would make you sick," said the Kid. "Listen to me! Don't be a fool, Ruth!"

"It won't make me sick," said she, "I'd like the adventure of seeing what you are."

A sudden vibrant humming came from the railroad track, then the puffing of the distant locomotive.

"Get back from here," said the Kid. "Don't make a show of yourself."

He waved his hand. She stepped back a little and waited. The locomotive came around the next bend, shuddering with effort.

"Ruth, you'll roll under the wheels if you try to jump that train. It's coming faster than you think!" he told her.

"If I can't jump a slow freight like that, I'm no good," she answered. "I'll try, anyway."

His face was bright with perspiration.

"You're trying to drive me crazy," said the Kid. "What's the matter with you?"

"I'm trying to find out; and I'm an optimist," she said. *"Todos non es perdos!"*

He started. A slow flame went up his face.

"Ruth," he said, "do you speak Spanish?"

"All my life," she answered. "How could I live in the Bend without learning the Mexican lingo?"

The engine roared up to them and past them. The Kid turned slowly. He saw the line of swaying empties go past, each roaring out in a separate key. The sliding-door of a box car opened and the startled face of Texas Charlie looked out at him.

The train gained the top of the grade, instantly gathered speed again, and so took itself and the bewildered face of Charlie out of view.

But still the Kid looked after it. It was very hard to turn to the girl again.

"That's why I had the courage to come," said she. "And this morning I asked Dick all about it. He told me, too. He told me all that he could remember and particularly about sitting there on the hilltop watching the men of Rubriz out on the desert. I knew you meant what you said to him then and that's why I came after you."

The Kid turned to her. Still it was hard to look her in the face. She made it unnecessary by turning at his side. They walked together from the railroad cut and back onto the road.

"Well," he said. "I don't know what to do. What do you say, Ruth?"

"You're the boss," said she.

"I haven't even a name. I'm a tramp," said the Kid. "Listen to me. If I didn't care so much, I wouldn't care what happened."

She smiled at this jumble of language. He became aware that her eyes were calmly taking possession of him.

"To go back to the ranch without horses makes me seem like a fool," said the Kid.

"Then we won't go back," said the girl.

"We've got to go back," said the Kid.

"All right, then we'll go back," said she.

"You talk as though you don't care a rap what happens!" said the Kid.

"I don't," said she. "I don't care a rap."

"There's your mother. Breaking her heart doesn't matter, I suppose?"

"Nothing matters," said the girl.

"Well," said the Kid, "I don't know what to do."

"We'll wait till you've found out," said she. "I don't want you to go back to a desert island of Laverys. They're nothing to me."

"What do you mean by that?" asked the Kid, frowning.

"Well, I'm Mrs. Montana, or Mrs. Mexico," said she. "What *is* your name, first or last?"

"I don't know," said the Kid. He flushed. "Nicknames—that's all I've had, or synthetic names that people gave me when they took me in when I was a brat."

"Well," she said, "names don't count."

"How did you happen to see me leave the ranch?" asked the Kid.

"I wouldn't have known. It was Dick who said you were looking at the sky and ready to fly. He knows wild birds."

"Geese particularly, eh?" said the Kid.

She said nothing.

"We'd better start," said the Kid.

"All right. Where?"

"For the ranch, of course. It's a long walk. But—what will your mother think?"

"I don't care what she thinks. Would you be happy there on the ranch?"

"Happy?" said the Kid. "Why, I'd rather be in that valley than in the best pasture lands in heaven, and learn how to throw a rope like Buck, and how to run cattle, like Stew Ransome."

They stepped on briskly along the trail.

"That won't last," said the girl.

They climbed a slope. When they came to the top they could see nothing but the great green waves of the hills with the wind flooding wildly across them.

"Why won't it last?" asked the Kid.

"But *I'll* last," said the girl.

He put his arm around her. He made a great gesture.

"D'you know something?" he said. "I feel as though I owned the whole green world!"

He began to laugh and she laughed with him.

Center Point Publishing

600 Brooks Road • PO Box 1
Thorndike ME 04986-0001 USA

(207) 568-3717

US & Canada:
1 800 929-9108
www.centerpointlargeprint.com